MURDER BY LAMPSHADE

An absolutely gripping cozy murder mystery full of twists

JEAN G. GOODHIND

A Honey Driver Murder Mystery Book 5

Originally published as
Deadly Nightshades

JOFFE BOOKS

Revised edition 2022
Joffe Books, London
www.joffebooks.com

First published by Accent Press Ltd
in Great Britain and the USA as *Deadly Nightshades* in 2014

This paperback edition was first published
in Great Britain in 2022

Cover art by Dee Dee Book Covers

ISBN: 978-1-80405-392-8

CHAPTER ONE

Reception at the Green River Hotel was having a makeover and Honey Driver was as excited as a kid at Christmas. 'I've put up with Dracula's drawing room for three years now. The old place is due for enlightenment.'

She'd opted for the Louis XIV look: all china blue and French cream with sparkling chandeliers and ornate, Frenchified mirrors.

The red carpet had gone, the wood had been rubbed down and the crème de la crème of Bath's interior designers, Philippe Fabiere, had ordered the necessary paint, wallpaper and furnishings. Much sought after in the industry, he was flamboyant, dictatorial and something of a fraud. His professional nom de plume was very *à la Française*, but in reality he was a black guy from the East End of London, and the name he'd been born with, Philip Fernsby, did not suit an interior designer with towering ambitions, dyed-blond hair and *very* colourful clothing.

All that apart, Philip — or Philippe as he preferred to be called — was the interior designer of choice for Bath's more cultured hoteliers. Honey had had to have him, but she also had to have everything completed within two weeks. She had a business to run and money didn't grow on trees — and Philippe's bill would need to be a towering pine.

Glowing with satisfaction she cast her gaze over the bare walls, the exposed oak floorboards, the rubbed-down dado rails. At present the place was more Fred Flintstone's cave than Louis XIV's Versailles — a bit depressing really. Luckily she had a vivid imagination.

'Just wait till it's all done,' she sighed to herself.

A decorator wearing off-white overalls splashed with myriad colours used a palette knife to open a paint tin. The lid opened with a reassuring *pop* — not exactly champagne but certainly something of a celebration. The first roller full of china blue was applied to the wall, and the smell of fresh paint came with it. She congratulated herself on being sensible enough to decline any room reservations. Guests didn't like upheaval, even when it was in their interests; it would only lead to complaints. So she'd given Philippe two weeks to complete the job and stopped taking bookings.

She voiced her satisfaction out loud. 'Glad we didn't take any guests.'

Lindsey grunted an inaudible response. Her daughter's rear was sticking out from beneath the reception counter, a large built-in affair with many compartments, drawers and shelves. She was attempting to extricate the computer wiring from the tangled mass it had got itself into. The reception counter was also being revamped into something more elegant, more in keeping with Philippe's artistic vision.

'That blue was definitely the right colour,' Honey added dreamily, folding her arms as a wall of bare plaster turned blue.

A dust-covered Lindsey backed out from under the counter and got onto her knees. She wrinkled her nose. 'Strong smell.'

Honey took a deep breath of the paint-tinged air. 'It's a clean smell. A new smell.'

The same red carpet fitted in the reception area had also adorned the sweeping staircase leading up to the guest rooms. The deep red would be replaced by a durable but luxurious carpet of the deepest harvest gold. In the meantime she heard the *clomp, clomp, clomp* of descending footsteps. Mary Jane, the only resident left in the building, was coming downstairs.

'Good morning,' Honey called to her, fully expecting Mary Jane, professor of the paranormal, to be her usual exuberant self.

'I've got a complaint,' said Mary Jane.

Honey blinked. It wasn't much past eight o'clock and Mary Jane's apple-green tracksuit was guaranteed to shock anyone into instant wakefulness. The vividly colourful item had been purchased at a car boot sale at a knock-down price. Mary Jane had knocked the price down even further. The collar and cuffs were trimmed with shocking pink, as was the jacket zip. Given its still vibrant colour, the previous owner must have been glad to get rid of it. Mary Jane's multicoloured trainers matched the wooden parrots swinging from her earlobes.

Honey was a picture of sympathy. 'I'm so sorry to hear that, Mary Jane. Tell me all about it.'

Face powder floated down from Mary Jane's face as she spoke. Mary Jane favoured using a lot of face powder. She left a trail of it everywhere, including an imprint of her face on her pillow.

'It's Sir Cedric,' she said in a low voice, glancing over her shoulder.

'Oh dear,' said Honey. She had great patience with Mary Jane. She was after all a very nice person. After a while, talk about long-dead ancestors calling in on her ceased to be shocking. Sir Cedric lived in the wardrobe in Mary Jane's room, so Mary Jane had told them.

'He's upset at the smell of paint. He doesn't like things changing. This old place has changed too much over the years.'

Mary Jane was also a full-time resident. She'd kind of landed in the room when visiting one year and had decided that was the place she should be. In no time at all she had exchanged Californian sunshine for the more variable English weather.

Honey had learned to talk about Sir Cedric as though he were merely another guest — one who didn't pay the going room rate, but then he didn't use the hotel facilities as such. She was suitably apologetic. 'Please render him my sincere apologies, but it just has to be done. I'm sure he'll appreciate the improvement when it's finished.'

Honey presumed that Sir Cedric went wandering around at night. It didn't do to go into great detail. Show the slightest interest, and Mary Jane would go on for hours about her family tree.

'You don't understand,' said Mary Jane, her eyes shining with that strange glow that always came about when she spoke of Sir Cedric. 'Resident spirits hate having their routine disturbed and tend to show their displeasure.'

Honey glanced at her watch. 'Well, I'm sure that if we open the windows, he shouldn't be too disturbed.'

Mary Jane looked unsure.

'Look,' said Honey, wondering why she was swallowing this. But, feeling obliged to placate her one and only guest, she made a promise.

'Tell you what, as soon as Philippe gets here I'll have a word with him about this. I'm sure we can sort something out — even if it's only to acquire a less pungent paint.'

Mary Jane frowned. 'Will this Philippe guy be very long getting here?'

'No,' said Honey shaking her head vehemently. 'I'm expecting him at any minute. Leave it with me. I'll sort something out.'

Mary Jane's scepticism was palpable.

'Have you had breakfast?' Honey asked, keen to change the subject.

At the mention of food, Mary Jane's expression shifted.

'Doris did room service. It's waiting for me up top. I'll get back up there and do it justice. I expect your interior designer will have come and gone by the time I'm finished.'

'No doubt he will,' said Honey with more assurance than she felt. It was gone nine and Philippe had promised to be there at eight. Up until now he'd never been late. But there was always a first time, she told herself. Wasn't there?

Mary Jane's long legs took her back across reception and up the stairs.

Honey looked down at Lindsey, who was still on her knees. 'Sir Cedric doesn't like being disturbed.'

'So I heard,' said Lindsey, getting to her feet and swiping the dust from her hands. 'Does this mean he's checking out?'

'That's fine as long as his bill's up to date. Two hundred years or so at an average of fifty pounds a night — that's about fifty grand, give or take a thousand or two . . .'

'The least troublesome guest we've ever had,' murmured Lindsey on her way back down beneath the desk, where the tangled wiring awaited her.

Honey picked up a pen and inspected a few requests for reservations. Some had arrived by Royal Mail, the others by email. Luckily they were all for some time after the refurbishment was likely to have finished. She spent a while on these, then she checked her watch and the old-school clock ticking away high on the wall. Ten o'clock. Philippe Fabiere had still not arrived.

The decorators had been on their tea break. On their return, one of them came strolling over.

'Sorry to bother you, love, but Phil was supposed to be bringing us some more size.'

'Size?' What was size? Honey tried to look engaged.

'The sealant we need to put on the old plaster before painting the walls. Just to seal it. Know what I mean?'

'Leave it with me. I'll give him a call.'

She did just that, dialling Philippe's home phone. There was no answer. His answering service clicked in at the eighth tone. She didn't leave a message but dialled his mobile phone. No answer there either. She put down the phone. A steady supply of junk mail was threatening to take over her desk. It had to go. Forming a pincer attack with her hands, she was just about to bundle the lot of it up and throw it into a bin bag, when the phone rang. Philippe Fabiere's mobile number flashed up on the screen.

'Hello, Phil? What's happening? You're supposed to be here?'

'Who's that?'

She recognised Steve Doherty's voice. 'Me.'

'Honey?' He sounded surprised. 'What are you doing ringing this phone?'

'Why shouldn't I be?'

His tone of voice gave her a bad feeling, but she explained anyway.

'I was after my interior designer. He was supposed to be here this morning. Hang on.' She took a deep breath. 'I'm getting bad vibes from you, Steve. Let me gaze into my crystal ball. You're going to tell me something bad. Right?'

There was a pause — a very pregnant pause.

'He won't make it to your place today. In fact, not ever.'

When they weren't on a case, Doherty's voice was super macho and sensually enticing. It wasn't like that now. This was business — very grim business.

'This sounds bad.' Her voice faltered.

'As bad as it gets.'

'Murder?' Her voice was hesitant and hushed.

'You said it, babe. Did you know him well?'

She felt a lump forming in her throat. Philippe was, or rather had been, a nice guy that she'd grown quite fond of. He'd had such energy for his chosen profession, his eyes lighting up at the sight of a particularly luxurious piece of fabric, an interesting paint colour, a scintillating wallpaper pattern. He threw things together seemingly with no thought at all, yet it always worked.

She sighed a heartfelt sigh. 'He was a nice guy. A great interior designer too. Everyone used him. He wasn't the cheapest, but he was certainly the best. The rest trailed in his wake.'

There was that pause again. Doherty thought big thoughts in those pauses.

'Steve? I can hear you thinking.'

'Yep. So he had rivals? Do you know who they were and whether there were any fallouts of late?'

She bit her lip hard but managed to pull herself together and think logically.

'I can soon find out. I'll make a few calls.'

'Come back to me.'

'Where are you?'

'St Margaret's Court.'

'Leave it with me. I'll catch up with you as soon as I know something.'

Replacing the phone, she sensed Lindsey was looking up at her, waiting for an explanation.

'Philippe's been murdered.'

'By who?'

Honey shrugged. 'They don't know yet, but I'm going to look into his competitors.'

'Try Casper. He would know a few.'

She was right. The chair of Bath Hotels Association was a fount of knowledge, especially when it came to the aesthetic. Art and culture were abundant in the city of Bath. She rang him and told him what had happened. His sigh was as heavy as hers had been before he expressed comment.

'The poor boy,' he exclaimed. 'He wasn't just the best interior designer in our small corner of the world, he was the best in the country.'

Honey had to agree with him.

'Was there much jealousy in the trade?'

Casper gave a gasping, choking laugh. 'Of course there was! These people are *artistes*! Creative people, my dear Honey, have insecurities the rest of us cannot imagine. Reputation is their lifeblood, and not just good reputation. Undisputed reputation as the very, very best.'

'Where should I start?'

'Julia Porter for one. Dylan Sylvester of the Sugar Moon Design House for two. I'll let you know if I think of anyone else.'

'That's good of you.'

She hadn't meant to be sarcastic, but it did seem to come out that way. Casper expected great things of her in keeping crime to a minimum in the city, but did not sully his carefully cultivated hands with the nitty-gritty. He left that to her.

His voice turned gravely grim. 'I want the culprit incarcerated as quickly as possible. I don't care how you do it. Just see to it.'

Casper hung up, and Lindsey voiced exactly what was on Honey's mind.

'My bet is on professional jealousy.'

'What makes you so sure?'

'They'd strangle a rival if they thought it would enhance their reputation. A damask cord, of course. Something suitably tasteful.'

Honey considered her short acquaintance with Philippe, his drooling over materials and colours, his defensiveness in the face of criticism, his jealousy when a rival's name had been mentioned.

She looked down at her daughter, who was once again burrowing beneath the desk.

'You're right,' said Honey. 'You're absolutely right.'

CHAPTER TWO

It was the worst possible scenario. Things might not have been so complicated if the coach hadn't drawn up outside. The big shiny tour bus was a classy shade of beetroot, or more poshly termed burgundy; the company name was emblazoned in gold Roman lettering along the side.

Doherty eyed the motley collection of tourists piling off despite having been told to stay on board. By the looks of them and the babble of languages being spoken, he could almost believe that the coach had just got back from a whirlwind trip around the world, picking up passengers at every stop along the way. A lot of them were seniors. The moment he clapped eyes on them, Doherty knew they'd be trouble.

They'd alighted from the coach and were now being held at the bottom of the majestic steps leading up to the equally imposing front door of the St Margaret's Court Hotel. It was obvious from the raised voices and walking sticks that they weren't happy about it. Like a flock of angry geese they gathered around the tour guide and the two uniformed constables who were expected to keep the public at bay. The coach party did not consider themselves 'the public'. They were tourists. They were guests who'd paid a pretty penny to stay at an original

Elizabethan mansion. Now they were being told that they weren't allowed in.

A carpeted ramp had been set in place over one half of the steps, principally for the use of disabled guests. One of the constables, wearing a worried expression, came striding up it in Doherty's direction. He pushed his cap back slightly before speaking.

Doherty eyed him sidelong. Constable Shaun Jones, mostly known as Jonesy, was young and fresh faced. Doherty felt a stab of envy. He himself had been young and keen once, excited to be on his first murder case. Just like the fresh face and the youth, the initial enthusiasm would disappear in time, to be replaced by a sardonic acceptance that there was as much malice in the human race as there was goodness.

'They're not happy, sir.'

'Neither's the bloke in there,' snapped Doherty, having not quite shaken off the flash of nostalgia. He nodded in the direction of the arched doorway behind them. 'In fact he's a damn sight less happy than they are, seeing as he's dead!'

The young copper had guts if nothing else. He persisted. 'Yes, sir. They're saying that they've paid their money and you can't stop them from coming in.'

Doherty raised one eyebrow in disbelief. 'Oh, do they now!'

A sheepish expression came to the young police officer's face. 'Thing is, sir, they've got to stay somewhere overnight, and they can't sleep in the coach. They do have a point, sir. We have a duty of care. After all, some of them are getting on a bit.'

Doherty scowled. There had to be a solution, though it was hardly his job to find them all rooms for the night. He wasn't a hotelier, for Christ's sake!

Jonesy paused. 'I hear that this place belongs to a Russian, sir.'

'That's right,' returned Doherty. Tanya, the girl in charge of reception, had told him so.

'They seem to be all over the place nowadays, don't they — owning football clubs and that.'

Doherty didn't answer. So the Russian preferred a hotel to a football club? There was nothing wrong in that.

He thought then about the many hotels that he'd stayed in himself in his time — professionally and for pleasure. Looking up at the sixteenth-century facade, he thought he wouldn't mind staying in this one. He loved old places. They had atmosphere, better than a modern place with plate glass and minimalist décor. He wanted to stay here. That was why he'd defied his usual decorum and bought a raffle ticket at the reception desk, the proceeds going to charity. The prize was a night's luxury accommodation for two with all the trimmings.

Constable Jones was nothing if not observant.

'Did you see the raffle tickets, sir? A fiver. Wouldn't catch me paying all that for a raffle ticket. Mad!'

'We're not here to discuss the price of a raffle ticket, Jonesy,' said Doherty. Eyeing the near-to-rioting senior citizens, he swiftly shoved the ticket he'd purchased into his pocket. A night of luxury for two! Now, what would Honey think about that? The hotel was running on low revs at the moment, what with the refurbishment. She had no excuse to say no.

Standing on top of the steps outside the main entrance, he had a good view of the single-track road winding up through St Margaret's Valley. It was a beautiful scene — the narrow, green valley was sparsely dotted with large upmarket houses, complete with big driveways and a stable or two at the rear.

The view at this moment couldn't be better. In fact what he saw made his jaw — which had clenched almost painfully — now relax.

A pink Cadillac was speeding its way none too carefully up through the valley. The cavalry had arrived.

* * *

Mary Jane stayed at the bottom of the steps. Once the Americans on board recognised one of their own, she was swamped with complaints and questions.

Honey was accompanied by the young constable to where Doherty stood at the top of the steps. She tried to read the look on his face. Not possible. It was serious, as it always was when there was a job to be done.

'You're looking pale,' Doherty observed.

'What do you expect? My car's in for a service. Mary Jane brought me here. I'll be fine after a few seconds on terra firma.'

Mary Jane and her car were becoming famous. It was a simple little Cadillac coupe dating from 1961. And pink — a delicate shade of pink. Mary Jane's driving was infamous in its own right. So far she'd been lucky. Either that or the local traffic police didn't want the hassle of filling out a load of forms. The fact was that Mary Jane's driving was hair-raising, but the car had never been involved in an accident. In fact it seemed to lead a charmed life, and Mary Jane took great care of it. She loved her car. She wanted it to last.

Honey was OK with that. She merely wanted to live longer.

She followed Doherty through the oak-panelled reception room over black-and-white Dutch tiles. Spotlights were trained on medieval tapestries, suits of armour and pewter plates. St Margaret's was Grade I listed. In the right light, at the right time, it was easy to imagine ladies in Elizabethan bodices and bearded gents in doublet and hose peopling the hall.

'This way,' said Doherty.

She followed him along a panelled corridor, their footsteps accompanied by the squeaking of ancient oak floorboards.

Forensic had just finished. The bathroom was luxurious in the old-fashioned way. The tub was enormous and supported on lion's claws. The tiles were dark green and looked Victorian. A polished brass water pipe connected the willow-patterned lavatory pan to its overhead cistern

— beautifully period, though perhaps not too practical on the cleaning front. She noticed the pull chain was missing.

The window was wide open. A panel of glass had been broken, and the bits were scattered on the floor. Doherty pulled it closed.

'The manager was called to open the door with his set of keys but the bathroom was bolted from the inside.'

'So who discovered him?'

'Scaffolders. They were putting up scaffolding in this section so the stonemasons could repair some of the mullions. The bloke nearly fell off when he looked through the window.'

'Method of death?' she asked.

'The victim was choked with the handle of the lavatory chain. It was lozenge shaped, made of willow-patterned china from the Wedgwood factory — according to Forensics, that is.'

Visualising Philippe — someone she knew quite well — choking to death sickened her. As a result she said something stupid.

'No chance of him having done it himself, then?'

Doherty looked at her askance.

'Not unless he had an odd penchant for eating vitreous china. Someone bent him backwards over the pan and tore the handle off. Somebody strong. There are bruises at the side of his neck. Loads of fingerprints, of course. It is a communal lavatory.'

'What a shame! Philippe directed his revamps like the theatre producer he used to be. He had a full cast. And the bolt?'

Doherty was examining the bolt that had been so firmly locked. He frowned as he shook his head. 'Wiped clean.'

'So definitely murder, but how come the door was locked and the bolt pulled across?'

Honey could see that Doherty was not best pleased. He was scowling at the bolt as though it, and it alone, was responsible for the dastardly deed. He muttered, 'A bolted empty room except for a dead body. Reads like a bloody

Agatha Christie novel.' He slid the bolt backwards and forwards then rubbed finger against thumb. 'Grease.'

'Vaseline,' said someone from Forensics. 'Helps it run more smoothly. Not that it didn't run smoothly anyway. It's a pretty old bolt. A new one would be a bit stiff. But not this one.'

Honey shrugged. 'So?'

'No doubt somebody will inform me exactly how it was done,' said Doherty. He said it as though the police had all the answers — which she doubted.

Honey had her own ace of wonders. 'I'll ask Lindsey. She's good at puzzles.'

'I'll find out before you do.'

'Would you like to bet on that?'

'Ten pounds.'

'You're on.'

She shivered as she walked back through the elegant reception hall. Being choked to death with a lavatory handle — even an antique one — was pretty macabre. Thank goodness the body had been removed before she'd got there.

'So how about his competitors?'

'Two main ones.' She gave him the names Casper had given her. 'He expects an early arrest,' she added.

Doherty eyed her wryly. 'Casper always expects an early arrest.'

Things were pretty bad. She couldn't have possibly guessed that they'd get worse.

Mary Jane was standing at the head of the group of aged tourists looking downright smug.

'Honey, these poor folk have been told that they can't possibly stay here until the day after tomorrow. The police want to continue their questioning and their investigation without guests tramping around the place. Understandable, of course . . .'

'Of course,' returned Honey.

'And they need somewhere to stay . . .'

'I expect they do,' said Honey. When her fingertips touched the door handle, it was as though the car had been electrified. A bolt of something similar to electricity shot through her. Her fingers tingled. But she knew it was not electricity. Suspicion. A deep, worrying suspicion that Mary Jane had done something she should not have done — not without asking.

She turned a jaundiced eye on her slightly dipsy friend.

Mary Jane smiled. 'I've sorted them out,' she said in no-nonsense fashion, slamming the car door behind her. 'I've told them that all your rooms are empty and they can stay there as long as they don't mind the smell of paint and no carpet on the floor.'

Before Honey had chance to object, Mary Jane was waving to her new-found friends.

'It's OK, guys and gals. I've got everything under control. Just get your bus driver to drop you and your stuff at the Green River Hotel.'

Hands and walking sticks were brandished above wrinkled faces and a big cheer went up. Mary Jane had done her good deed for the day. Honey still had reservations. No one was as critical as a hotel guest on the wrong side of sixty-five.

The drive back to Bath passed in a blur of horns, sounded by other road users. Mary Jane, driving as furiously as ever, was totally oblivious. As she drove she wittered on about something to do with Tarot cards, though Honey, more concerned with Mary Jane's road sense, couldn't work out what.

Honey tried to focus her mind on what she'd just witnessed. It was bad enough that Mary Jane had been outside playing the Good Samaritan while she'd been inside playing Hercule Poirot. Her main thoughts were with Philippe Fabiere. She couldn't help dwelling on what had happened. Who on earth would do something so macabre, something so . . . original?

* * *

They beat the coach back to Bath. Honey entered reception in a dream. It wasn't until Lindsey asked her for details that she got round to telling her about the locked bathroom. That was after she'd wailed about a whole coachload of people being foisted on her.

'Are you getting paid for having them?' Lindsey ventured.

'Well . . . yes . . .'

'Then it isn't all bad. Now for the brainteaser. How much have you bet Doherty?'

'Ten pounds.'

'Easy peasy,' said Lindsey, a smile cracking her face. 'Follow me.'

Lindsey trotted into the men's lavatory. Puzzled and curious, her mother followed her into one of the three cubicles.

Squashed between the washable walls, Lindsey slid the bolt across. She was wearing one of her very serious looks. Lindsey was good at deep thinking. Honey hadn't a clue where she got it from. Not from her. Nor from Carl, her father. Carl had been a party animal. Lindsey was far from being that. As for taking after her grandmother, neither of them had been tarred with that particular brush. Honey preferred jeans to Jaeger and Lindsey preferred casual to classic. Neither kept their nails in good order and painted to match their outfits. Only Gloria Cross, Honey's mother, did that.

Lindsey slid the bolt to and fro. 'This one's a bit stiff, but as long as the bolt runs free it's quite easy, really. Strong thread or fishing twine.'

'OK, Professor Hawking, explain.'

'I'll do better than that. I'll show you.'

Back they went to reception. She snipped a length of cotton from the emergency sewing kit behind the reception desk and headed back to the cloakrooms — this time they opted for the ladies'. Lindsey ran a piece of cotton thread around the bolt handle, keeping the two loose ends in her hand.

Honey had noted that the bolt had been pretty loose and said so.

'It's Doris. She polishes everything with beeswax. It helps things run more smoothly.'

'As good as using Vaseline, I expect,' Honey observed.

Lindsey ordered her to close the door. Honey obeyed.

Using both hands Lindsey gently pulled on both ends of the thread. The bolt slid home. Once she was sure it was tightly secured, she pulled just one end of the thread. Slowly but surely the thread lengthened in her hands. She slid the thread out altogether.

Honey tested the door, pushing at it with both hands. It didn't budge.

'Amazing! It's locked.'

Lindsey grinned. 'Voila!'

CHAPTER THREE

Even now with the rooms occupied, the hotel seemed to echo with silence, though there was no time to dwell on the ambience. A number of staff had taken advantage of circumstances and booked their annual leave. Rumour had it that Dumpy Doris had bought a miniscule bikini and flown off somewhere sunny.

That was OK, although it did mean more for Honey and Lindsey to take care of. For Honey this included taking over the cooking of breakfast.

'I can hardly believe it,' she said as she struggled into the kitchen carrying the fifteen pounds of sausages she'd just bought at the specialist shop in Green Street. 'Doris sunning herself in a bikini.'

Smudger, her rugby-playing chef, made a puking sound. 'Dumpy Doris in a bikini. Disgusting! I just don't want to think about it.'

The sausages landed on the stainless steel table with a resounding thud. The sound echoed off the stainless steel shelving, cupboards and appliances that lined the kitchen walls.

'I hope you wouldn't say the same about me behind my back,' said Honey.

Smudger smiled and a mischievous look sparkled in his eyes.

'I'm a man that knows quality meat when I see it.'

'Charming. In that case you can check these sausages.'

Honey made her way along the corridor leading to reception. The painters and decorators were huddled in a group. Philippe's assistant, Camilla Boylan, was standing slightly apart from them. Honey surmised that some discussion had taken place.

She didn't stop to pry but headed for the stairs and the linen cupboard. Besides cooking immeasurable amounts of bacon, sausages and free-range eggs, there was housekeeping to attend to. Dumpy Doris kept a strict check on the laundry: the sheets, linen tablecloths and mountains of bath towels had to be dealt with. So far the fact that her empty rooms had been filled — thanks to Mary Jane — was not causing problems.

The restaurant was unaffected by the alterations, so it was business as usual. The seniors seemed to take everything in their stride, even when a sticky toffee pudding captured a set of false teeth. Finding bedding and making the beds had been more of a problem. Heating in the rooms had been turned off. They'd needed airing. A few grumbles had ensued about freezing English bedrooms, but they'd got over that. Thanks to the tourist guide travelling with them, plus some input from Mary Jane, Honey's visitors were settling in.

Making the beds was quite therapeutic for the most part and helped her deal with Philippe's murder. Who would do it and why?

She was smoothing a pillow when Doherty phoned.

'I thought you might like an update.'

He sounded subdued. She was feeling that way herself, and he possibly knew that.

She sighed deeply and let the pillow fall on to the bed. 'I cannot believe it. I think even Casper is dumbstruck. He hasn't phoned me yet today to check on our progress.'

'No,' replied Doherty. 'He phoned me, but he's far from being dumbstruck. He's downright vocal, in fact. Wants me to go out and arrest somebody right away.'

The news that the exuberant and self-centred Casper St John Gervais was moved enough to phone Steve Doherty before phoning her was news indeed.

'I could do with a break. How about you come to my place for dinner tonight? I'm good at dealing with stuff like this. I've got the experience.'

'You can't tell me you've had victims throttled with a toilet handle before.'

'It is rare.'

His cynical attempt at humour almost made her laugh — almost, though not quite. Familiarity might breed contempt; familiarity with crime led to more than contempt. In Doherty's case he'd developed a kind of immunity over the years. He had to in order to cope.

She looked towards the window, where the spring sunlight was attempting to coax lime-green buds from bushes and trees. A host of daffodils turned their bright yellow trumpets skywards as though they were sounding a silent welcome.

The sunlight made her want to emerge from winter too. 'OK. Casual or evening gown?'

'Whichever one shows off your figure best.'

The call was interrupted. Philippe Fabiere's partner was waiting for her in reception. She made her excuses to Doherty and signed off.

Camilla Boylan had a heart-shaped face and jet black eyes. She also had red lips and brandy-coloured hair cut into a geometric bob. The distant look was at odds with her direct way of speaking.

'The men won't stay. It can't be helped. It's the probate situation. They won't get paid until it's all sorted out.'

Honey swore under her breath. 'Why the hell didn't Philippe make a will?'

Camilla shrugged her narrow shoulders and shifted the meagre weight on her equally narrow hips. 'Because he didn't expect to die. None of us do, do we?'

'But I paid a deposit!'

A £3,000 deposit — not much in the grand scheme of things but enough to make her bank manager blink before allowing the overdraft. She eyed a particular spot where the blue paint finished and the bare plaster began. The shape of the plaster against the blue roughly resembled a humpbacked whale. A small splash of paint had created what looked like an eye.

As Camilla went on to explain about the probate and that Philippe's bank account had been frozen, Honey's face froze too. She did not wish to be left with what amounted to a rough-and-ready mural.

'Wait,' she said, raising her hand, palm facing Camilla's china-doll face. 'Have you any idea how this is affecting my business? I refused room bookings for the next two weeks presuming everything would be finished, including the mink suede settees and scumble-glazed coffee tables. Now you're telling me that I can't even get the basic paintwork done.'

She told herself that there was no point in mentioning that she'd relented on her decision with regard to room occupancy. The action had been forced on her in dire circumstances.

'I suppose I could run it past the solicitor.' Camilla blinked and for a fleeting moment truly seemed to sympathise before the distant look returned. 'There again, it can't really prevent you from letting the rooms, can it?'

'Of course it can!'

An elderly couple speaking German were coming down the stairs. Camilla glanced at them before turning back to Honey, raising a querulous eyebrow. 'You have guests?'

'It was an emergency,' Honey said swiftly. 'They can't stay at St Margaret's Court until the police have finished. It's only for one night.'

Camilla jerked her ever-so-pert chin. It was difficult to tell whether she believed Honey or not. Camilla was the sort who made a career out of always being right. Not the sort with many friends, thought Honey.

The German couple waved to her. 'So nice here,' said the man.

'A lovely room,' said his wife. 'We have a four-poster bed,' she added, directing her comment at Camilla. 'Isn't that wonderful? It's just like being on honeymoon all over again.'

Judging by the smug expression on her husband's face, she was telling the absolute truth.

'I'm glad you like it,' said Honey, refusing to turn pink in response to Camilla's querulous expression.

'Lovely colour,' said her husband, indicating the half-painted walls as he followed in his wife's footsteps towards the door. 'This should not take too long now before it is complete.'

'I'd like to think so. Now,' she said, turning back to Camilla once the old couple had gone, 'how about I pay the painters' wages and then reclaim it when probate is granted?'

Camilla pursed her blood-red lips as she thought about it. 'I would have to consult the solicitors.'

'I'd rather you told the decorators first,' returned Honey, noticing that said crew were swiftly packing up their equipment rather than spreading paint on the walls. 'If you don't, I will.'

'That's fine. You tell them. I'll ask the solicitor whether that's in order.'

'Great!'

Camilla swung her bag over her shoulder. 'Right. I'll be off.'

'Not yet,' said Honey, cupping the girl's elbow and edging her to one side. 'There's a question I need to ask you.'

A slight frown came to the porcelain complexion. 'Really? What's that?'

'Had anyone threatened Philippe? Was there any member of the competition with an axe to grind?'

Camilla shrugged. 'There always are. It's a very competitive profession. Philippe was very good at what he did and a good businessman. People get jealous at the success of others. That is a fact.'

'Who inherits Philippe's estate?'

Camilla turned defensive. 'I don't know that it's any of your business . . .'

'I'm not speaking to you as Honey Driver, owner of the Green River Hotel. I'm speaking to you as Honey Driver, crime liaison officer. I'm working with the police on this. Either I ask you the question or the police will be calling you in to answer the same question down at the station.' She shrugged. 'The choice is yours.'

The distant look turned hard. The corners of her bright-red mouth turned slightly downwards.

'It's a foregone conclusion. As the surviving partner of the business, I get everything.'

'Nobody else?'

'He has no family. Will that be all?'

Honey folded her arms and eyed the girl with a mix of amusement and malice. Camilla Boylan was too perfect for words.

'Forget what I said about the possibility of the police calling on you. You're now prime suspect. It's a dead cert.'

CHAPTER FOUR

It came as something of a relief for Doherty to arrive at the Green River Hotel even though it was unannounced.

Honey waved the coffee pot? 'Coffee?'

'I'm here in an official capacity,' he said.

Honey poured coffee.

'How well did you know Philippe Fabiere?'

'This well,' said Honey, indicating the ongoing paintwork with a sweeping wave of her right hand. 'Well enough to believe I was going to get this place fixed up, but not well enough to know he was earmarked for such a remarkable death.'

'Top marks for originality, whoever it was.'

Despite the dark subject matter, Doherty looked amused. He rubbed at his day-old stubble. He wore plain clothes, of course, but having stubble was part of the uniform. Plain-clothes cops liked to fit in with civilians.

She explained about the deposit and about Camilla Boylan being the sole beneficiary in the absence of a will.

Doherty looked surprised. 'But there is a will. Miss Boylan phoned me to say one had been discovered, so the granting of probate shouldn't take very long at all.'

Honey pulled a face. 'How very convenient for Ms Boylan.'

The dotty German couple waggling their fingers and smiling at her as they came through the door failed to lift her spirits, but she waved back all the same.

'You looked a bit down, my dear,' said Frau Hoffner. She had twinkling blue eyes and fluffy white hair that looked as though the slightest puff would blow it away.

'We brought you a cake,' added her husband.

He was tall, broad shouldered, and had a shiny face that looked as though it got a regular coating of beeswax.

'It is called a *cream horn*,' said his wife, her smile undiminished.

Aware that Doherty was hiding a grin behind his hand, she thanked them and said she would eat it later.

'We knew you English like cakes with your tea,' said Herr Hoffner.

Honey didn't enlighten them that her preference was for black coffee. English tea drinking was not what it had once been.

The couple paused on their way back up to their room to speak to the decorators.

'When's the job supposed to be finished?' Doherty asked.

Honey's attention was brought back from the Germans to him.

'Two weeks. I was lucky to get Philippe to do it. He's in such great demand, but he managed to fit me in with this big job he'd been doing at St Margaret's Court. His exact words were, "Them dudes are heavy going. I need a little light relief."' Just for a change he'd dropped the French accent. Honey was as grounded as he was.

Doherty made a puzzled frown. 'So you were the light relief?'

Honey shrugged. 'He referred to the people overseeing the St Margaret's project — the accountant, the project manager and the architect — as the three little pigs. Snouts in a trough come to mind.'

Doherty took out his mobile and scrolled down. 'I've been trying to make notes on this thing. Seemed a good idea, seeing as I'm always mislaying pens.'

Honey nodded. 'That's a very good idea. I wouldn't be without mine.'

'So you'll know how to use this?' he asked.

She ignored the hopeful look on his face. 'Mine's a different make than yours.'

She also ignored the sceptical glance. Lindsey was the one who sorted hers, though she wasn't about to admit that to him.

'Here goes,' he said, rightly convinced that she knew as much about the damned thing as he did.

She watched as he scanned the glowing screen. 'It's very smart,' she remarked, feeling that she had to say something.

He shook his head. 'It might look that way, but it isn't easy to operate. I don't know that I'll ever get the hang of this!'

Honey sniffed knowingly. 'Do you want me to summon the technical department?'

The answer had to be in the affirmative. Lindsey came along and sorted it out.

'Press this, this and this. And there you are!'

Although he nodded as though he understood her perfectly, there was a blank look on his face.

Honey handed her daughter the box containing the cream horn. 'I'll have it with my tea.'

'You don't drink tea.'

'I'll make an exception — in honour of Mr and Mrs Hoffner.'

Doherty suggested she accompany him to interview the architect in charge of the St Margaret's project.

'One of the three little piggies. Ferdinand Olsen. His offices are at Laycock.'

'There's a nice tea shop in Laycock,' Honey pointed out.

'As good a reason as any to go there.'

CHAPTER FIVE

A shiny brass plaque adorned a red brick mill, now converted into the offices of Ferdinand Olsen Associates. The mill dated from the time of William and Mary, when William Penn had given his name to Pennsylvania on the A46 just outside Bath and men had worn stockings and had buckles on their shoes.

There was a lane running to one side of the property and space to park outside on the cobbled street. The shop serving home-made scones with butter, jam and a choice of tea was just across the way. Honey's mouth watered as she eyed it covetously. But they were here on business, and that came first.

Plate glass doors opened into an atrium of old brick and huge roof trusses. A fountain tinkled in one corner next to a couple of mill stones and an oak mill wheel. Ahead of them people worked behind smoked glass in a ground floor drawing office. A flight of stairs led to more offices above.

Mr Olsen's office was on the first floor. Presuming the name was of Scandinavian origin, Honey had expected a blue-eyed blond. Standing before her was a swarthy man with a mass of shoulder-length curls and velvet-brown eyes, the kind usually described in romantic novels as 'smouldering'. He held out his hand and gave them both a firm handshake.

'Terrible thing to happen,' he said. The timbre of his voice was deep but not loud. But then, he was expressing his remorse at what had happened.

After offering them refreshments — which they both declined — he offered his help.

'In any way I can. Although I don't pretend to know that much about what happened.'

He smiled affably. For someone so swarthy he *was* quite handsome — rugged, though slim rather than heavily muscled. He'd cut quite a dash as a swashbuckling pirate, she thought — jerkin, red sash, white shirt and a sword dangling against his tight breeches.

The mental vision must have shown in her eyes.

'Are you feeling ill, madam?'

She was mortified to find she was gripping his hand too tightly.

'Sorry.' She turned scarlet. 'You weren't quite what I was expecting.'

Impossibly white teeth flashed against his tanned skin when he smiled.

'You're surprised I don't look like most Scandinavians. My mother was Spanish.'

Honey nodded. 'That would do it.'

'How long had you known the deceased?' The question brought the reason for their being here back into focus. Doherty had clearly noticed her attention had drifted.

Olsen obliged. 'Only since he was taken on as interior designer by the project management team. My company merely designed the alterations, drew up the plans and applied for permissions where needed. You may not be aware that St Margaret's Court has a Grade One listing. Modernising and improvement is a very delicate operation with such an ancient edifice. There are strict rules to be followed.'

As Honey listened her gaze dropped to his hands. They were big and lay flat on the desk, fingers splayed. Whoever was responsible for Philippe's cruel demise must have had strong hands, like Olsen's. She felt her throat constricting.

Doherty continued with the questions. 'Where were you the day before yesterday between the hours of ten p.m. and twelve midnight?'

'Certainly not at St Margaret's Court. I was attending an event at Bath Abbey. A Welsh choir was singing there.'

'Can anyone vouch for you being there?'

Honey knew instinctively what the answer would be.

'My wife. I'm not terribly keen on choirs, tone deaf in fact, but my wife bought the tickets and it pleased her for me to attend.'

'I may need to speak to your wife. Is she at home now?'

'Not in the house. She'll be in the field at the back. Just go round. She won't mind.'

The meeting yawned with disappointment. There would be no early solution to this case.

Olsen gave Doherty a list of the members of the project committee. 'There are basically three of us overseeing the project and a lesser committee attached to that.'

Doherty was impressed by the sumptuous offices. Such premises cost a great deal of money to maintain. He'd also seen the Ferrari parked at the front.

'Is that your car outside?'

Olsen nodded. There was a wary look in his eyes. 'Yes. There's no law against owning a Ferrari is there?'

'How much is the project worth?'

Olsen shifted slightly. The leather chair creaked. 'A little over five million.'

Honey swallowed. The Green River wasn't worth five million altogether. The St Margaret's Court Hotel was spending that amount on a refurb! Phew! The mind boggled.

'A lot of money,' Doherty remarked.

'Yes, but there are extra considerations with old buildings that do not arise with new builds. Special permissions have to be applied for.'

'The other people on the committee . . .'

'There are . . . or rather there were three of us. The owner, of course, myself and Joybell Peters of Mackintosh

Neate. They're the accountants with overall charge of project management.'

Joybell Peters would be interviewed. Apart from that they'd learned nothing except that Ferdinand Olsen had big hands.

'Did you notice them?' asked Honey as they settled back into Doherty's sporty little Toyota MR2. She gave him a visual image, placing her own hands around her neck. 'He had maulers the size of shovels.'

Doherty was trying desperately to avoid looking in the direction of the bright-red Ferrari.

'They didn't need to be big,' he said, sliding the gear stick into first. 'The victim wasn't strangled with a pair of hands. He was throttled with a lavatory chain.'

There was something about Ferdinand Olsen's big hands that fascinated — that and his smouldering good looks. He had such a lithe romantic look about him — tumbling black hair and brandy-brown eyes. The hands seemed somewhat out of place, almost as though they'd been borrowed from someone bigger and stuck on as an afterthought.

'Mrs Olsen first, then,' said Doherty.

'I'm with you.'

For some obscure reason, Honey had assumed that the Olsen residence would be similar to his office building — a tasteful mixture of old and new, plate glass windows stretching from floor to gable held within frames of green oak. Instead they were crunching up a gravel drive to a Jacobean monument. From its mullioned windows to its sturdy gables, Four Winds was the epitome of period pieces and the opposite of what Honey had expected.

'Heavenly,' said Honey, lowering her head so she could better see the full height of the place through the car windscreen.

'Must have cost a pile,' Doherty remarked.

'After seeing his office I did wonder how come he was involved in the refurbishment of a historic building. He lives in one.'

'Wish I did.'

'You do,' said Honey.

'Only part of one. I have a flat.'

'Lucky you.'

Doherty's apartment was part of a subdivided house in Cavendish Crescent, about a mile from the city centre and uphill all the way. Walking up there was hard work, but the view was to die for. The whole of Bath spread out in a panorama beneath it.

As instructed they made their way through a gate at the side of the house. A path led past the well-laid-out garden to another gate past a stable block, through yet another gate and into a field.

'Walk on! Walk on! Walk on!'

A woman stood in the middle of the field holding a lunge rein. A chestnut horse, neck arched and nostrils flared, was walking a circle around her. Every so often she flicked the tip of a long whip some distance from the horse's hooves.

Honey noticed the saddle on the horse's back and made comment. 'It's a young horse. She's training it to respond to the voice and get used to the weight of the saddle on its back.'

'Is she going to hit it?' Doherty asked.

'No. It's a lunge whip and it's only used for training horses. You'll also be pleased to know that I've never heard of it being used to chase away nosy policemen!'

'That is good to know.'

Doherty approached holding his warrant card high.

'Police,' he called out. 'I need to ask you a few questions.'

'I know,' she called back. 'My husband phoned to tell me you were coming.'

As she gradually brought the glossy-rumped horse to a standstill, Honey observed the wife of Ferdinand the Pirate. Mrs Olsen wasn't at all what she'd expected. For a start she wore a black-velvet Alice band holding back her pale-blonde hair. From all that she'd read, pirates' wives did not favour black-velvet Alice bands. Ribbons woven into tumbling ringlets were more their style. The jodhpurs, padded jacket and checked shirt didn't do the job either. A pirate's wife would wear a big dress with a low-cut bodice displaying her shoulders and a heaving bosom. Deirdre Olsen looked like a farmer's wife; though she might scrub up well — *just like you do*, Honey reminded herself.

The horse came into the circle in response to Deirdre Olsen's command of '*Whoa*.'

'He's a beautiful horse,' remarked Honey, stroking the soft muzzle between the flared Arab nostrils.

'Obviously a stallion,' said Doherty, as if he knew.

'Not for much longer. He's being gelded.'

Doherty winced. 'Ouch!'

Mrs Olsen threw him a wry grin. 'Don't worry, Mr Policeman. We only geld horses, not men — unless unduly provoked.'

Honey kept her head. 'He's an Arab. Right?'

'Right,' said Mrs Olsen, eyeing Honey as though to ascertain her horsy credentials — in other words, a wide behind and a devil-may-care attitude towards fashion. Seemingly liking what she saw, she opened up a little.

'This is the fourth colt I've had from his mother. I have three mares and one gelding — his half-brother, in fact.'

Mrs Olsen's first response had been cool and she had an ice cool voice. Her hairstyle was regrettable. Her face was devoid of makeup, her nose slightly red and her eyebrows straggly over pale blue eyes. She had great cheekbones, had possibly been a looker when younger, but had ceased taking care of herself. Perhaps Mr Olsen was no longer the love of her life, replaced by a love of horse flesh.

Feeling he didn't quite fit into this equine equation, Doherty stuck to the job in hand.

'Were you with your husband between the hours of ten and midnight the night before last?'

Mrs Olsen raised her straggly eyebrows. 'My husband's already told you that we were together.'

'I know,' said Doherty, showing no sign of impatience — yet. 'I need you to confirm.'

'Well, I wasn't with him! I went to a concert at Bath Abbey and he cried off saying he had a cold. Cold my *arse*!' She pronounced 'arse' with a great deal of emphasis. The upper class never dropped their aitches, thought Honey, not even in the middle of a word.

Mrs Olsen went on. 'I ride horses and my husband rides fillies, though his have two legs and they're usually wide open!'

Honey stifled a giggle.

It wouldn't be the first time that Doherty had dealt with a scorned woman whose husband was cheating on her. Getting even could become downright vicious.

'Are you sure about that, Mrs Olsen? And I want the truth. Perjury can be punished with a prison sentence.'

Mrs Olsen didn't bat an eyelid, continuing to stroke her handsome young horse.

'He phoned begging me to cover for him while promising that he wouldn't see that old trollop any longer. But in my husband's case I know that there will always be an old trollop — or a young one — whatever takes his fancy at the time. Well, I'm not going to cover for him. Let him stew. He deserves it.'

Now this was a turn-up. Sensing he was on to something, Doherty persisted. 'So who was he with?'

The horse rubbed his head against Honey's shoulder.

'He likes you,' said Mrs Olsen, beaming. Without needing to ask, Honey knew that the Olsens did not have any children.

Doherty gritted his teeth and asked the question again.

Mrs Olsen almost spat the reply.

'With Joybell Peters. She's one of the hotel directors who sits on the project committee with him. Sits on a lot more besides, if you ask me.'

Honey began feeling sorry for her. 'No wonder you prefer horses.'

Mrs Olsen turned suddenly prickly. 'Yes! And preferably gelded. Now, if you don't mind . . .'

She didn't wait for a response. Leading the horse by her side, she headed for the stables.

'Phew,' said Doherty, sighing with relief. 'That's one sore lady.'

Honey could have made some quip about Olsen getting his balls cut off at the same time as the horse, but something was troubling her.

'Why did Olsen need her to cover for him? Surely he knew she wouldn't. Why didn't he send us direct to this Joybell person?'

Doherty looked thoughtful. 'Number one, he truly believed she'd cover for him. Number two . . . well . . . I don't really know. I was going to say that he thought she was in the dark about him having another woman. Obviously she wasn't.'

Honey had been thinking the same thought. 'So someone must have tipped her off.'

Doherty swayed to and fro on his heels as he mulled it over. A light drizzle was beginning to fall. Honey stood throwing expectant looks between him and the hood of the sports car. At present it was folded back. The seats were beginning to collect a misty film of water.

Seemingly unperturbed, Doherty slid into the driver's seat.

Honey remained standing.

She folded her arms. 'Well?'

He blinked. 'Are you getting in?'

'How about putting the hood up, or don't you mind ruining your upholstery?'

He quickly flipped a switch on the dashboard.

'Sorry. I wasn't with it.'

'So where were you?'

He grinned. 'With you.'

'Where?'

'Somewhere special.'

* * *

The chestnut yearling nickered gently to his stable mates as Deirdre Olsen led him into his box. The horses were kept in spacious stalls divided by wooden barriers topped with iron railings. There was a loft overhead where hay and straw was stored. The wooden flooring was warped with age. Any movement overhead brought down a flurry of straw and dust. It fell now in front of her face. She backed out of the stall and looked upwards.

'I know you're up there. Come down. Now.'

The falling debris continued: bits of straw, bits of grain and plenty of dust. Footsteps sounded from those areas of the hayloft that were not covered with loose straw.

Deirdre moved slowly along to the ladder, the only access besides the overhead door where straw was taken in for storing.

She stopped dead when a booted foot appeared. The boots were tan and of the sort used by hikers. They had thick soles and metal hooks for the laces.

His jeans were baggy. A black-and-white-flecked sweater showed from beneath the waxed jacket he wore, and his chin was thick with grey stubble that matched his eyebrows. He had a rugged, rough look about him. Some might look at him and think him the salt of the earth. He was that all right. He was rough, he was rugged and he didn't give a damn about anything except getting by from one day to the next.

His smile was fleeting. 'That was lucky.'

Deirdre didn't respond. She was thinking.

'I think you'd better lie low for a while.'

He looked at her in disbelief and chanced a swift laugh. 'You're joking. I need the money. I've got a life to lead, you know.'

She raised her eyes without raising her head. For a brief moment the man's expression turned plaintive. It was a thoughtful, conniving kind of look.

'You can't go back there. Not yet. The police are nosing around.'

'But I need the money—'

The flat of her hand landed on his cheek with a resounding *thwack!* He stepped back.

'There was no bloody need for that!'

Face contorted with anger; she held a warning finger in front of his face. 'You will do as I say. You will not go back there until the coast is clear. Do you understand?'

He continued to rub the side of his face. A small spot of blood trickled from the corner of his mouth.

'Do you understand?' She glared at him more fiercely, the tip of her finger only inches from the tip of his nose.

He took his time responding, but at last he nodded, though the mocking smile stayed in place.

CHAPTER SIX

This was to have been a night of wine and roses and perhaps a nice juicy steak with all the trimmings. Before enjoying the fruits of their labours that evening, Honey and Steve had agreed to visit Joybell Peters in the afternoon and ask where she was on the night of the murder. Unfortunately things did not turn out as planned.

Doherty had only just picked Honey up from the hairdresser's when Lindsey rang to say that there was a problem. The chandeliers and French mirrors had arrived courtesy of an antique dealer named Fred Cook. 'That's not all,' Lindsey added. 'Some of the seniors want to stay on.'

This was better news. They'd already insisted on extending their one-night stay to three and now they wanted more. What a turn-up! Honey almost skipped with joy.

'They prefer a three star to a four star? Well, that's a result.'

'Don't get carried away thinking this is all good news,' said Lindsey. 'Herr Hoffner got bored. He's painting reception. I'm afraid he's upset the workmen.'

Honey groaned. Doherty dropped her off and went to interview Joybell Peters with a promise that he'd see her later.

As she swung into reception, the smell of paint and the sound of arguing came out to greet her.

Lindsey came steaming forward. 'They're not happy,' she said, indicating the two men in paint-splashed overalls. One of them came marching over purposefully, his bottom lip quivering.

'Do you see what he's done? *Do you see what he's done?*'

On repeating the words, his voice went an octave higher.

Honey looked. It seemed that Herr Hoffner had been very busy indeed. He'd finished what remained of the bare wall and was steaming into a second coat.

He saw her and without breaking stride called out, 'Don't worry, Mrs Driver. I will have this finished very quickly indeed!'

The two professional painters and decorators were not impressed.

'He's stealing the bread from our mouths! *The bread from our mouths*,' said the painter with the habit of repeating himself, the pitch of his voice worryingly close to becoming full soprano.

'It is all a fuss about nothing,' came the voice of Frau Hoffner. Until now she had made herself comfortable in the corner of a coffee-coloured sofa that had just arrived and was still covered in polythene. While her husband busied himself painting, Frau Hoffner knitted. On seeing Honey she got up, smiled and came tripping over.

'We have decided to stay on, Mrs Driver. The others are moving into a very smart hotel at our next stop — Stratford upon Avon, I think. But my husband does not care much for Shakespeare and he also gets very bored when we go on holiday. He likes to be busy, you see. It took me two years to persuade him to come on this trip . . . Men!' she finally exclaimed, and although she pretended to be critical of her spouse, it was obvious she absolutely adored him.

Honey thanked Frau Hoffner for her explanation while Herr Hoffner whizzed on with the paint roller.

The painter, whose name she'd recently found out was Warren, wasn't impressed, judging by his pink cheeks and glassy-eyed stare.

'Now look here, Mrs Driver . . .'

'He doesn't want paying,' Frau Hoffner added suddenly, fixing Warren with a sniffy lifting of her nose. 'So do not think that, my good man.'

There were many occasions in the everyday running of a hotel when tact and mediation were required — sometimes between guests, sometimes between staff, but most especially when the chef was about to brain the kitchen porter with a frying pan.

Herr Hoffner was something of a first. Honey had never had to accommodate a paying guest who didn't want to relax. So who was she to argue? The customer was always right. The next task was to placate the painter.

'Look at it this way, Warren,' said Honey. 'Herr Hoffner is bored. He doesn't want paying. Couldn't you let him help out? I'm desperate to have the job done as quickly as possible. I've got no objection to him giving a hand. I'll still pay the same rate. In fact, the sooner it's finished the better. Humour me. Please?' Her expression was as pleading as her tone of voice.

Warren seemed to consider this, one eyebrow drawn so deep that it was in danger of blinding him. 'And we'll still get the same amount of money, even if we finish early?'

It was a tough deal, but was she to argue? 'Exactly. Call it a sort of bonus.'

While he went off to chew it over with his workmate, Honey headed towards Fred Cook. She'd seen him out of the corner of her eye, standing with his arms crossed and an amused smile on his face. Having the advantage of great height he could see over everything to what was going on. His hearing too was probably better than anyone else's, seeing as he was so tall. He was as thin as a lamp post, round-faced, as bald as a coot and sported a thick moustache on his upper lip.

'You've got my chandeliers?' she asked breezily, looking hopefully at the large square boxes stacked around his legs.

'I have. I got them from France. And the mirrors.'

His amused smirk had all but disappeared. 'It's the two oil paintings I haven't got.'

Honey was disappointed. The two paintings were of genteel eighteenth-century ladies with pale skin and rounded breasts peeping above plunging necklines. She'd been a bit dubious about them at first, but Philippe had assured her that they would look quite wonderful in her blue-and-white reception area.

'So French. So typical of their century.'

She'd accepted his advice though she was not one-hundred-per-cent sure they would suit her clientele, most of whom were middle-aged and American with a smattering of European and Japanese. But there, she'd been persuaded to adopt this French look and at quite a pretty price. She'd assured him she could get something to suit at auction. He'd persuaded her otherwise.

'Not like these. They'll be an investment. Mark my words. I have a contact, a specialist in his field.'

So she'd marked his words and studied photographs of the two works of art he was attempting to sell her. The paintings, although no more than sixteen inches in length and destined to hang one above the other, had cost her a small fortune — or a large fortune by her standards. The money had come from the sale of some marine memorabilia her husband had left behind when he'd gone on his last sailing adventure. He'd sunk into the Atlantic and she'd been left everything. Most of the money had been put into the hotel. She'd forgotten about the bits and pieces relating to the boat. In all it had come to ten thousand pounds. Buying a couple of oil paintings — which Carl would have considered a ridiculous extravagance — had given her great satisfaction. After all, he'd never considered his sailing yacht an extravagance, so hey ho to it all!

Now there was a problem. Fred Cook looked very doubtful indeed.

'Monsieur Philippe's storeroom is empty.'

Honey thought about it. It made sense that Philippe would have somewhere to keep decorative items for use on specific jobs. Once the decorators had moved out, that was when he moved in to oversee the laying of carpets, the hanging of curtains and the embellishment of the whole work with paintings, antiques and carefully chosen pieces of furniture.

She pointed to the packing cases. 'But you have my chandeliers and my mirrors.'

'Yes, love. Monsieur Philippe delivered them before the . . . um . . . happening . . .'

'Before he got choked with a lavatory handle.'

'Is that what happened? Good grief. Anyway, he told me he was awaiting delivery of the paintings.'

Honey was puzzled. 'He told *me* they were already delivered.'

Fred Cook shrugged his angular shoulders. 'We won't ever know, will we, love? There's nothing in his storeroom now, that's for sure.'

CHAPTER SEVEN

Having been party to everything going on, it fell to Lindsey to impart consolation.

Honey sat behind the messy reception desk, her head in her hands. Nothing seemed to be going right.

'This could only happen to me!'

'Let's have a day out.'

Honey did not want a day out and said so. She spread her arms, indicating the confusion that was the Green River reception area. 'Look at this place! It's a mess!'

'Nothing that can't be overcome with a bit of tidying up.'

'Without my paintings,' Honey whined, her face screwed up like a cabbage patch doll. 'I can't possibly leave everything and go gadding about. I can't concentrate on anything except this place.'

'Precisely!'

Lindsey took each of her mother's arms in turn and shoved them into her coat.

'We're going out.'

'Like this?'

Honey was wearing jeans and a black sweater, the casual get-up she favoured when she wasn't meeting and greeting or out with someone she wanted to impress. She usually only wore it when she was doing the washing up or attending to the pot plants.

Lindsey looked her mother up and down. 'You'll do. Here. Put on your wellies.'

Giving in to her daughter was easier than resisting when she was in one of these moods. In that way, she was like her father. Carl had been very persuasive — so persuasive, in fact, that he'd got her into bed on their first date. No other guy had done that before or since. It still made her blush to think of it. And glow. Carl had been good at making a woman glow.

Honey found herself frog-marched out of the door to end up sitting in the back seat of Mary Jane's car.

'Your daughter reckons you need a day out, and I'm going to make sure you both get there,' declared Mary Jane.

Honey felt her stomach churning even before Mary Jane had started the car and bunny-hopped away from the kerb. Clutch control was not one of her finest skills. Neither was steering come to that.

The first thing that entered Honey's head was to wonder how long she would have to endure the ride.

'Where are we going?'

She resisted the urge to close her eyes, at least until they were out of the city.

'I'm going horse riding,' said Lindsey. 'And so are you.'

It was hard not to slide to the floor. What with riding in Mary Jane's 'vomit comet', plus the prospect of riding a four-legged brute with a mind of its own, today was going downhill at a rate of knots.

Deirdre Olsen was waiting for them outside the stable block around the back. Honey dragged her heels, head down. Mrs Olsen appeared not to recognise her as the woman who'd come calling with a police officer just a day or so before. Horses she remembered, it seemed. Humans less so.

She didn't enlighten her when Deirdre said, 'I've seen you around.'

'I expect you have,' Honey answered breezily enough. 'I ride as much as I can when I can.'

It was an absolute lie.

Lindsey rolled her eyes and mouthed, 'Wicked woman.'

Mary Jane stayed in the car. She was presently trying to write her memoirs about her time working as part-time help at a wedding chapel in Reno. That was when she'd had her first 'out-of-body experience', she'd told them. The minister had got drunk on communion wine — or he said it was communion wine. Though he was far from being minister of any mainstream church, more something off the cuff — the Church of Those Who Like to Do Their Own Thing. He'd stumbled in climbing up to his pulpit and knocked the lectern over. The lectern had hit the stiff cardboard cut-out of a married couple; this had tumbled over to hit a standard lamp, which in turn had fallen and knocked Mary Jane out cold. She'd been writing in the register at the time and reckoned she'd been flying above it while unconscious. She hadn't a clue what happened to the couple getting married.

One horse was black and the other was grey. Honey got the black one, a Welsh cob who seemed due for his afternoon nap. The grey one allocated to Lindsey was keener, but then she was a far better rider than her mother.

Although Honey had once had ambitions to be a top event rider, she'd never been very good at it. She said this to Lindsey as they made their way to the field.

'That's because you're top heavy and your legs are too short,' returned Lindsey. Sometimes daughters could be cruel.

They eventually reached the field.

'You seem capable, so I'll leave you to yourself,' Mrs Olsen declared, shutting the gate behind them.

Mother and daughter exchanged looks.

Honey didn't want to appear nervous, but she had to feel safe. Feeling safe was very important.

'It's been a long time. I wouldn't want it to run off with me.'

'Mother, you're riding a Dobbin.'

Of course she was right.

'Race you.'

Lindsey kicked her heels and off shot the handsome grey. Dobbin, whose real name was Mildred, played follow-my-leader without Honey having to do anything except cling on.

A little warning voice chimed in at moments like these. It did so now. *Try thinking about something else.*

A good idea. She couldn't have come to a more auspicious place, and not just to ride a horse.

'I'm hoping I'll learn something since I'm here,' Honey said breathlessly as she slowed from trot to plod beside her daughter. 'That woman's husband is one of the three on the project management committee at St Margaret's Court.'

'Uh oh! You're not going to dismount and go snooping, are you?'

'Well . . . not unless I see something interesting.'

Lindsey groaned. 'Mother . . .'

'Don't worry. I haven't seen anything of interest yet. Just horses, grass and the odd dollop of manure.'

'Good things come to those who wait.'

'Here's hoping,' grunted Honey, her fingers clawing at good old Mildred's mane.

It was just a case of resurrecting old skills. Eventually everything seemed to come together. Mildred finally got the idea that her rider was in charge and that breaking from a trot into a canter wouldn't result in a total collapse of the legs.

'I think I've got my sea legs,' shouted Honey while in the process of a slow canter past her daughter.

Lindsey, who had been doing wondrous things with the haughty grey, had slowed to a walk and appeared distracted.

Honey turned Mildred's stubborn head and went back.

'Did you hear what I said?' she cried gleefully, bouncing up and down at a rising trot.

'Sea legs are for people in boats, Mother. I think you mean you've got your seat.'

Honey looked over her shoulder in the direction of her derriere. It seemed stubbornly stuck to the saddle. She decided that having a reasonably sized bottom probably helped in the process of staying in the saddle.

'It looks OK. What do you think?'

Receiving no reply, she looked up. Daughter and horse were motionless.

Lindsey's eyes were fixed on a shallow copse and the smoke from a bonfire. 'I think we're being watched.'

'I don't see anyone.'

'There was someone there just now. I saw him — or her — dive for cover.'

Honey peered again in that direction and repeated that she couldn't see anyone.

'Well, there was someone watching us. He was standing next to the bonfire.'

'Let's go and see if he's still lurking around. Ask him what the game is.'

After dismounting and tethering the horses' reins, they climbed over the fence and into the copse. The trees were little more than saplings, their leaves rustling and making a sound like tin foil in the breeze.

'Yoo-hoo! Anyone around?' yelled Honey.

'Ye-es! Me-ee!' Lindsey yelled back.

'No need for sarcasm.'

Lindsey eyed her mother reproachfully. 'Really, Mother. Don't you know that undercover cops never draw attention to themselves?'

'There's no one around.'

'You don't know that for sure. Someone with something to hide isn't going to shout back, "Here I am. Come and get me!"'

Honey strode on until they were standing in front of the fire. The fuel on the fire had obviously been too damp to burn furiously. Instead, it smouldered, hence the plume of smoke.

'It's a stack of boxes,' said Lindsey.

'Boxes?' Honey frowned. Bending down she examined one of the boxes. 'There's an "ais" on the side.'

Honey was thinking about the familiarity of the box and the lettering when Lindsey broke into her thoughts.

'*Français*. Something in French or of French provenance.'

Honey straightened. 'That's just what I was thinking. Still,' she shrugged, 'it's only a box. A lot of things come from France nowadays.'

'Like your paintings?'

Exactly what Honey was thinking. It had always been something of a trial having a daughter who was too clever for her own good. Now she was being a mind reader too.

Honey seethed to think that someone was enjoying the provenance of the paintings she'd paid for. 'Let's go and have a word with Deirdre Olsen.'

Mrs Olsen was dishing out bran mash into buckets. She looked up when they wandered back into the yard.

'Had enough already?'

Honey mentioned about the man watching them. Mrs Olsen pulled a face.

'I don't employ any men, only girls. They love horses more, and they work better under a female boss. Men tend to get a bit shirty when you tell them they've done something wrong.'

Honey was inclined to agree with her. Smudger wasn't too good at taking criticism. For the most part she avoided giving it. Good chefs were hard to come by. Tact was the name of the game.

'He was burning some rubbish over by the trees,' offered Lindsey as she led her horse to its stall.

'I told you. I don't know who he is,' returned Deirdre Olsen, more gruffly now, her eyes shifting uneasily from the horse to Honey as she led Mildred into her stall. She swiftly shut the stable door behind the horse before Honey had a chance to enter. Not that she wanted to. The riding was fine; removing tack, brushing down and cleaning hooves was bloody hard work. *Still*, thought Honey, *shutting me out was a bit drastic. I've got nothing against Mildred and I don't think she's got anything against me.*

She persisted with her line of enquiry.

'I thought I recognised one of the boxes. I had some stuff from France arrive in a box like one of those being burned.'

'Did you now!'

There was no doubt that Deirdre was being deliberately offhand. Honey had a terrible urge to slap her broad backside with the riding crop she still carried. It certainly presented a large enough target as she bent down to clean out Mildred's hooves.

'You've already paid. No need to hang around,' Deirdre said over her shoulder.

'No problem,' said Lindsey. Her eyes met those of her mother over the back of the horse as she ably removed the saddle. She jerked her head sideways, a signal for Honey to wander a little, nose around if she wished.

Gingerly she backed away from the stall, sidling past the one Lindsey was hanging around in, making for the very end of the barn-like building.

The stall next to the grey Lindsey had been riding was empty. So was the one after that. In the gloom at the far end of the building where the light hadn't been switched on she thought she saw something move. It might only have been a shadow, but she moved to investigate anyway. According to Lindsey someone had been watching them outside in the field. Was that same someone watching them now?

Softly placing her footsteps, she inched her way closer and closer. Her heart began to race with the kind of excitement that only comes with apprehension — and fear.

Straw bedding was heaped to one side, and bales of hay were stacked immediately in front of her. Someone could have been hiding there, looking out at them.

Narrowing her eyes she leaned forward, attempting to peer behind the stacked straw. Slipping on a patch of muck, she reached out for support.

A chestnut head darted out over the top of a stall, knocking her off balance. The horse screamed and reared, nostrils flaring, hooves flailing.

Honey flattened herself against the wall opposite, her breath tight in her chest.

Deirdre Olsen came running.

'Captain! Captain!'

She didn't attempt to help Honey up. Lindsey was left with that job.

Once she'd calmed the horse down, her expression was less than pleased. 'Look! You stupid woman! See what you've done. You've upset him terribly!'

Honey tried to apologise, but Deirdre wasn't listening. She was talking to the horse.

'There, there, Captain. Mummy will kiss it better for you, darling.'

Honey swallowed her temper. The bloody woman was fussing over the bloody horse! Those flying hooves might have killed her.

'I think we'd better go,' Honey muttered as Lindsey helped her brush the dirt and debris from her clothes.

'Mother, you're shivering.'

'That horse scared me.'

'Seems to me like he was pretty scared too.'

Honey noted her daughter's frown. 'We scared each other.'

'Are you sure there was no one else here?'

In all honesty she couldn't be sure. She might have seen more if the horse hadn't gone crazy. She said so to Lindsey.

'Horses don't go crazy for nothing. Something has to spook them.'

'Our friend from the bonfire?'

Had she detected the smell of smoke? She tried to remember but the crazy horse had sent all logical thoughts scuttling from her head. She remarked on this to Lindsey as they made their way back to the car.

Lindsey was thoughtful. 'Horses can scare at the smell of smoke.'

They took one last look at Deirdre and her horse. The former was bending over, aiming a hosepipe into the fitted water butt. Her rear obscured the view.

'They say that people get to look like their pets,' Lindsey remarked. 'That includes horses. Do you think she resembles her horse?'

Honey glanced over her shoulder. 'Only from the rear end.'

Lindsey looked, nodded and agreed with her.

CHAPTER EIGHT

Joybell Peters was in her late thirties, had platinum shoulder-length hair and wore a red suit with black tights. She also wore big earrings and a painted red smile. Strong perfume wafted from her clothes each time she waved a hand to emphasise something she said. A diamanté elephant sparkled from the collar of her suit jacket and vaguely matched her earrings.

She smiled and straightened in her chair as Doherty entered.

He liked to think he'd made an impression. Perhaps she was expecting an older bloke. He heard the unmistakable *hush* of nylon stockings as she crossed one leg over the other. This was a gal who knew how to entice. Another time, another guy. He was here on serious business.

After clearing his throat, he introduced himself. 'Detective Inspector Stephen Doherty.'

'Steve!' she gushed with open-mouthed exuberance. 'What can I *do* for you?'

The sound of rasping stockings was repeated. Different leg.

She said the word 'do' as though it encompassed a whole variety of likely services. Doherty kept to the script and outlined the basics — she'd been having a fling with Ferdinand Olsen.

'We understand he was with you at the time in question.'

The inviting smile froze. 'Did he tell you that?'

'No. His wife did.'

She shrugged as though it were the most normal thing in the world. In a way, it was. Men and women being what they were, regardless of marriage vows, sometimes one attracted the other. And with Mrs Olsen preferring horses, it was only to be expected.

'Yes. We were together. Ferdinand's good company. Good looking too.'

'He's married.'

'So?' She tossed her silvery mane, her eyes and her earrings flashing in unison.

Doherty gave her the 'casual but tough street cop' look, folding his arms and eyeing her as though she were the biggest liar he'd ever met — which she might very well be.

'Don't you think it's a bit out of order for you to be screwing another woman's husband? A business associate at that. Conflict of interest and all that . . .'

She shrugged her elegant shoulders. 'Not at all. She spends more time with her horses than she does with Ferdy.'

Though he had not intimated the fact, Doherty had been jealous of Ferdinand Olsen. He was smooth, sophisticated and most definitely a ladies' man, the sort who had no problem picking up women. Now it seemed he wasn't that irresistible. His own wife preferred her horses. Poor bloke!

He focused on the line of questioning. 'Regardless of that, surely Mrs Olsen wouldn't have been that pleased when she found out.'

The light of exuberant sexuality suddenly dulled the exquisitely made-up face. Folding her silky-smooth hands before her, nails slicked with gleaming red varnish, Joybell sighed.

'Poor Philippe. He had such exquisite taste and flair. Everyone I know went to him for his interior design skills. He was the best in Bath. His father wanted him to join him in the family business. Philippe toed the line for a while, but it didn't last. He was such an artistic man. Goodness, it would have killed him to stick to making concrete blocks for a living.'

'He helped his father make concrete blocks?'

Joybell interlocked her fingers with their red varnished nails. 'His father made block-making machinery for manual operation in developing countries. Philippe — or George as he was then — made the blocks as a sideline. He hated it. So I am reliably informed.'

'So you admit to being with Ferdinand Olsen on the night in question?'

'Of course I was.'

There was something about Joybell Peters' attitude that bothered Doherty. He couldn't put his finger on it, but he'd come across enough love triangles in his time to know an odd one when he saw it. However, she'd confirmed Olsen's alibi, so there was nothing more he could say.

Once he was finished, she followed him to the door.

'Is a policeman ever off duty?' she breathed as he opened the door. Her chin was almost resting on her shoulder. She was standing close. Too close.

'Of course.'

'Perhaps we could meet up when you're free.'

He regarded her for a moment before shaking his head. 'I'm afraid that isn't possible. You're a witness, Ms Peters. You might even be more than that.'

She jerked her chin back in surprise. 'Pardon?'

'Everyone's a suspect until the case is solved.'

He left her looking stunned. Somehow it pleased him.

Once outside he studied the names on the list of other people besides the main three responsible for managing the refurbishment of the St Margaret's Court Hotel. The builder contracted to do the job was a big firm that had a long association with Bath and historic buildings in particular: Paul Paling and Sons Ltd. Making an instant decision, he headed in that direction.

Honey's call came just as he'd reached the rather plain building that served as the company's headquarters at the bottom of town close to the river. She told him about the missing paintings and the empty storeroom.

He pulled a face as he thought about it — bottom lip out, eyes piercing the toes of his shoes. 'Could he have moved the stuff somewhere else, somewhere Fred doesn't know about?'

Honey was climbing the walls. 'No way! Philippe trusted Fred. He would have told him. Philippe's stock has been stolen, I tell you, and my paintings with it.'

Doherty didn't need to be told that Honey was frantic.

'Now, calm down. They were only paintings.'

'Ten grand's worth of paintings.'

'Shit!'

'I know the money came from selling off some of Carl's old junk, but that's not the point. I need them to finish off the Louis Quatorze look.'

'Can't Louis Quatorze sell you something else to suit?' Although Doherty liked old places, he didn't know much about British history and hadn't a clue about French.

Honey snarled. 'It's not a high street chain store! Louis Quatorze — King Louis the Fourteenth — of France. It's a specific look based on the period of his reign.'

'Sorry. Look, leave it with me. I'll get a team round there. In the meantime, if you could ask around . . .'

She said that she would.

'I'll be with you as soon as I can.'

'I would appreciate that.'

'Leave it with me. I'll think of a way you can show your appreciation.'

* * *

Honey was still fuming after she put down the phone. On the plus side, the refurbishment of the reception area was going well, thanks to the intervention of a German tourist who didn't know the meaning of relaxation.

Herr Hoffner had turned the Green River Hotel into a hive of activity, though at present there was something of a lull. The German was sharing sandwiches with the workmen. His wife was nowhere to be seen, though her knitting was bundled into the corner of the polythene-covered sofa. Once the decorating was finished, the polythene protection would be whipped off and the true beauty of the sofa fabric finally exposed.

Honey admired the brightening walls. The second coat had been applied and was drying nicely. Now Herr Hoffner and his team were undercoating the woodwork. The kindly and diligent gentleman appeared to have taken over supervision of the project, and the decorators had fallen in line. Their pace was slower than his, but he didn't seem to mind.

After the problem with the paintings, the area was now a little oasis of calm, and Honey's blood pressure steadied. That was, until Mary Jane came down the stairs.

Wearing a wrinkly, worried expression, the tall, gaunt American stopped halfway down, leaned over the banister, and beckoned her over with a loud hiss.

Honey tried not to frown. Frowning caused wrinkles. Deep inside she felt stirrings of apprehension. Problems usually came trotting along behind when Mary Jane wore that expression and hissed like that. Winding her way between paint pots and over dust sheets, she found herself looking up into Mary Jane's very blue and very worried eyes.

'We have a problem,' said Mary Jane. 'I think I've done something I shouldn't have done.'

Honey's apprehension grew from a stirring to a torrent.

Just for once there was no twinkle in Mary Jane's eyes. This was worrying. And she'd interlocked 'we' and 'I' in the same statement.

'What?'

Honey considered the possibilities. Frau Hoffner was not around. Was she in Mary Jane's room threatening to teach her how to knit? Mary Jane wasn't the knitting kind. Neither was Honey for that matter. *Drop one, stitch one* never happened with her knitting. She tended to drop everything and end up with a knitted scarf that could loosely be termed *perforated* and might be more suitable for catching fish in the North Sea.

As Mary Jane was in secretive mode, voice barely above a whisper, Honey leaned closer so she could hear better.

'What appears to be the problem?'

Mary Jane's words tumbled out machine-gun style. 'It's Gerda. The German lady. She's gone into a trance. I was only doing a demonstration. She was quite keen, but circumstances arose and caused a problem. Help! What do we do? Help!'

Visions of being sued gave speed to Honey's feet. She almost vaulted over the banister but settled for a more conservative dash up the stairs.

Frau Gerda Hoffner was sitting in an antique armchair, her eyes vacantly staring at the corner cupboard. Her hands were resting on the chair arms.

Honey bent down in front of her, waving her hands across Frau Hoffner's eyes. Frau Hoffner didn't even blink.

As a cold sinking feeling dropped from her throat to her knees, Honey looked at Mary Jane. 'You got her into it. You must know how to snap her out again?'

Mary Jane hunched her shoulders and spread her hands. Her expression was of total confusion, if not helplessness. 'How can I? I didn't mean to get her into something this deep in the first place!'

Honey rolled her eyes and briefly thought about hiding in the dry goods store, adjacent to the jar of glacé cherries and the sweet little Virginia amaretti biscuits they served with coffee. There should be enough amaretti to keep her going until Frau Hoffner came out of her trance. Or the men in white coats came — for one or both of them.

The fates were responsible for an act of gross unfairness. There was Herr Hoffner doing his bit for European working relations by assisting decorators who hadn't initially wanted his assistance and doing it pretty well by the look of things.

Locking his wife out of her own body was no way to repay him.

Drastic situations called for drastic measures. But what? 'You have to do something.'

Mary Jane's eyes were bulging. 'What?'

Honey shrugged helplessly. 'I don't know. Isn't there some procedure to get people out of trances? You know, like some words that have to be spoken or potion to be drunk.'

'I do beg your pardon!' Mary Jane looked quite insulted. 'I am a professor of the paranormal, not a witch. My name's Mary Jane not Morgana le Fay!'

Honey just about remembered who Morgana le Fay was before opening her mouth and putting her foot in it. Mary Jane got very touchy about anything to do with King Arthur and the Knights of the Round Table. She'd regressed there at some time. Honey had made the mistake of asking her if she'd been a serving wench. She'd snapped back that she'd been no such thing. 'I wasn't a servant! I was glorious. I was handsome and tall in the saddle. I, my dear Honey, was Sir Lancelot!'

Visualising a very tall Californian woman of senior years as the lover of Queen Guinevere and sword fighting with the best of them was pretty hard going.

Frau Hoffner had not moved from the chair. She hadn't blinked either. A sudden terrible thought struck her.

She bent down again and stared into the woman's face. 'She's not dead, is she?'

Mary Jane leaned down beside her, looked and shook her head. 'No. I can see the breath from her nostrils disturbing her moustache.'

It was true. With each breath the fine hairs on Frau Hoffner's upper lip fluttered slightly.

Now what?

'Sometimes a big shock can jolt them out of things like this,' offered Mary Jane. 'Sometimes it's just the presence of somebody who happens to be their opposite in terms of soul and body.'

'And that person is?'

Mary Jane shrugged. 'Search me. We won't know until it happens.'

'But that could take for ever! And what if her opposite never turns up? What then?'

Being sued for millions now seemed a very distinct possibility. Panic set in big time. She fought to regain control. Thinking straight was what was needed — logical thinking, the first rule of which was to retrace your steps and see where you may have gone wrong.

'But how did this happen in the first place?'

'I introduced her to Sir Cedric. She shook his hand.'

This was getting crazy. Sir Cedric was a ghost and Honey didn't believe in ghosts. Not really. Only sometimes when she didn't want to upset Mary Jane's feelings.

'Right. Now think back. How did you get her into this in the first place? Is there a possibility that you can reverse the steps you took and get her back to normal?'

Mary Jane heaved a huge sigh, her bony shoulders seeming to sag under the weight of it.

'I'll try.'

'Good.'

The urge to run away and play at being an ostrich was now too powerful. There was nothing Honey could do. Mary Jane had got Gerda Hoffner into this situation; only Mary Jane could get her out. Her own presence was superfluous. She told herself she'd made an executive decision.

'I'm going out.'

She headed for the door.

Mary Jane pointed out the obvious. 'There's no point calling for a doctor.'

Keen to avoid a situation she neither understood nor had a clue how to remedy, Honey was taking the coward's way out. She made her excuses.

'I've got some important things to deal with regarding the murder of Philippe Fabiere.' She didn't add that she might also check her Public Liability policy. Hopefully the premiums were all paid up.

Heading for the door, she couldn't help rolling her eyes to heaven. 'I'll leave Frau Hoffner in your capable hands,' she added, hand tightly wound around the door handle.

Honey skedaddled. She knew nothing about trances and out-of-body experiences and all the other stuff Mary Jane believed in so fervently. What's more, she didn't want to know. All she knew was that she couldn't stay in the hotel while this was going on.

Grabbing a Jaeger velvet jacket with braided trim, she tore through reception and hit the street running — or at least walking very quickly.

She was in urgent need of a diversion. The day was bright and breezy, so she was glad of the coat. The air had a bite and a smell to it. The bite was a remnant of winter. The smell was of new buds breaking out into a mild spring.

By the time she'd got to the auction house her footsteps were not quite so speedy. The problems of the Green River Hotel were behind her, though their after-effects were never more than a few steps behind. The questions were like noisy butterflies fluttering around her head.

The problem with Frau Hoffner didn't seem quite so serious. Perhaps it had something to do with the amount of oxygen she was breathing in. She kept telling herself that Mary Jane would sort it out. Hopefully.

Thinking of more weighty matters should help her get things in perspective. The number-one question was, who would want to kill Philippe Fabiere? A rival, came the resounding answer, and according to Camilla Boylan, Philippe had had quite a few. Who was his greatest rival?

'Julia Porter,' she muttered. Julia had given her a quote for the reception area in competition with Philippe. Julia had come across as rather domineering, intent on impressing her style without regard for the client's point of view.

What else did she know about her? Not enough, she decided. She took out her phone and dialled someone who did.

Casper answered.

'What do you know about Julia Porter?'

'Do you want me to dish the dirt or merely give you a potted biography?'

'Start with the biography. We'll see where we go from there.'

Casper related what he knew.

Julia came from a wealthy background — very wealthy, her father being a baronet and her mother an ex-showgirl with long legs and a history of showing much more than that on the stage of the Moulin Rouge in Paris.

Julia was what those of her social class would call a fine-looking filly: blonde, blue eyes and immaculately turned out. She'd also had the benefit of a private education, and although some strings had been pulled to facilitate a place at a top university, she had opted to start her own business.

Easy peasy. Daddy provided the money. She'd gone into interior design. She wasn't bad at it and for a time got all the plum jobs in Bath — until Philippe came on the scene. She'd hated him on sight, though she smiled through her hostility. But you could see it in her eyes. Honey mentally ticked her name.

'That's the basic biography,' said Casper.

'And the dirt?'

'Ah! She's been around the block with a few brickies, bankers and polo players. Not married. Not even engaged. I did hear that she was having an affair with the Russian who bought St Margaret's Court.'

'A serious affair?'

Casper hummed and hawed. 'Depends what you mean, my dear girl. Let us settle for calling it a *career relationship*.'

'She was after the interior design contract.'

'Correct.'

She thanked him. What he'd told her was certainly food for thought.

Members of the hotel staff were also a possibility. Then there were the other people on the project management committee other than the three pigs — the interior designer, the architect and the accountant. And what about Camilla? She was definitely a suspect. She stood to inherit everything he'd left, including the storeroom full of antiques — which weren't there anymore. So that in turn could mean that it might have been someone coveting his hoard of valuables, in which case . . .

'Here!'

She blinked as a cup of hot tea was placed in front of her.

'I've even brought out one of my finest china cups. There's only three left of a set of twelve. They're the office specials. You look as though you could do with a cup of hot tea, hen.'

Her mind came back from its flights of fact-based fantasy. She was standing at the counter in the reception area of Bath's premier auction house. Now, how the devil had she arrived here?

'How did I get here?'

'You walked, hen.'

She frowned. 'I was doing a lot of thinking.'

'Thinking too much causes wrinkles. I've also heard it said that if you're having worried thoughts your mind will take charge and guide your steps to a place where you feel comfortable. So here you are!'

Alistair, a red-haired mountain of a man, was eyeing her from behind the counter of her favourite auction house. It was Alistair who had plonked the tea in front of her — in a Royal Worcester cup with mismatched saucer, no less.

'Do I really look as though I've taken leave of my senses?' she asked, trying for a glimpse of her reflection in the glass-fronted cabinets behind him.

He made a disapproving clicking sound. 'Would I have got out my best china if you didn't?'

She shook her head woefully and took a sip. A thought suddenly hit her. Alistair had his ear to the ground in the antiques trade. Here in the heart of antique auction land was as good as anywhere to start in the pursuit of Philippe's killer and her bare-bosomed ladies.

Folding his arms on the counter, he eyed her speculatively. 'Well, come on then, hen. Spill out whatever you're holding in. Ask me what you want to ask me.'

She raised her eyes. Alistair had a huge red beard, so it was difficult to know whether he had a mouth in there at all — it was that well hidden. She was sure he was grinning.

She took another sip of tea. It warmed her as well as loosening her tongue.

'You know that Philippe Fabiere was killed.'

'Aye,' he said, one hand rising to stroke his beard. 'I did hear the news. What a way to go.' He tutted as though Philippe had been careless to die like that.

'Fred tells me his store has been cleared out of all the good stuff. There's only bits of furniture left.'

'As in tidied up or stolen?'

'The latter, I'm afraid.'

He raised his eyebrows. 'That's very unfortunate.'

'We could be jumping to conclusions. Perhaps he'd merely cleared it out and not told Camilla. Do you know whether he had another store somewhere?'

'One he'd want to keep secret from the bonny wee girl?' He shook his head. 'I don't believe he did, but you never can tell. Interior designers are different from antique dealers. They're not secretive about what they've bought and how much profit they're likely to make. The items are only pieces of a whole, the icing on the cake of a project. Blokes like Philippe — bless the wee man — are very artistic. They count the aesthetic value of an item above money . . . on the whole, that is — generally speaking.'

He seemed suddenly to have second thoughts. 'Of course, I could be wrong. You say that there was only furniture left?'

She nodded. 'Does that have any significance?'

He gave a so-so shake of his head. 'Could be that they only took what they could carry. Porcelain, silver — that kind of thing. The more expensive stuff as it works out. The value of antique furniture has dropped these last years. Porcelain is still highly collectable. A different market to interior design, but still . . .'

She told him about the paintings she'd bought. 'All I've got left are the photographs he showed me.'

'Is that right, hen? Well, in that case, how about you bringing them along and showing them to me? If I've got them imprinted here,' he said, pointing at his forehead, 'maybe I'll notice them if they come up for auction. Then we'll know, won't we, hen?'

She agreed to do that.

The tea was almost gone. She eyed the bottom of the cup.

'Would you like another?'

She wanted to say yes but her thoughts had returned to another pressing subject. The thought of going back to the Green River was giving her the heebie-jeebies. What if Frau Hoffner wasn't out of her trance? Would her husband run amok with the paintbrush? She could just about handle that. But what if he sued? What would she do then? Of course, in the liability stakes Mary Jane was more liable than she was. But could it be said that she'd been allowing her premises to be used for questionable purposes?

She imparted her concern to Alistair.

He raised his eyebrows. 'Questionable purposes? I don't think that's illegal. It's immoral purposes you have to watch out for.' He winked.

It made her smile, but worry was still there.

'Any chance of a job?' she asked.

If he was surprised by her question, he didn't show it.

'If you ever need one, I'm sure we can fit you in.'

The response gave her hope and made her feel better. There was a light at the end of the tunnel, a future doing something if all else failed.

There was nothing for it but to bite the bullet and go back, though she'd take it slowly. She might even stop for a bag of home-made fudge on the way. Fudge helped calm her nerves, besides which it might be the last bag she could enjoy if all her money and property went to recompense the Hoffners.

It came as something of a surprise to hear the clicking of knitting needles the moment she hit reception. The fact that everything seemed so calm and back to normal stopped her in her tracks. Frau Hoffner had reclaimed the corner of the sofa. She beamed sweetly, her cheeks pink as sugared plums.

'Good day, Mrs Driver.'

Honey worked her jaw to prevent it from seizing up in the down position. She managed a weak 'good day'. She hoped she didn't look like a goldfish.

Mary Jane once again appeared halfway down the staircase. She was wearing a sky-blue outfit with fluffy blue shoes. Just for once her expression was more shocking than her outfit, though the glassy-eyed look was gone. The panic was obviously over. Leaning over the banister, she whispered into Honey's ear.

'Everything is fine. It was so easy. So quick.'

Honey sighed with relief as the burden of the worst-case scenario fell from her shoulders.

'There. I'm no expert in these matters, Mary Jane, but I did think reversing what you'd done would work.'

The fact that she'd seemingly been proved right made her feel smug.

Mary Jane punctured her smugness.

'Remember I told you about how an opposite soul appearing could jerk her out of it?'

'Ye . . . sss,' Honey said slowly.

'Well, it happened. Your mother appeared!'

Honey weighed up the immensity of this pronouncement.

So! Her mother was the exact opposite of Frau Hoffner. She glanced between the two Germans — Frau Hoffner knitting contentedly while her husband made himself useful. Her mother on the other hand had never knitted in her life; never, ever had she looked, nor would she ever look, homely. On reflection it seemed totally logical. Of all the people in all the world, her mother had come flouncing up the stairs and into

Mary Jane's room demanding to know where her daughter was. Lindsey had gone to the gym. Her mother had learned not to interrupt a chef when he was at full throttle with his meat cleaver so had steered clear of the kitchen. Mary Jane was the next port of call when it came to enquiring about her daughter's whereabouts.

'Hannah! I need to speak to you.'

Just for once Honey was genuinely glad to hear her mother's voice.

'Mother! I wasn't expecting you. Are you stopping for coffee?'

This morning Gloria Cross, Honey's mother, was a vision in a black-velvet jacket braided in dark blue, a yellow, red and green patterned blouse with a black background, and dark-blue trousers. Her kitten-heeled boots were a shade of silk green. It was also a fact that she had never, ever looked on while her husband painted walls; all her husbands had been more Wall Street than wall painters.

'Of course. I'll see you in the conservatory. Get the coffee taken there.'

'I will.'

Usually she would have muttered something under her breath. Her mother threw orders around like confetti at a wedding. On this occasion Honey owed her a debt of gratitude. But first she had to find out a few details from Mary Jane.

'Does she remember seeing Sir Cedric?'

Mary Jane shrugged. 'Shall I ask her?'

Honey slammed a restraining hand on Mary Jane's arm. 'Let's let sleeping dogs lie, shall we?'

She was about to join her mother when she noticed something. As was the way of things in the hotel trade, another day, another problem. The secret was to anticipate problems before they happened or alleviate their effect. She could see a problem developing before her very eyes.

Two extra men were attempting to install one of the crystal chandeliers. On her way to the conservatory, her mother had paused and was proceeding to give them directions as to how it should be fitted.

At present she was standing directly beneath the sparkling and very heavy objects. Judging by their expressions, the electricians didn't seem too happy about it.

'Not too high,' her mother was shouting up at them, one painted talon pointing to the exact position she wanted it to hang from. 'Lengthen the chain. Lengthen the chain!'

The two men were straining for all they were worth to get the light exactly where her mother wanted it. She saw the lips of one man move in a silent mutter. It wasn't difficult to guess what he was saying.

'Mother!'

Honey grabbed her mother's arm. 'Leave the men to get on with their job, Mother.'

Gloria Cross pouted with pink-lipped petulance. 'Give me one good reason why I should!'

Honey pointed at the men. 'See that chain they're lengthening?'

Her mother nodded.

'If they make it much longer, they're likely to hang you with it.'

CHAPTER NINE

Camilla Boylan marched determinedly between the iron railings bordering the checkerboard apron in front of a Regency town house in Henrietta Street. A woman draped in Gucci was about to put her key in the door.

'Julia!'

The shout made the woman stop in her tracks. All traces of a pleasant welcome fell from her face when she saw who was approaching.

'Camilla!'

On sighting Camilla, Julia turned the key quickly and leapt over the threshold, meaning to slam the door.

Too late. Camilla had the foresight to jam her foot in the gap.

'I want to talk to you.'

Julia was her usual sniffy self. 'Well, I have nothing to say to you whatsoever!'

Camilla flinched. When it came to cut-glass voices, Julia's could slice a jugular.

As the daughter of an ex-showgirl, Julia towered over her would-be rival. Camilla was made of sterner stuff and refused to be intimidated. Her acid-green eyes narrowed as they peered upwards into Julia's frozen face.

'I know what you did,' she snarled.

Julia's eyes reflected her disquiet, blinking as though suddenly blinded by a bright light.

'I don't know what you're talking about.'

Camilla raised her voice. 'Shall I shout it out for the whole street to hear? Shall I shout out to everybody that you use underhand means to further your career? Besides Daddy's money, that is. Shall I also tell them that some of your dealings are downright illegal? Who else would buy stolen goods from a Warsaw museum?'

Attracted by the raised voice, a few passers-by looked in their direction.

Julia's face turned red. 'You'd better come in,' she said, her voice lower now but maintaining a distinct tone of unwelcome.

Julia's house was a monument to Regency splendour and the world of interior design. As a designer she was known for blending old with new, shiny surfaces with old masters. She was also a great collector of Chinese and Japanese pottery. A whole battalion of the stuff sat on a long walnut sideboard that had once done service in a stately home. A gilt-framed mirror caught the minimalist beams of overhead spotlights.

Camilla picked up a blue, orange and white sweet dish. The design was known as Imari. The piece was not hugely valuable but expensive enough. She let it fall. Julia caught it. She hugged it to her chest, her face white with alarm.

'I'm going to screw you into the ground,' hissed Camilla. 'Your business depends on knockers, thieves and how good you are in bed. But it didn't work with the Russian, did it, Julia? I wonder, does your father know what a tart you are?'

'You've got no proof,' Julia hissed back. Her voice was steady, but the clichéd retort showed just how unnerved she actually was.

Camilla smiled. 'You don't fool me, Julia. Not like you fooled Philippe. He's left everything to me and now you're going to have real competition. Philippe was an artiste not a businessman. It was easy to convince him that entering into a loose partnership was a good idea. Just take it as read that the partnership is dead and buried and I'm no longer restricted by a bloke who was too soft for his own good.'

'We had a good working relationship.'

'You screwed him. He lent you stuff from that storeroom and you never gave half of it back. And now the goods have gone, or at least the decent stuff has. Where are they, Julia? What have you done with them?'

'I don't know what you're talking about.'

Julia proceeded to throw her keys in a dish and take off her jacket, her eyes flickering nervously between her treasured porcelain and Camilla's menacing presence.

'You took Philippe's stuff.'

'It was mine. Half mine, anyway. Philippe said that if anything happened to him I would put it to better use than his parents.'

'Whatever, you cannot deny that the other half is mine. I was his business partner, not you!'

Her scowl deepening, Camilla ran her fingers over a Chinese figurine of a reclining mandarin. With one sweep of her arm the porcelain figures and dishes were sent crashing to the floor.

'I want the stuff back, Julia. I know you have it.'

Julia was on her hands and knees gathering up the bits of broken china. 'You cow! You fucking cow! Look what you've done!'

'I'll smash more and I'll smash you,' snarled Camilla. 'I want everything from the storeroom returned. Now!'

'I haven't got it!' Julia screamed. 'I don't know where it is!'

Camilla grabbed a bunch of Julia's sleek blonde hair, using it to tug her head back so she could glare into her face. 'Once a liar, always a liar. Now get it back for me. Pronto! Or else.'

CHAPTER TEN

Steve Doherty sat considering the implications of the raffle ticket in his hands. The *winning* raffle ticket . . . He could hardly believe it. He'd actually won something. The manager at St Margaret's Court Hotel had phoned him that morning to say he had won a five-course dinner with champagne and the honeymoon suite for the night. Now all he had to do was pluck up the courage to ask Honey if she'd join him. Honey accepting his invitation for a night of luxury and unbridled passion he could cope with. Rejection was another matter entirely, and although he'd never admit to it, his pride would be dented.

His phone's ringtone caught him on the point of ripping the ticket into tiny pieces, halting his hand. The decision could wait.

'Doherty,' he said tersely as he tucked the ticket back into his inside pocket.

Mathison, the new Forensics guy, was on the other end.

'Guess what?' He sounded breathlessly excited.

Doherty was in no mood for guessing, but Mathison was new, and as such each piece of the crime jigsaw was incredibly exciting; you could hear it in his voice.

Doherty was less than forthcoming. Excitement wasn't his thing in the world of solving crime. Only facts mattered.

'Enlighten me.'

Mathison's deep breathing was clearly audible.

'He didn't just choke to death. A little poison helped him on his way.'

'Christ!'

'Belladonna. A nice old-fashioned poison.'

'I see.'

'We don't know how it was administered.'

'Well, there's a thing.'

'But we're looking into it.'

'That's good to know.'

'He'd also been drinking,' said Mathison, sounding as though he'd ballooned to twice his normal size. 'Poison and alcohol are a lethal combination.'

'You don't say.'

'I'm terribly pleased at the outcome.'

Doherty pointed out the obvious. 'We haven't found the murderer yet!'

Mathison was deflated. 'No, but we've at least identified the poison. I mean—'

Doherty severed the connection. Now he had two things to worry about. Number one, who the hell would use belladonna to poison Philippe Fabiere? And why the china lavatory handle? Why poison the poor chap in the first place?

Number two, Honey's reaction when he told her he'd won the raffle prize.

CHAPTER ELEVEN

Despite the empty rooms, the smell of fresh paint and the crumpled dust sheets spread over the bare floorboards, Honey was in a pretty good mood. And at the rate Herr Hoffner was breezing through the reception area with a full paint roller, it wouldn't be long before the mess was far behind.

So it was quite a shock when Doherty phoned to tell her that Philippe had been poisoned.

'Isn't poisoning a woman's weapon of choice?' she asked.

'Notable murderers have used it. I suppose you'd consider them creative types.'

'I see.' She was currently in the kitchen, thoughtfully watching Smudger sprinkling spices and herbs into a risotto mix like there was no tomorrow.

Doherty assured her it was true. 'On the other hand, whoever shoved the piece of china down his throat was fairly strong. It's not easy to do whether the victim's living or dead.'

Honey took an involuntary swallow of the warm cookie she'd pinched from a tray. 'What was the murderer trying to say?' she wondered out loud. 'And why lock the bathroom door?'

'I'm presuming it was just a delaying measure. Someone wanted time to get away before the body was discovered.'

Honey sighed heavily. 'Poor Philippe. He was such a nice guy. He was so . . . vibrant.'

Doherty made the usual mumbling sounds acknowledging that he'd caught her drift. Philippe was bright, funny, artistic and — in Doherty's eyes — unashamedly flamboyant. Doherty had always shown his discomfort with the latter. He couldn't help it. He was the product of a certain upbringing, though Honey was convinced he would have liked Philippe if he'd known him better. Everybody loved Philippe — or so she'd thought. Obviously, someone had not.

'When and how was he poisoned?'

'According to my information it was tasteless, odourless and slow acting. Our victim had knocked back a crème de menthe one hour before dying. We're working on the poison being in the drink, though it's difficult to be absolutely sure.'

'So questions are being asked at St Margaret's Court?'

'Exactly. We're checking backgrounds too. One waiter has already done a runner, chap by the name of Aloysius Rodriguez. We're checking on him with the immigration authorities. You know how many foreign workers there are in Bath. Low wages and all that . . .'

Honey was perfectly aware that the catering and hospitality trade would grind to a halt if it weren't for the influx of foreign workers. Most of them were here quite legitimately. Some were not. It was logical to assume that Aloysius Rodriguez was here unofficially and police activity had made him nervous, so he'd done a runner.

Doherty's voice broke into her thoughts and took them back to the murder victim. 'Can you think of anyone who disliked the guy enough to kill him?'

Honey licked some biscuit crumbs from around her mouth. 'I'm working on the professional rivalry angle — Julia Porter's name has come up. I'm looking into it. Other than that, I'm not sure. Some people might not have liked his brocade swathes or deep coral upholstery swatches, and clients can get pretty hostile if a colour scheme doesn't match up with their personal vision. I don't think it makes them mad enough to kill — hold a grudge, perhaps . . .'

'Really?' Doherty sounded genuinely surprised, then abruptly changed the subject. 'Look, I wondered if you were free tonight. We could go over things . . .' His tone was cautious, almost secretive.

Although she detected the hesitant tone, Honey went on to picture how it would be, perched on stools against the bar of the Zodiac, their knees touching. It was a nice thought. She nodded into the phone.

'Same place, same time.'

'Honey . . .' Doherty sounded as if he wanted to say something but didn't know how. 'See you there.'

What was up with Steve? Never mind. Honey had her timetable to tend to. First, she wanted to check on the painters. Things seemed quiet in reception. She went to investigate.

CHAPTER TWELVE

The silence in the crisply painted reception area was broken only by the sound of Frau Hoffner's knitting needles. Herr Hoffner was nowhere in sight. Neither were the painters. The paint pots remained where they'd been left the night before. The dust sheets were still spread across the floor.

'Is your husband having a lie in?' she asked Frau Hoffner after wishing her a very good morning.

Frau Hoffner's bright eyes twinkled above her half-moon spectacles. Her smile was instant.

'The painters have gone to another job while they're waiting for the paint to dry here. They asked Hans if he would like to go with them. He jumped at the chance.'

She sounded incredibly happy about it.

'You don't mind?' Honey asked.

'I have no objection.'

Honey found this refreshingly pragmatic. 'Some wives would sue for divorce if their husband went off doing other things without them when they were on holiday.'

'I don't mind at all. I am having a nice break. I can sit here knitting and thinking. Hans is also doing what he wants to do. We are both happy.'

'You've been married a long time,' Honey pronounced. It was a statement rather than a question. They were incredibly tolerant of each other. Being happy had to be the only reason they were still together.

'Forty years,' said Frau Hoffner. 'We are very happy.'

Yep! There it was.

Honey left her there with the click-clacking needles. She met Mary Jane on the first landing at the top of the stairs.

'Are those needles disturbing your psychic vibes as much as they are mine?' Mary Jane asked.

'Um . . .' Honey hesitated. It wasn't every day someone asked you about the wellbeing of your psychic vibes. She didn't know if she'd even had any to begin with. 'I'm not sure.'

'They sure are messing about with mine,' whispered Mary Jane, her eyes darting from side to side as though a giant had taken hold of her by the shoulders and was giving her a good shake.

'Ah,' said Honey. 'That must be a bit of a nuisance. Can you do anything about it?'

She was envisaging that Mary Jane might make herself a cup of herbal tea or something. Her assumption couldn't have been further from the truth.

Mary Jane's eyes narrowed in a manner that could best be described as threatening.

'I thought I might try a spot of hypnotism again to make her stop knitting. If all else fails I do keep a book of spells with my things. You never know when you might need one.'

Honey was overcome by a sense of panic as a thought took hold of her.

'That isn't what you did when she went into a trance before, was it? Cast a spell, I mean.'

'No! What do you take me for? Some kind of charlatan? That was her. She got drawn into something by some ethereal presence — either that or she ate something that disagreed with her. So many things can throw a spanner into the paranormal system.'

Hoping that the something Frau Hoffner had eaten had not been prepared in the Green River kitchen, Honey sighed with relief. 'Phew. Thank goodness for that.'

'If I put her under, then under she'd go until the time was right to wake her. Last time was a one-off. I'm sure of it. I'm off for brunch.'

Honey stood as stiff as a petrified tree trunk. Mary Jane had the ability to confuse and confuse she did. Honey quite often had problems getting her head around what Mary Jane was about. She would have asked how come Frau Hoffner had entered a trance in the first place, but one psychic puzzle was enough for one day. Besides, she had things to do. Dumpy Doris was away sunning her broad backside in a faraway place. It was down to Honey to step in and give a hand. All hoteliers had to do chores at some time or another. Except Casper, of course, but then, Casper was a notable exception in a lot of respects. He had elegant fingers and exquisitely polished nails. Not for him making beds or wielding a toilet brush. For Honey it was a different matter. Doris was away. She had work to do.

CHAPTER THIRTEEN

On the landing Anna was heaving piles of clean sheets from the linen cupboard and onto the chambermaid's trolley.

'Ah!' she exclaimed at the sight of Honey. 'I'm going for a tea break and to feed Bronica, but I have to make a phone call first.'

Barely awaiting a reply, she darted off brandishing her phone. Anna had Polish relatives in Swindon. She was on the phone to them all the time, more so than when they'd lived in Kraków.

'I won't be long,' Anna shouted over her shoulder.

She disappeared too quickly for Honey to insist she kept to that. Ten minutes. No more. Hopes on that one weren't too high. Anna was an ardent cigarette smoker. Honey guessed she was gasping for a smoke. Despite serious misgivings, she reassured herself that Anna would come back for Bronica as soon as she was through and she didn't mind keeping an eye on the baby until she did. It happened on those days when she had a gap in childcare. Smoking and speaking to distant relatives was very important to Anna. Not that her daughter wasn't important. Of course she was. It was just that to Anna everything she did was important. She was a very intense young person.

Gently opening the door so as not to disturb the wee mite, Honey peered into the linen cupboard. The carry cot was balanced on the bottom shelf next to the spare pillows and mattress covers. The little sweetie, no more than three months old, was sound asleep. Honey couldn't resist smoothing a tiny hand with her finger.

'Now be a darling little angel and stay quiet while I get on making the beds. Auntie Honey has a hotel to run. Though sometimes I wonder whether anybody notices that,' she added in a low voice.

Bronica obviously had very good hearing. She began to snuffle, her little mouth screwing up into a demanding moue while emitting small, cough-like grunts.

'Ah!' Honey swiftly removed her offending finger. 'Bronica, you're letting me down. If you could just wait . . .'

It had been a long time since she'd taken on the responsibility of a baby — nineteen years, in fact. They did say that it all came flooding back to you. Quite frankly she didn't want it flooding back at all. Feeding, winding and wiping a baby bottom were all behind her, and she'd prefer that it stayed that way, thank you very much.

She glanced worriedly in the direction Anna had disappeared and proceeded to tell herself a host of reassuring lies: that she would smoke only one cigarette, make only a very short phone call, have only one cup of tea. And, of course, she would not forget the baby . . . right?

The baby began to wail loudly.

'Shhh!' She proceeded to gently rock the carry cot from side to side. 'Mummy will be back in a minute. If you could just hang on . . .'

Bronica took no notice at all. The wailing increased in volume.

A door opened some way along the landing. A guest poked out her head. 'Do you think you could keep that child quiet, please? My husband's having a lie in after his medication.'

Typical! Not all the seniors had gone sightseeing.

'I'm sorry,' she called back, poking her head out from behind the linen cupboard door.

The mauve-haired lady wearing the Dame Edna glasses and sporting a flowery dressing gown grunted something about children being seen and not heard. Mary Poppins she was not.

Perhaps if she closed the cupboard door . . . No. Somehow that wouldn't be right. She tried making soothing sounds interspersed with *lickle, tickle, you must go to sleepies.*

'Shhh,' she said again in her most soothing voice. 'Mummy will be back soon.' She smiled hopefully into the bonny pink face.

Bronica was not for soothing. She wailed even more furiously between sucking sounds, pursing her rosebud mouth ready for feeding.

Honey was pretty certain that Bronica was breastfed. 'Look,' she said, laying both hands on her breasts. 'These here are for show only. No milk bar.'

To no avail.

She resorted to rocking the cot once again. 'There, there. Mummy will be back shortly.' The child chortled.

Honey was pleased with herself. 'Good girl. I'll just go and—'

The moment she tried to exit stage right, Bronica was off again.

She rolled her eyes to heaven. 'Shit!'

No help was coming from above. Hands on hips, she looked down at the child and shook her head. 'You aren't going to let me go, are you?' She felt kind of privileged at being wanted. It was oddly touching and made her feel quite smug. She hadn't lost the touch after all.

The child didn't reply as such, though her expression said it all. Funny how fat little faces can say a multitude of words without the need to speak. However, feeling privileged that baby Bronica enjoyed her company would solve nothing.

Carry cot bumping against her side, sheets tucked beneath her other arm, Honey struggled along to each room.

Running round each side of the bed, turning down sheets, rocking the carry cot, running into the bathroom, wielding the toilet brush, replenishing tea and coffee stocks — it all took longer with a baby in tow.

But every baby has only so much patience. At last Bronica was crying lustily, face resembling one of those wooden Russian dolls with scarlet cheeks.

There was no alternative. Honey picked her up. The child made sucking noises in her ear. The pillow the child's head had been resting on came out with her. That was when she saw the bottle tucked beside the pillow. So Anna wasn't a slave to the know-it-alls who said breast was best.

Recognising instant relief when she saw it, she swooped on the bottle. There wasn't much milk left in it, but enough. Satisfied at having something to suck at last, Bronica went willingly down into her cot.

Honey breathed a sigh of relief.

Finishing the rooms went quicker after that. She began to hum to herself, pleased that she was doing so well. Who needed staff anyway?

'Pssst!'

Mary Jane appeared around the door.

'She's still knitting, you know. Can't you hear it? Doesn't it just make you want to stab her with one of those darned awful needles?'

She said this just as Honey was bent double over a large canvas laundry bag. Obviously, Mary Jane had finished her brunch. Honey had to admit she was looking a little pale, the lines in her face swirling deeper than they usually did. But this comment — well, wasn't it a little out of character? Gerda Hoffner was only knitting, not swinging naked from the chandeliers.

'Couldn't you confiscate them?' Mary Jane asked hopefully.

Honey pulled the straps tight on the canvas bag. The men who came to collect the laundry complained if the soiled sheets and bath towels slipped out on their way to their van.

But that wasn't the only reason for appearing immersed in what she was doing; she was visualising what confiscating a guest's knitting needles would do for her reputation.

'Mary Jane, you really shouldn't let it get to you. How about you give me a moment to finish here and we talk this over out in the conservatory?'

Mary Jane clenched her jaw in the act of gnashing her teeth. 'I hear that click-clacking in my sleep. It follows me down the hall and out into the street. I wonder how her husband puts up with it. No wonder he's gone off with the decorators.'

'Is that so?' said Honey, taking hold of Mary Jane's elbow and steering her towards the stairs. 'We'll have refreshments in the conservatory. I'll open the door. We can hear the birdsong.'

'Dandelion for me.'

'Dandelion tea it shall be.'

Besides birdsong, it was also quite probable that the sounds of the city might filter in and blot out the sound of persistent knitting.

Her suggestion seemed to have the desired effect. She nodded thoughtfully and her jaw slackened a little.

'You're probably right. I shouldn't let this get to me. A cup of dandelion tea might steady my nerves.'

Determined to steer Mary Jane away from the offending needles, Honey left the bed linen and accompanied her down the stairs. She made a detour away from reception, through the staff rest room and out into the conservatory. On the way she rang through to the kitchen to organise tea. Lindsey brought it out to them.

'Now,' said Honey as she poured. 'Let's sit here a while and enjoy the view.'

The view wasn't panoramic, but the old brick walls surrounding the walled garden gave off a warm glow even when the sun wasn't shining. Just as she'd visualised, the birds were singing.

Mary Jane took a little twist of paper out of her pocket, untwisted it and poured its powdery contents into her cup.

Honey eyed it with misgiving. 'What is it — that powder?'

'Oh, this,' replied Mary Jane after taking a sip or two of her tea. 'Belladonna. It helps with my hot flushes. Calms me down. Like with like. You know?'

No, Honey didn't know it helped with hot flushes. It shook her even to think that Mary Jane still needed something like that. What concerned her most of all was that Mary Jane was knocking back what she understood to be a deadly poison of her own free will. Was her obsession with the knitting needles a sign of something deeper? Something distressing? Had her mind become unhinged?

She grabbed Mary Jane's wrist. 'It's deadly nightshade! A poison!'

Mary Jane only barely managed to stop her knocking the cup from her hand. She looked at Honey as though she were seven years old.

'Honey. Calm down. Belladonna, or deadly nightshade as it's known, is far more than a poison. Carefully administered, it has quite intriguing therapeutic powers and is used in homeopathic medicine. A little does a lot of good, from calming you down to inducing a much-needed sleep.'

Honey was shaking. She'd been ready to see Mary Jane fall comatose — or worse still — onto the floor.

Mary Jane repeated what she'd said.

'It's not just a poison, Honey. It's a very useful medicine, a beneficial herb when used in the right way.'

Honey fanned her hand in front of her face in order to still her racing heart. The cool air coming in from the open door helped.

'Have a little. It stops hot flushes,' said Mary Jane helpfully.

Honey shook her head. 'I'll pass, thanks.'

She was about to question Mary Jane in more depth when Anna came bursting in.

'Oh, Mrs Driver, I am so sorry. I was talking to my cousin in Swindon and I forgot what time it was. She has problems, you see, with her husband. I was trying to advise her. I hope Bronica was not too much trouble.'

Honey sprang to her feet. She'd had the child with her. Where was she now?

'Oh, Anna. I'm so sorry. I forgot.'

'I will fetch her from the linen room,' said Anna.

'Oh, she's not in there,' replied Honey. 'I took her with me around the rooms. We are expecting guests after all now everyone else has cleared out . . .'

Her voice petered out as the realisation dawned that she couldn't remember which room she'd left Bronica in.

'Which room?' asked Anna.

Honey's mouth hung open. 'Ah! Now let me see . . .' She was playing for time. She hadn't a clue.

Before Anna had a chance to bound out and up the stairs, Lindsey came in carrying the cot and a sleeping Bronica. She was smiling.

'Mr and Mrs Stopes said they only booked a room with en-suite bath and shower, not en-suite baby.'

CHAPTER FOURTEEN

'See this?'

Honey looked. Smudger was showing her a small piece of porcelain — a sweet dish by the looks of it.

'Is it Spode?' Honey asked.

Smudger knew enough about collectables to turn it over and scrutinise the base.

'Yep! Says so right here.'

'It's very pretty. Let me guess what you paid. Fifty pounds?'

'Get off! Course not.'

'Go on, then. Tell me.'

He beamed in the deeply smug way beloved by chefs and people who've got themselves a bargain.

'A tenner!'

'Ten pounds?' Honey was seriously surprised. 'Where did you get it?'

'Car boot sale. Pretty, ain't it?'

Honey studied it and decided someone had made a very big mistake. Spode attracted good prices. It wasn't usually found at car boot sales, those odd get-togethers that had started life in the USA as swap meets.

'Very. Someone didn't know its real value, that's for sure. Lucky you. Must have been a good stall and a dumb seller. Was there much else there?'

It was only logical to enquire. After all, a collector is a collector, even if Honey's particular interest was antique underwear rather than porcelain.

Smudger was still radiant with smugness, polishing the dish on his sleeve.

'Quite a bit, as a matter of fact. All the stuff on the stall was donated for charity — retired horses or some such thing.'

His reference to a horse charity sparked a response in her brain.

'Horses, you say? Who was running the stall?'

'Two women.' He grinned. 'Young and gullible.'

He proceeded to wrap his valuable purchase in greaseproof paper before placing it into an empty ice-cream container.

'You didn't steal it from them?'

Smudger looked deeply insulted. 'I will treat that comment with the contempt it deserves,' he said pompously.

'Sorry. You paid a tenner. Their mistake.'

'It weren't like that. As it turns out they weren't supposed to sell it at all. They'd picked it up by mistake, according to the woman in charge of the stall. She'd gone off to get herself a cup of tea or something and came running after me wanting to buy it back.'

'I expect she would,' said Honey. 'It's worth fifty to sixty-five, any day of the week. But you kept it.'

'Even when she offered me a hundred. I said I liked it and that was it.'

Honey was genuinely surprised. 'A hundred! For such a little thing.'

'Little things mean a lot,' said Smudger. He gave her a knowing wink.

OK, it was a long shot, but Honey couldn't get one particular thought out of her mind. Why had the woman offered more than the dish was worth? Sentimental attachment? And who was the woman? Her conversation with Alistair came to mind. Heavy stuff was left in store. Smaller items were easier to steal and sell.

Being suspicious was a prerequisite of the amateur sleuth, but a name had popped into her mind. She pushed Smudger for a description.

'Oh, you know. One of those horsy types with big pants and a padded jacket. They all look the same to me.'

'You sure she didn't have silvery blonde hair and an Alice band?'

He made a so-so face. 'Now you mention it . . .'

CHAPTER FIFTEEN

Like a high-spirited thoroughbred, Honey almost pranced her way to her meeting with Doherty. She felt cocky, clever and cute because she had something exciting to report to him. She'd worked it all out by herself and felt good, good, GOOD about it!

Someone had been stealing things from Philippe's storeroom and selling them for cash. Philippe had found out, confronted them, and *hey presto!* An argument had ensued. Rather than resort to blows — Philippe was no brawler — the parties concerned had agreed to meet and settle their differences. Unfortunately, one of said parties was not going to play fair. A little something extra entered the interior designer's cocktail and — *whack!* — he went down.

The vitreous china handle was still a bit of a problem though. Why bother with that? Was it some kind of symbol?

Never mind. She had a basic map of what might have occurred; Doherty could no doubt fill in the details.

So there it was! She'd solved it!

A few more skips drew the bemused smiles of overseas tourists before she arrived at the Zodiac.

The Zodiac night club had become their place of choice from the very start of the acquaintance between hotel owner and detective inspector. It was crowded, suffused with the smell of sizzling steaks, rich with noise and abundant in atmosphere. Every hotelier and innkeeper in Bath congregated there in the hours following pub closing time or when paying hotel guests were all safely tucked up in their beds.

In response to her knock a small shutter opened and a pair of eyes blinked at her.

'Let me in.'

No introduction. She'd know that pair of shifty eyes anywhere. The door swung open.

'Hi, Clint.'

Honey didn't know how he did it, but Rodney 'Clint' Eastwood filled in as doorman-cum-bouncer on his nights off from other work. He had a whole range of jobs, including helping out with general kitchen duties at the Green River. What was most surprising about his stints at the Zodiac was that he always seemed to fill in on theme nights, when he was required to dress accordingly. Tonight was 'Fruit Night', and Clint was dressed as a gooseberry. The outfit appeared to be made of some kind of inflatable pale green cellophane to which thousands of nylon hairs had been attached. A twig and green leaf arrangement sat on his head and around his neck.

Honey tried to recover herself after doubling over with laughter. 'Nice outfit,' Honey quipped as she wiped the tears from her face.

'You're not dressed,' he responded hotly.

Honey spread her hands, indicating her crisp jeans, navy-blue sweater and silk scarf.

Clint was unimpressed. 'You haven't made much of an effort. It's not really entering into the spirit of things. You could have come as a banana or an apple.'

'I could pretend to be an aubergine, right? Given the colours I'm wearing.'

Clint was unimpressed. 'Give over. They're a vegetable, not a fruit. And they're purple not navy blue.'

'Never mind. This is business. I'm meeting Doherty. What do you expect him to come dressed as?'

A slow grin spread across Clint's face. It was no secret that he and the police were not exactly bosom buddies, mainly because some of his income was derived from less-than-reputable sources.

His smirk stayed fixed to his face. 'He's already at the bar looking like a right lemon!'

'You mean he's alone. Does my lack of costume mean I'm denied entry?'

He hesitated only briefly. Clint knew which side his bread was buttered. If he wished to continue washing up at the Green River, he had to let her in.

Doherty was sitting on a bar stool looking like an island of solitude. He was glancing at his watch.

'I'm not late,' said Honey, taking it that the visual rebuke was meant for her.

He saw her. 'I didn't say you were.'

'You were looking at your watch.'

'It's allowed.'

He ordered her a drink. She took a sip before filling him in on Deirdre Olsen and the boot fair.

'I think the item of Spode was stolen, and that Mrs Olsen didn't want it falling into anyone else's hands and the trail leading back to her. And Philippe was killed because he found out somebody was stealing from him.'

Doherty was lukewarm about it. 'It's a long shot.'

'Have you by any smidgen of a chance got hold of a list of contents with regard to the stuff taken from Philippe's storeroom?'

'Sort of. That Camilla woman is working on it. She vaguely remembers him keeping a list on his computer. Apparently she's having trouble getting into the system. I've given her another two days before I contact our own computer bods and get them to break into it.'

Honey eyed her glass, twirling it between her fingers. 'When can we expect them to arrive?'

He shrugged. 'I have to put in a requisition for service. Shouldn't take any longer than four days before they arrive and then . . .'

On seeing the sneaky way she narrowed her eyes and looked at him sidelong, he paused.

'Go on,' he said cagily.

'Lindsey could do it in no time.'

His mouth curved appreciatively. 'I had a feeling you were going to say that.'

She felt his eyes on her as she swirled the ice cubes around in the bottom of her glass. She looked up quickly, meaning to take him unawares. His look surprised her. He was eyeing her like a cat about to take a final leap on a particularly juicy-looking mouse.

'What?' she asked.

His look turned defensive, as policemen are wont to do if they feel threatened. 'What do you mean, "What?"'

'You look as though you want to ask me something. Anything important?'

He shrugged and immediately turned casual. 'Nothing specific. I was just thinking that I'll be glad when this case is over. We'll celebrate with a glass or two of champagne. How's that with you?'

It was fine with her and she said so. The problem was that she still felt he was holding something back.

'Are you hiding something from me?' she asked pointedly.

He spread his hands in the disarmingly time-honoured way. 'Hey, Hon. Would I do that? Are we a team or what?'

Honey found this a little condescending. On the other hand she liked being regarded as one of the team. It made her feel so very professional.

Steve was supposed to be the professional, bound by the rules of the Home Office. She was the amateur, brought in because she knew the tourism industry, the lifeblood of the city. But she was sure she'd cracked the case.

'How about we do a return visit to Mrs Olsen, her of the knee-high boots and cut-glass accent?'

She could see he wasn't buying her theory. He clearly had his own idea of the whys and the wherefores. 'My money's on Camilla.'

Her hand shot forward. 'Bet you fifty pounds you're wrong.'

He took her bet. 'Done.'

His hand lingered longer than it should. His smile was cagey. 'Anything else you'd like to bet on?'

She sensed where this was going. 'That would have to be one hell of a celebration.'

'Fifty pounds would buy the champagne.'

Dropping her head, she trained her eyes on him, playing the seductress.

'I'm worth more than that.'

'I agree . . .'

It seemed to her that he'd been about to say something else but had chickened out. It didn't matter. It wasn't important. The light of victory was shining in her eyes and doing wheelies in her heart. Everything seemed cut and dried.

And so it remained — until the following morning.

CHAPTER SIXTEEN

Back now from her holiday and tanned the colour of a crusty loaf, it was Dumpy Doris who informed Honey that Herr and Frau Hoffner had disappeared. They hadn't come down for breakfast and they weren't in their room.

'I gave the door a good hammering,' Dumpy Doris reported.

Honey glanced at her enormous fists and believed her.

Shortly after that the painters came calling for their eager comrade.

'Perhaps he's already out at St Margaret's Court,' Honey suggested.

'He shouldn't be. We told him we were working here this morning.'

Honey shook her head. 'Well, neither of the Hoffners is here. We've checked and they haven't been down for breakfast. Perhaps he liked St Margaret's better.'

'Very possibly,' said Peter, a tall skinny painter with a thread-veined nose and a slack mouth. 'And we get a cordon bleu lunch,' he added.

It struck Honey that workmen were so choosy nowadays. In the past a cheese and pickle sandwich would have sufficed. She sensed this could turn competitive if she didn't watch out, egging her on to outdo the repast the upmarket hotel dished up for its subcontractors. She was pretty certain that he was angling for her to offer an even classier meal than St Margaret's Court. She wasn't going there.

'Are you sure you don't know where he's gone?' she asked.

He grunted. 'We wouldn't be here if we did.'

Honey frowned and stroked her chin. Two hairs had sprouted there without her noticing. Middle age sprang surprises all the time. The tweezers would take care of them. In the meantime, what reason could the Hoffners have for checking out? Without paying, she reminded herself.

First things first, she said to herself. Secure the crime scene and ask the relevant questions.

It turned out that the Hoffners had dined the night before, and the servers noticed that Frau Hoffner had knitted while waiting for the next course.

'But they were acting very strangely,' said Pallo, one of the waiters. 'Their heads were very close together — as though they did not want anyone to hear. They looked a bit . . . het up,' added Pallo.

'You didn't hear what they said?'

He shook his head. 'No. They were speaking in German.'

'And you don't understand German?'

'No. I am Portuguese.'

'Did you see them leave?'

'Yes. They didn't hear me when I asked them if they wished to put the bill for their meal with the rest of their stay. They seemed engrossed with each other and whatever it was they were talking about.'

'Just one thing,' said Honey. 'Did you know Aloysius Rodriguez? He worked at St Margaret's Court.'

'Yes. We came over at the same time.'

'Was he reliable?'

'Absolutely.'

'Would he go off without telling anyone where he was going?'

He shook his head adamantly. 'No. No, he would not do that.'

'I believe he had a family in Portugal.'

'A wife, I think, and two children. He adored them. He said he was working here in order to pay for his children's future. He was very proud of his girls. He wanted them both to go to university.'

'You heard about the murder, I suppose?'

Pallo nodded. 'Mr Fabiere was a nice man. Aloysius showed him his drawings. Mr Fabiere told them they were very good.'

'Really?'

So the missing waiter and the dead man had known each other.

CHAPTER SEVENTEEN

By mid-morning Anna had reported that she couldn't get into the Hoffners' room to tidy up. It was decided they must be having a lie in. It was by pure chance that the night porter strolled into the foyer dressed in tartan golfing trews and a green polo shirt. He'd left behind a blockbuster he'd been reading in between doing his nightly rounds and unlocking the front door for those who'd left their keys behind.

Honey was discussing the Hoffners with Lindsey, who had assured her mother that the room key had not been handed in, so they couldn't have gone out.

'Oh yes they have,' he assured them. 'They borrowed the spare and went out last night at around midnight.'

Honey's first thought was that they'd absconded without paying their bill; it wouldn't be the first time that seemingly nice people had flown the nest without settling their account.

Sid, the night porter, put her mind at rest.

'They didn't have any luggage with them.'

Lindsey handed her mother the bunch of master keys.

It didn't sound as though they'd done a runner, but Honey was resolute in her mission. Luggage left behind would be evidence that they had not left without paying their bill but had merely . . . she fought for the right word. There was only one. *Disappeared.*

Still, she thought, jutting out her chin. *Early days yet, Honey.*

She marched straight to their room. Mary Jane tagged along behind her, giving her the lowdown on how much quieter her head seemed to be without Frau Hoffner's needles clicking like clockwork castanets.

Honey opened the door and entered the room. Mary Jane shadowed.

Some guests junked their rooms, unjustly reasoning that someone was being paid to clear up after them. The Hoffners were not of that persuasion. The room was pristine: bed made, luggage stowed where it should be, and both clean and dirty clothes stored in their proper place. Even the knitting was where it should be, safely secreted inside a tapestry knitting bag with wooden handles.

Mary Jane made the observation that they weren't the sort of people to stay out all night.

'Midnight makes seniors turn into pumpkins,' she muttered dolefully.

Honey was of the same mind. 'They may just have taken it into their heads to hop on a train or a bus to somewhere they wanted to see. They'll probably be back later.'

'Have they left their passports?' asked Mary Jane. 'People can go off without their luggage, but they sure as hell can't travel without their passports.'

Honey didn't like the eerie tone that had crept into her voice, but she had to be positive.

'Oh, yeah,' she responded and tried to sound flippant, as though she was not even a teeny bit concerned. All the same, she made a thorough search for passports. She found Frau Hoffner's but not that of her husband.

Honey was getting more and more nervous. Neither Mary Jane's tone nor the direction of her remarks was helping.

'Do you know what I reckon happened?' said Mary Jane, her eyes round as saucers, her voice hushed like she was telling a creepy story.

‘Hmmm?’ said Honey while she checked beneath the pillow. Ridiculous! What was she expecting to find? A loaded .45?

Despite Honey’s apparent lack of interest, Mary Jane proffered her diagnosis.

‘I reckon that Mr Hoffner was as fed up with that infernal clicking sound as I was. I reckon he did away with her. I reckon he lost his temper and stabbed her with one of her own knitting needles. That’s why her passport’s still here and his is gone.’

‘I don’t think so,’ said Honey shaking her head, though she had to admit it was a distinct possibility.

‘I bet you . . .’

Mary Jane dived into the tapestry bag with the wooden handles.

‘There!’ she said, bringing out one needle on which a slate blue item hung in thick folds. ‘Only one needle! I tell you, Honey, he did for her. I’ll bet my last dollar on it.’

Honey stared. The needle was lime-green with a black knob at one end. She eyed it warily. What if Mary Jane was right and Herr Hoffner had snapped? The thought of it sent a shiver down her spine. People had snapped thanks to a lot less.

But Mary Jane had a point. Two people and one passport missing. A swift departure. What had happened to her German guests?

CHAPTER EIGHTEEN

The painters had touched up a little paintwork before taking themselves off to the St Margaret's Court Hotel for the rest of the day. Honey asked if they could check whether anyone there had seen Herr Hoffner, and one of them, Peter, had had the presence of mind to leave a mobile number.

Halfway through the morning, the disappearance niggling her, Honey gave him a call.

'Herr Hoffner wasn't upset about anything, was he?'

Peter gave a noncommittal grunt. 'Don't think so.'

'Or perhaps he was upset with someone,' Honey needled. She wanted to ask whether he'd had a set-to with his wife. But that would be leading the witness, she decided. Besides, it would be gossip and not based on fact.

'Couldn't say,' Peter finally said. 'He were all right with us,' he added in his gruff Somerset accent. 'What shall I do about his wages?'

It struck her then that no one would forego their hard-earned cash. She hadn't thought to look for cash or credit cards. *How dumb can you get?* she chastised herself. Anyone who'd truly done a runner would take both with them, surely.

She ended the call and went straight back to the Hoffners' room to check for financial support. There was no money. No wallet.

Peter dropped in around five o'clock in the afternoon. He'd brought Herr Hoffner's wages with him.

'Shame he's gone off like that,' he commented. He tilted his head back as he said it. For a moment Honey thought he was eyeing the painted ceiling. On reconsideration she realised that this was his thinking stance, like some people sit with their head in their hands.

'He was downright reliable was old Wilhelm. But that's it with the older generation. You can leave them to get on with a job without supervision. Can't leave any young whippersnapper on site like you can older folk. They'd be lounging around with loud music booming out and eyeing up the girls the moment your back's turned.'

He gave her a brown envelope with *W. Hoffner* written on it. She nodded a trifle dolefully and thanked him. The Hoffners' disappearance worried her. She would never have guessed that they were the sort to leave without paying their bill. It just wasn't . . .

A light came on in her head. It lit up her mind like neon on a dark city night.

She sprang at Peter the painter without realising she was doing it.

'Are you saying that Herr Hoffner was there by himself?'

Excitement and overenthusiasm for the job had got the better of her. She wasn't aware that she was twisting the neckline of his sweater and that he was swiftly turning puce.

'Is it that important?' asked Peter between gasps that should have told her he was fighting for breath. The bloodshot eyes either side of his red-veined nose were viewing her with outright alarm.

'Of course it's important! He was there by himself. Who knows what he might have seen? And a man would claim his wages, wouldn't he? Yes! Yes! Of course he would. He wouldn't forego his just desserts.'

'Do you think . . .' croaked Peter, his fingers desperately involved in trying to loosen hers from his throat.

Realising that she'd been overcome by her Eureka moment, Honey apologised and dropped her hands.

Peter cleared his throat and flattened his sweater.

'I got carried away,' Honey said, still apologetic, but keen for Peter to confirm that Wilhelm Hoffner had indeed been working by himself at St Margaret's Court Hotel.

He accepted her apology.

'So he was there alone — out at St Margaret's Court, I mean.'

'Peter nodded cautiously, as though afraid his head might fall off following her rough treatment.

'Yeah. That's right. It weren't much of a job. Just a long back passage only used by the staff and tradespeople.'

'Below stairs as they used to call it,' Honey stated.

'That's right. Just a bit of paintwork. Nothing much, really. They said one bloke would be enough. Someone discreet. I told them that Wilhelm was the height of discretion because he didn't speak a word of English. They were happy about that. Said it suited them fine. I lied about the English, obviously.'

'Curiouser and curiouser,' Honey muttered.

'Pardon?'

She shook her head. 'Nothing to concern you. It's just that I sometimes feel that I've fallen down a well in pursuit of a white rabbit.'

He looked at her as though she'd taken leave of her senses. 'Right. I see.'

She could tell by his expression that he didn't see at all. Judging by the look on his face and the way he was taking backward steps to the door, he thought she was quite mad and was best left alone.

Any concern for what he might think about her passed immediately. She was wondering about St Margaret's Court. Her belief that someone had been stealing from Philippe remained firm. It still seemed a safe bet in the absence of any other explanation. But the disappearance of the Hoffners had thrown a spanner in the works. Were the two events connected?

She fingered the brown envelope. She didn't know. She just did not know.

CHAPTER NINETEEN

The man looking out of the upstairs window had the kind of eyes any sane person would avoid looking into. In one light they seemed a very pale blue; in others they appeared to have no colour at all and were defined only by a black pupil and a dark grey edging to the cornea. The greyness of his eyes matched his hair and the thick eyebrows throwing shade over his eyes.

His shoulders were broad, his facial features as hard as chiselled marble and just as cold. His hands were clasped behind his back. There was no looseness to his mouth, no emotion in his eyes. He was standing perfectly still like something dead. His name was Ivan Sarkov and he owned the St Margaret's Court Hotel.

The upper-storey rooms above the main entrance were his domain and luxuriously appointed, yet still encompassing the air of great antiquity. Although he very much wished to integrate with the country he had made his home, he carried memories with him of Russia — though a very different Russia, from a time when it was known as the Soviet Union. Keeping one's private life just that came very high on his personal agenda.

Joybell Peters had been contracted to pick the architect and interior designer for the envisaged project. He had a lot of respect for her. She was a woman who knew what she wanted from life, both on a professional and a personal basis. So far he had not got involved with her sexually, mainly because he liked to be in control of a sexual relationship. He sensed that Joybell was of a similar nature. She was also a damned good accountant who would keep a tight check on the figures.

Ferdinand Olsen was sitting in a large leather armchair with cabriole legs, its arms decorated with polished brass studs. Unlike Ivan Sarkov, he could not maintain a cool exterior or keep from interweaving his fingers or shuffling his feet. He was nervous and wished he hadn't told Ivan that Tanya, his head of reception, had said more than she should have to the police. His palms had become unbearably damp. He rubbed them on his trousers. His gaze stayed fixed on Sarkov and there was a lump of lead in his stomach.

Even when the door behind him opened, Sarkov did not turn to acknowledge those who had entered. The door was closed as quietly as it had opened. Nobody hearing it would have guessed that three people had come in. The door opened and closed so smoothly, so beautifully was it crafted. The carpet was thick and made of pure wool.

One of the three new arrivals was Tanya. She looked nervous. A man stood on either side of her.

Olsen knew they weren't so much her companions as her guards, escorting her in case she ran away. He was pretty sure that if they hadn't been there, she would have.

Tanya was employed as hospitality manager at St Margaret's Court. The title was open to interpretation. She took care of the guests, providing them with everything they might require, and was typical of the pretty girls Sarkov employed.

Olsen swallowed. No licking of lips could moisten the dryness of his mouth. He wished he wasn't here but reasoned that he had to take the bad with the good. Sarkov had made him a rich man — at a price. Olsen had understood the Russian to be a bona fide businessman, a guy who'd made good following the collapse of communism. He kept telling himself that everything about Sarkov's rise to success was above board. The illusion was beginning to dim; Sarkov was frightening and, worse still, ruthless. He'd only that morning flown in from Kiev.

The Russian was speaking in English. His voice had a sharp edge to it like broken glass.

'What do you have to say, Tanya?'

'I couldn't put them off . . .' The girl's voice trembled. Her eyes were round with fear. 'They were booked in by the previous owners—'

Sarkov cut across her. 'I'm not talking about the coach party, though it would have been better that you had put them off. However, the police did your job for you. I'm glad about that. I'm talking about Mr Fabiere. You gave the police a list?'

'They insisted . . .'

'You should not have done that. I value my privacy. You should not have given them this list without my express permission. You should not have told them that I was the owner and given them my name.'

'I thought—'

'You are not paid to think!' he shouted.

Olsen noticed the girl tremble. His own palms were clammy. Sarkov had that effect. But he paid well. And on time.

He'd become wealthy following the fall of the Soviet Union despite his less than salubrious background. Now he sought to become a civilised gentleman. However, the ruthlessness with which he had carved out a criminal empire was still evident.

The girl turned pale. 'I did what I thought was right. I couldn't refuse. They are the police!'

Sarkov approached the girl, and there was a loud cracking sound as his palm slapped her cheek.

She gasped. Her hand shot up to cover the red handprint that had swiftly blemished her snow-white skin.

Olsen gasped.

The bodyguards were unmoved.

Sarkov clutched the girl's chin.

The girl eyed him pleadingly. 'Ivan. You know I would never do anything to hurt you. You know this.'

Her voice was turning into a whine and her eyes were watery. Olsen took on board the plaintive beseeching; Tanya was not just an employee. There was a relationship here. Funny he hadn't noticed that before, thought Olsen, though he really should have done.

Sarkov's voice cut into his thoughts.

'Get out!'

Olsen sat, not sure who Sarkov was addressing.

One of the bodyguards opened the door. They both went out but left the door open.

'Out!' Sarkov repeated, louder this time.

There was now no mistake about it. Sarkov wanted him gone. He was up from the chair and out of the door like a shot.

What about the girl? he wondered.

He shut the door behind him. Some semblance of guilt made him stay outside, his stomach tightening with apprehension. Sound travelled. Another slap. A scream followed by pleas for forgiveness.

A movement at the end of the landing drew his attention. The two thugs who'd escorted the girl were loitering and looking directly at him. The silent message was obvious. Get away from there. Get out. Get lost!

He didn't hang around. He left hastily, a sickness heavy in his guts. He had to get away. He had to tell someone what was going on — or at least, what he thought was going on. There was one person he could trust, or believed he could. He was welcome there, or at least that was the way it seemed.

CHAPTER TWENTY

'It's Cybil,' said Honey's mother. 'She's very upset.'

The woman to whom her mother was referring had large bony hands covered with age spots. Tendons pressed against the shiny skin like the twigs of a gnarled old tree.

The comparison between her mother's sparkly exuberance and Cybil Camper-Young's antique gentility was incredibly compelling. It actually made Honey quite proud that her mother was so dapper in her pin-striped trouser suit with crisp white shirt and green silk tie. Her handbag and shoes matched the green tie. Glitzy gold jewellery that owed more to *Dallas* or *Dynasty* than Dior gleamed like gaslights at midnight.

In contrast, Cybil wasn't so much dowdy as long, angular and unfeminine. There were no soft lines to her shoulders or her body and she strode along as though she were auditioning for a place in the changing of the guard at Buckingham Palace.

Seemingly in an effort to play down her masculine plainness, she'd favoured wearing Laura Ashley prints when they were the height of fashion and still wore the originals. Her straight-up, straight-down figure was swathed in a multitude of chintzy roses; her shoes were flat and classy, and her hair was bobbed too squarely for her square face. She was gawky and ungainly in comparison with the neat smartness of Gloria

Cross, but looked athletic, even strong. She mended her own car and did her own gardening, except for on Wednesday afternoons when a retired local gentleman came round to give her a hand. It was also rumoured that she'd replaced her own roof tiles following a particularly bad winter storm. In short, Cybil was a force to be reckoned with.

She lived in St Margaret's Valley, just a stone's throw from St Margaret's Court — in fact, immediately opposite the main gate of the hotel. The cottage she lived in was built in Victorian Gothic style of the famous honey-coloured Bath stone. The stone's colour had become muted over the years, but the house was still imposing — though not, of course, anything like the size of the hotel just across the way.

They were sitting in the little room at Secondhand Rose — immediately behind the serving counter and next to the changing room — where tea and sympathy were given out. The shop dealt in the recycling of top-quality designer clothing. Gloria ran the shop in tandem with three other women of similar age. Cybil was not one of these, but was acquainted with them, Gloria most of all. They went back some years.

Cybil had a bright strangeness to her eyes as she chatted over her second cup of tea and dunked her chocolate-coated digestive.

Honey's mother explained that Cybil's relatives lived a fair distance away and could do nothing about the dilemma she was faced with. As her family were not on the doorstep, she had turned to the next best thing — her friends.

'Gloria! I am not helpless.'

'But my daughter can help.'

Honey had dropped in meaning to trawl the clothes rails in the hope of finding something casual to wear in her moments off duty from the hotel. She'd been in the middle of pulling up a pair of Betty Barclay navy-blue trousers when she'd heard Cybil recounting how she was being intimidated by foreigners in big suits.

The trousers hadn't been coming up over her hips too well, so she'd had time to pause and listen. The plummy voice, cultivated as much by social status as by finishing school, went on to describe the foreigners in more detail.

'They have terribly short hair and do not appear to be gentlemen.'

'You mean they have buzz cuts?'

Honey recognised her mother's voice.

'I wouldn't know the correct terminology. Terribly short hair and a very suspicious manner.'

Honey relinquished the struggle to pull the offending trousers up and tried instead to take them off. That wasn't easy either. 'More elastane needed,' she muttered to herself.

Cybil carried on outlining her problem. 'I am not averse to having foreigners as neighbours. I will tolerate them if they tolerate me. However, what has happened is quite, *quite* impolite and, what is more, they came on my property to do it! It is quite intolerable. In fact, I regard it as illegal.'

Honey had sat down on the small chair provided and was proceeding to pull off the trousers. She paused in the effort, becoming ever more curious to know exactly what these suspicious foreigners had done.

Eventually it came out. 'They cut my wires! That's what they did.'

There were indrawn breaths.

Gloria Cross asked for more detail. 'What wires did they cut and why?'

'They cut the wires to my security cameras. I wouldn't have noticed if I hadn't been due for a service. I phoned the company that maintains them immediately. I'm not terribly technical, you know — not on electronics, anyway. But the culprits were caught in the act. The engineer told me so and showed me the film.'

There were gasps of indignation from the other ladies.

'That is totally out of order,' said Honey's mother from the other side of the curtain.

'You see? I think someone should have a word with them,' Cybil went on. 'Someone who has official backing.

Perhaps the police, or at least someone connected with the police. That's where your daughter comes in.'

'Hannah!' The curtain swished as it was pulled back. 'You've got to help Cybil.'

Luckily her mother had caught her in the act of doing up the button on her waistband. Not that the ladies present would have worried about that. They were absorbed in the story of Cybil and her brush with the foreign devils, twittering among themselves with various suggestions on how to deal with the problem.

Her mother glanced at the trousers lying crumpled on the floor. 'Those are designer, you know.'

'I know,' Honey replied grumpily.

'Then treat them with some respect.'

Indignation pouted her apricot lips as she snatched them from her daughter's hands. The solution to the crisis was delayed minimally while her painted fingernails smoothed each leg out before fixing the trousers back on their hanger. 'I take it you don't want them.'

'They don't quite fit.'

'I could have told you that.'

Honey was taken aback and it showed on her face. 'You make it sound as though I dine on doughnuts.'

'You could be a little more discerning in what you eat.'

Counting to ten in order to refrain from exploding was something Honey had learned to do well. Her mother would never have cut the mustard as a diplomat. Opinionated might be the kindest description; downright tactless otherwise.

'How are you, Miss Camper-Young?' asked Honey once her temper was under control. 'Or rather, what can I do for you?'

Beaming more brightly than the faded roses that covered her dress, Cybil repeated the same story Honey had heard from behind the curtain.

'The Russians cut the wires to my security cameras.'

'And they work for the owners of the hotel opposite you?'

Cybil nodded while taking a genteel sip from her rose-patterned tea cup. The cup and matching saucer matched her dress. Perhaps that was why she visited the shop so much.

'They do indeed. A Russian owns the hotel.' Her bottom lip curled out at the mention of the Russian.

Besides turning the Grade I listed building into a fabulous hotel, the previous owners had been antique dealers on the grand scale, dealing in architectural stonework and things from antiquity.

'They retired to the Cayman Islands,' her mother informed her.

Honey raised her eyebrows. 'I didn't know that. How come you knew?'

A secretive smile came to her mother's beautifully made-up face, coupled with an undeniable sparkle in her eyes.

'Evan Meredith has invited me to enjoy some sun, sea and something else when I get the chance.'

'I thought he had a wife,' said Honey, feeling somewhat shocked and surprised. Her mother loved men but had old-fashioned principles — those whom God has joined together and all that.

'She likes to see him enjoy himself,' said Gloria. 'It gives her time alone to do the things she wants to do. We're all getting older, you know.'

Honey refrained from asking exactly what Evan's wife — whose name she recalled was Primrose — did in the time she allotted to herself. This was no time to ask such a question. Her attention returned to Cybil.

'Why do you think they cut the wiring to your security cameras?'

'My man who comes in to garden on Wednesday afternoons went over and asked them why. They said they believed I was spying on them!'

Honey's mother exploded with indignation. 'Imagine that! As if Cybil would be interested in what foreign people were doing!'

There was something about Cybil's face that made Honey think she took a lot more interest in what her neighbours did than she let on.

'I just like to keep an eye on things,' said Cybil.

Honey nodded. 'I see.' She certainly did, and wondered if Cybil was observant enough to read her thoughts.

'So you'd like me to have a word with them?'

Cybil smiled appreciatively. 'That would be so kind.'

There was something about her facial expression that was almost contrived, as though she'd been trained to smile in the days when debutantes were still introduced at court and taught how to curtsey.

'How about these?' said her mother suddenly.

She was holding up a pair of good-quality burgundy trousers for Honey's inspection.

'There's plenty of room in these, especially if you intend spreading out some more as you get older.' To her gathering of friends she added, 'Hannah's a little bigger than I *ever* was.'

It was in moments like these, when her mother performed without the brakes on, that Honey wanted to murder her. Perhaps that was why she so relished this amateur sleuthing business. She couldn't bring her mother to justice, but pursuing the dire and deadly was a satisfying alternative.

CHAPTER TWENTY-ONE

Ferdinand Olsen hated living with his wife. Likewise, she hated living with him. They had separate lives and separate bedrooms. They rarely dined together and only attended the same social events when it was absolutely necessary to the maintenance of the income from his architectural practice, which was quite substantial. For the rest of the time Ferdinand dined out and stayed in luxury hotels with attractive women. Deirdre immersed herself in anything to do with horses. By the time this state of affairs had set in, younger couples would have parted — amicably or otherwise. Ferdinand and Deirdre had spent years together; cohabitation had become a habit. Sex had flown out of the window sometime after Deirdre had bought her third horse.

Ferdinand left the office early in order to catch Deirdre before she went into the stables to bed the horses down for the night. He didn't want to go in there if he could possibly help it. He hated the smell and harboured the fear that one of the beasts might stretch its muscular neck and take a nip of his arm. It wouldn't be the first time. He hated horses and they hated him — a bit like Deirdre and him, really. The other problem was that he didn't want to get his tan Gucci shoes eyelet-high in manure. Even when the concrete floor had received one of its twice-daily scrub downs, his feet usually still managed to find enough muck to stick to his soles and stain the hem of his trousers.

Keen not to chip the paintwork, he brought the BMW to a gentle standstill in front of the house. As with his car, he liked to see the house pristine, the gravel bright yellow, the grass borders and shrubs trimmed and blooming to the best of their ability. It was true to say the front of the house reflected his personality; the back was Deirdre's domain. His expression soured at the thought of it: dogs, cats and horses. Deirdre had been a typical English rose when he'd met her. He hadn't realised back then that English women become keener on animals and ditch their interest in men as they grow older. He wished he'd known sooner. He'd never have married her. But at least they could talk. That was something at least.

His feet crunched on the gravel as he made his way through the side gate and along the path running at the side of the house. A Welsh Springer spaniel came bounding out to greet him, tail wagging, tongue lolling around its dribble-soaked jaw.

'Piss off!'

Ferdinand aimed a kick. The dog squealed and retreated.

To his amazement the sounds the injured mutt was making did not attract Deirdre's attention. So! She wasn't in the vicinity of the house.

He carried on round to the neglected rear garden and the tree-trunk fence beyond, through the vegetable garden and into the stable yard.

The stalls ran in a line along one side. A wide concrete walkway ran in front, allowing easy access for cleaning and getting the animals in and out.

Brushes leaned against the wall to his left. The horses were stabled to his right. A hosepipe lay on the ground spewing water.

Ferdinand swore. He hated waste.

'Deirdre?'

The horses made soft nickering noises, except for a big bay named Lord John. His stall was at the very end of the rank. Ferdinand frowned, his dark eyes trying to discern if the animal was securely shut in before heading in that direction.

On the way there he had questioned why it was still to her that he came to air his fears and his failings. The answer was, of course, that his other women were merely that — women. They were good for sex but not to talk to. Women gossiped. Deirdre did not. She merely formed opinions. Most of the time her opinions were pretty sound. He wanted to tell her about Sarkov, how frightening this all was and how he wished he hadn't got caught up in it. She'd call him a fool and accuse him of being paranoid. But at least she'd listen when he told her that if he jumped ship his life could be in danger. And if his life was in danger, it might also come to pass that hers was too.

'Deirdre?' His mouth was dry. He didn't know why he suddenly thought about slasher movies, but he did. Fearsome Freddie was going to jump out at him if he went much closer. He told himself not to be stupid, though not all his fear was so easily curtailed. At best, Lord John might take a nip at his arm.

'Steady on, boy,' he said as soothingly as he could.

The big bay fixed him with a menacing eye. At the same time it blew noisily down its nostrils, backed away, spun in its stall and came charging back to the gate.

Luckily the stable gate was strong and made of galvanised steel. It shook on its hinges but didn't give.

He tried soft talking again.

'Whoa, boy. Go steady there.'

The horse didn't seem impressed. It rolled its eyes, one hoof pawing at the ground.

'You swine,' he muttered, eyeing the bad-tempered beast ruefully.

Deirdre had accused him of having a harsh voice. He'd told her he'd never had any complaints. She'd reminded him that this was a horse he was talking to and it was sensitive, not like the cheap slappers into whose ear he breathed terms of endearment.

Various horsy things hung from hooks on the wall behind him — halters, lead reins and lunging whips. He took one of the latter, folded the fine leather tip into his palm along with the handle and pointed it at the horse.

'Now, you beast! Get back when I tell you!'

The horse snorted and half reared as it backed into the stall.

'That's better . . .'

His feeling of power was short-lived. The horse's rear hooves disturbed what at first looked like a bundled-up horse blanket at the back of the stall. One of the creature's hooves caught in it, dragging it forward. The more it dragged, the flightier it became, snorting and lashing out with its back legs in order to disentangle itself.

Ferdinand lashed out. 'You stupid creature!'

The horse reared and came crashing down on the gate, its front legs over, its back legs still entangled.

That was when Ferdinand saw the pale-blonde hair and the Alice band. He had no chance to scream. The horse's flailing hooves came down on his head. He lost consciousness, not feeling the kicks that continued until the animal had freed itself and run out into the paddock.

CHAPTER TWENTY-TWO

The St Margaret's Court Hotel had taken on the appearance of a building site. There were workmen everywhere: stone-masons, glaziers and men in yellow coats and matching yellow hats. For the most part the latter were carrying rolled-up drawings beneath their arms, pointing and gesticulating as they discussed the ongoing work.

Gardeners were working in the areas outside the hotel where scaffolding hadn't been erected. Honey wished them a good morning. They nodded in response, their eyes warily regarding her from beneath frowning brows. Their busy hands never paused, and although nobody stopped her from treading around lumps of stone and piles of sand and cement, she got the impression her presence was tolerated rather than welcomed.

Still, the old place refused to be made less grand by all this activity. Its facade oozed history, one of those places that if it could speak it would have an extraordinary story to tell.

Wish it were mine, she thought, sighing enviously as she entered the magnificent portico. Huge oak doors, weathered by the centuries, framed the arched entrance. At least no modernist designer had suggested painting these magnolia or off-white — yet!

The interior of the hotel was visible and warmly welcoming on the far side of the inner doors. Amber lighting gleamed, seeming to swim over the polished plate glass.

The change inside only served to unsettle her further. She recalled the skeleton crew manning reception under dire circumstances. They were a typical team, each keen to assist no matter how awkward the customer. The police, Doherty in particular, didn't come much more awkward. How awkward was murder?

Beaming expectantly, she greeted them as exuberantly as she had the gardeners and the builders working outside. Not one single face was familiar.

'Oh! You're all new. Where are the old team?'

Their faces remained impassive, yet she detected that her comment had made them feel uncomfortable. It was down to the front-of-house staff to give a favourable first impression of the establishment. Even though everything was upside down — dust sheets everywhere, the carpets taken up, the oak boards exposed and dusty — the ones she'd met previously had coped well.

A pretty blonde girl with immaculate teeth and a polished face seemed to be in charge. She smiled broadly and asked if she could help. Honey was certain that she was as new as the rest, yet she seemed confident for all that. She recalled the other girl's name badge as saying 'Tanya'.

'Are you new?' Honey asked.

It was not pertinent to her enquiries, but one didn't usually see such a swift and total changeover of personnel in one area all at once. One or two faces might change on a shift, but not every single one.

'Can I help you?' the girl repeated without answering her question.

Honey tossed up whether to ask her again. *Hell, no*, she decided. That wasn't what she was here for.

'I would like to speak to the manager.'

A regretful look soured the beautiful face. 'I am afraid that Mr Parrot is very busy. There is very much work to organise.'

'So I see. But I think he will see me,' Honey persisted.

'I do not think—'

'Well I do!' Throwing caution to the wind, she made the decision to attach some authority to her visit. 'I'm working with the police on the murder that occurred here. There are a few questions I need to ask.'

The girl looked taken aback. She mouthed a single word. 'Oh!'

It said everything as far as Honey was concerned. Seeing Mr Parrot was a dead cert. OK, she'd used her words carefully, *implying* that she *was* police. She hadn't actually lied. Another option had been to say that she was here representing the Hotels Association, but working for the police was better.

It worked. The girl's smile tightened.

'The police?'

She looked nervous.

'Yes. Regarding the murder. I'd like to talk to the manager, Mr Parrot?'

The girl nodded. 'Mr Parrot. I will ask if he will see you.'

Was it Honey's imagination or did the girl's finger shake as she stabbed at the key pad?

She turned casually away as the girl used the telephone. Resting her elbows on the desk she pretended to eye what was going on, when in fact she was merely congratulating herself. This was good. It made her feel as though she were in a Mickey Spillane book, from an era when private dicks were the stuff of film noir and wore trench coats and broad-brimmed hats that shielded their eyes. Getting into character was no problem at all. She was no longer Honey Driver, hotel owner who did a bit of sleuthing in her spare time. She was on the case and the case was on her; logical thoughts kept finding their way into her mind.

The fact was that she wasn't at all sure that Cybil's problem with the security cameras had anything whatsoever to do with the murder, but on the other hand, what if they'd been cut *because* there was going to be a murder? What if the perpetrator had been hired in, and in order for him to make his escape in secret, Cybil's wires had been cut just before Philippe Fabiere had met his very untimely end? It was too much of a coincidence. She couldn't wait to tell Doherty. Wiping the smirk from her face, she turned a suitably grim expression back to the girl.

Sonia — according to her name badge — blinked nervously. 'Mr Parrot, there is a lady here to see you . . .' Her voice faltered. Obviously Mr Parrot had cut her short before she could finish. He was probably ordering her to politely tell the 'lady' to shove off.

'The police,' the girl blurted.

'Hannah Driver,' said Honey.

'Hannah Driver. She is from the police.'

That was good enough for Honey. She didn't correct her. The girl's outburst had grabbed the manager's attention.

'Yes,' she said in a crisp voice as she returned the phone to its station. 'He will see you. Will you take a seat, please?'

Honey guided her feet to a comfortable winged armchair big enough for two. Her feet were aching following a morning shift in the kitchen. Dumpy Doris had claimed more leave and was staying with her sister for two days. Someone had to grill the bacon. Fate's heavy hand had fallen on her.

Once again she assured herself that she was not impersonating a police officer. The girl had misunderstood. Studying the fine oak frieze above the marble fireplace helped focus her mind. Culture and history could really take you to different places. Each panel was a picture and each contributed to an overall story.

The one that particularly caught her eye appeared to portray a kneeling courtier announcing to Elizabeth Tudor that her sister was dead and she was now Queen Elizabeth I of England. Well, that was big news in platefuls; it certainly beat ending up in the Tower of London prior to getting your head chopped off.

'Hannah Driver?'

The sharp voice pierced the bubble of thought.

'Ah! Mr Parrot. Delighted to meet you.'

He was about five feet eight, had a narrow face and a very shiny forehead. His hair was fast waving goodbye to the rest of his scalp, clinging only to the back of his head. Three large moles and his head would resemble a bowling ball. He was dressed as a typical manager, a mustard-coloured waistcoat showing from beneath his dark, businesslike suit. His manner was abrupt, as though he were seeing her only on sufferance.

Honey stood up swiftly, sending a velvet cushion sliding to the floor.

Head stiff above spotless shirt collar, the manager glanced disdainfully at the fallen object. He shot a stern look at the receptionist she'd been speaking to and pointed at the cushion without a word. The girl scurried out from behind the desk to do his bidding.

Honey introduced herself, careful to use her given name. 'Hannah. Hannah Driver. I've a few questions.'

Luckily he didn't ask her for any identification or declaration of rank. For that she breathed a sigh of relief.

'Now,' said Mr Parrot once they were safely installed within his office. 'What can I do for you, Inspector Driver . . .?'

'Honey,' she gushed desperately. 'Just call me Honey. It's about a report I've received from a neighbour across the way. I wonder whether you can throw some light on the little problem she came to see me about.'

She told herself that she wasn't really being dishonest; she wasn't really guilty of impersonating a police officer — just not admitting to anything otherwise.

He looked puzzled. 'I'm not following your drift. What exactly are you talking about?'

'Miss Camper-Young across the way. Members of your staff took it upon themselves to cut the wiring to her security cameras. Can you firstly tell me who was responsible, and secondly why they would do that?'

His facial muscles froze. She could almost hear the cogs of his mind grinding and clunking like rusty clockwork as he sought a logical — though not necessarily truthful — excuse.

'There must be some mistake. I know nothing of this.'

'You do know Miss Camper-Young?'

'I'm not sure that I do.'

Was he kidding? He'd just crossed the dividing line between an excuse and an outright lie.

'Mr Parrot! Are you pulling my leg?'

She folded her arms, looked at him snake-eyed and didn't hold back on the sarcasm. 'The lady in question lives in Lobelia Cottage just across the road there. You can't miss it. Large, detached and very old. I think it's been there since Bonnie Prince Charlie was a boy. It's got lobelia tumbling out of the garden wall. Hence the name. And it's directly opposite your main entrance. You can't miss it. See?' She pointed at where the gravel drive swept out through the main gate. A cottage chimney could clearly be seen above a curved arch of wrought ironwork and the rear aspect of the Shaddick coat of arms — the name of the family who had long ago built the house. The gates had been added at a later date by a descendant of the original owner.

Her attitude and change of tone didn't go unnoticed.

'Ah, yes,' he said slowly, the tightness of countenance loosening a little. 'No one from here, of course. Vandals, I think you'll find. Teenagers out to cause trouble, I expect. We have problems like that every now and again, despite being over three miles from the city centre.'

This was absolute rubbish. She wanted to say just that, but she was also mindful to maintain something of a professional aura. She shook her head. 'No, Mr Parrot. Miss Camper-Young still has the very last tape. The two thugs on there are definitely not teenagers. She swears they're your employees.'

'Can you prove that?'

Honey took out the USB stick Cybil had given her and slammed it on to the desk. 'Shall we take a look?'

His eyes met hers in a frozen stare before he snatched the thumb drive from the desk. Without comment he crossed the room to a plinth-mounted monitor and playback unit, slid the stick into a slot and stepped back. A fuzzy picture flickered into life. Two thugs with wide shoulders and number-one crew cuts blundered into view. One was clearly carrying a pair of secateurs. The cheeky devils had even brought a step ladder with them. One set up the ladder. His pal climbed up, reached up with the secateurs and the screen went blank.

'Not teenagers,' said Honey, her tone reminiscent of that invariably used by TV policemen prior to making an arrest. The policemen on television were acting. So was she. The glare she flung him was full of meaning. *Tell me the truth or I'll take you downtown and beat it out of you*. She couldn't really do that, of course, but it didn't hurt to hint just a little.

'I take it they are your employees?'

He blinked. Blinks were always a sign that someone was cracking. She didn't know where she'd got that idea, but it seemed good to her. Hallelujah! She'd cornered him. They both knew it. Now, would he come clean or not?

'Indeed,' he said giving a curt nod. 'I remember them. They were temporary staff.'

She did her best not to crow with triumph, settling for a smile that glowed with satisfaction.

'Ah! Then perhaps I can have a word with them, if it's not too much trouble.'

Smug of expression, she waited for Mr Parrot to squawk an apology. He did — though it wasn't quite the one she expected.

'I'm afraid I can't do that. As I told you, they were only temporary staff. They are no longer in the hotel's employ.' She wanted to wipe the smug expression from his face, but she couldn't do that. You couldn't carry out police brutality if you didn't belong to the police in the first place.

He was the one crowing now. Honey seethed but resisted the urge to grind her teeth. There was one last card to play.

'Do you have a forwarding address for either of them?'

He shook his head. 'I'm afraid not.'

The old scenarios from private eye movies wouldn't go away. She wanted to kick him, purely to drive that sickly sweet look of triumph from his face; it was too similar to the one she'd been wearing just a moment before. She sensed he was about to say something that she wouldn't like. She was right.

'They've gone back to Russia.'

She paused.

'That's a long way. That's just too bad, Mr Parrot. That means the responsibility and the cost of repairing the old girl's security system rests with you.'

'I'd have to check that with my superiors.'

'Do that. Now!'

The aloof expression returned to the oval face, the pale lips tight, the high forehead gleaming like a gold-plated Buddha. He opened his mouth as though he were about to refuse when, just as suddenly, his whole demeanour changed.

'I'll do it right away. I'll have a man from the electrical contractors go over and fix it.' Even his tone was different. Pleasant, even.

'Good.'

The sudden change of heart was strange; a hotel manager's first priority was to control costs. Never mind. She'd got what she wanted.

He picked up the phone, punched in a number and barked orders. 'I'd like it done today, tomorrow at the latest. Can you do that? Good.'

'There,' he said once the call was finished. 'They're very reliable people. They do quite a lot of work for the group.'

'Miss Camper-Young will be pleased.'

'Please render my sincere apologies and inform her that the matter will be rectified forthwith.'

'Fine,' Honey quipped lightly, turning on her heels. 'Forthwith is good for me.'

Justice! She'd got justice for a defenceless old lady — well, not quite defenceless. Cybil was quite a formidable character. In her youth she'd worked for some very shady department at the Ministry of Defence. She wasn't sure what she worked as, though the roles of women in such a department must have been pretty mundane back in the sixties and seventies. She'd probably typed out secret service reports, she decided. Agile as Cybil seemed to be, she couldn't really see her doing anything else. People who wore chintzy Laura Ashley dresses were too ladylike to do parachute jumps into enemy territory and spy for their country.

No matter what her history, she's old and defenceless now, Honey reminded herself. The thought of someone being defenceless brought Philippe Fabiere to mind.

Parrot escorted her to the door.

Honey paused before leaving.

Parrot stopped abruptly when she stopped.

'Where were you when Philippe Fabiere was murdered?'

'The interior designer?'

He spoke as though he were only vaguely aware of the man's existence, when in fact as hotel manager he must have been in close communication with him. His expression was blank. Hotel people were good at looking blank. They had to be. They had many occasions to lie.

'Of course.'

'I was attending a meeting at the village hall.'

This was something she found hard to believe. The hotel was a world apart from the village. Some of the families living in the cottages and farmhouses hereabouts had been here for centuries. They didn't take well to outsiders coming into the village.

'What was the meeting about?'

'SSG International wish to extend the hotel's facilities. There are plans to build a leisure centre in the grounds, plus conference and nightclub facilities. We've applied for planning permission, but there some factions of the village opposed to progress.'

Honey pulled a face. 'That should go down well. I suppose you're going to tell the planning authority that the locals can use the facilities if it's passed.'

'Of course.'

‘And pigs might fly,’ muttered Honey. She’d seen big groups do that before: get the permission on a promise of the facilities being open to all. Hogwash!

Honey had one more question. ‘You don’t happen to have a German couple staying, do you?’

He frowned. ‘We have no one staying at present, not while the refurbishment is taking place. The coach party were a mistake. An unfortunate oversight.’ He glanced at his watch. ‘Look, I do have a very important meeting . . .’

‘Of course. I won’t take up any more of your time.’

There was nothing else she could learn — not from him. He was telling her only what he needed to. Whatever else she wanted to know she must find out for herself.

CHAPTER TWENTY-THREE

The girls behind the reception desk were stowing stationery in large boxes. A step ladder leaned against the wall behind them, likely the same one the men had used when cutting the security wires at Lobelia Cottage. Two men in high-visibility nylon waistcoats opened the doors for them.

Honey looked around at the mayhem. She practically had the place to herself. There was nobody around to see what she might get up to. She wouldn't be noticed doing a little snooping, now would she? And anyway, they all thought she was a police officer — right?

Naughty, naughty, said a little warning voice in her head.

'Get lost,' she muttered under her breath.

Her feet took her to the left, through a grand doorway which presently had no doors and along an empty passageway that echoed to her footsteps. Pots of paint were lined up at skirting level. Out of curiosity, she bent to take a look, fully expecting them to be of the required type and colour for use in a Grade I listed building dating from the time of Elizabeth I. The colours on the labels were evenly divided between Moroccan Orange and Egyptian Sand. They were also labelled as acrylic emulsion — hard wearing, of course, but not recommended for old plasterwork. The listed building inspectors would not approve. In fact, using such materials could very well result in a heavy fine.

She told herself they were destined for somewhere else, surely. Though if that were the case, they wouldn't be here in the first place, would they?

Suddenly she heard voices coming her way, echoing in the long emptiness. A set of stone steps went off to one side. She darted down those and, feeling like Alice in Wonderland, charged through the door at the bottom, stopping dead and closing it quietly behind her. It was dark. Her breath turned to steam. The sound of her every movement seemed to echo off the curved ceiling.

Ahead of her the passageway had a lower ceiling and was narrower than the one above. At some time in the past, it had been the domain of the army of servants employed to look after the family. She could imagine them scurrying around like busy mice, carrying out the labour that kept a stately home running like clockwork.

It was certainly not like that now, but instead was cold and empty. The only sound besides her footsteps was a long, low whine as though a draught was limbo-dancing beneath an ill-fitting door. The sound was unnerving, in fact a little ghostly, but Honey lived with ghosts, according to Mary Jane. Sometimes Honey believed her.

The coldness emanating from the walls was bone-chilling and made her shiver as though a fingernail had traced down her spine.

More tins of paint lined the walls at floor level. Terracotta this time. Someone obviously had it in mind to lighten things up. For centuries the walls must have been lime washed, the paint flaking in places. Where the paint brush had been, the walls were terracotta but peeling. The modern paint was obviously ineffective at covering the old lime wash, the old paint reacting with the new.

Three pots of paint sat in a row, one with the lid off. A brush had been left balancing on the rim. On a whim, she picked it up. The bristles looked stiff. She tapped them on the side of the can. Yep! They'd be easier to stab someone with than paint with.

She put the brush back, straightened and eyed the gloom ahead. Right! Now what?

She went forward. The kitchen and storage areas went off on either side of the passageway. At present there were no lights on and not a living thing — except for the odd spider, perhaps — trod this lonely place. Pushing open a swing door, she peered into the kitchen. The stainless steel was scrubbed down and not a pan, plate or cooking pot was left on view. It smelled as though it hadn't been used for a while; the odour of old plaster and acrylic paint outdid that of old cooking.

Daylight beckoned at the far end where the tunnel — it was best described as that — finished.

Satisfied that there was nothing in the kitchens or storerooms of interest, Honey headed in that direction.

As she gained the daylight, a sudden draught hit her, sending her hair flying across her face. She found herself outside looking up at the sky. A set of whitewashed steps to her right led upwards. Immediately ahead and above her, wrought-iron railings stopped anyone falling into the boxy void between the building and the world without. The railings were plainer than those framing the elegant main gate, but then this was the servants' entrance.

She was just about to let the door slam shut behind her and go up the steps when she heard raised voices. Cautiously she looked upwards. Two figures were silhouetted against the skyline, animated, rattled and ready for a fight. She recognised them immediately. Camilla Boylan and Julia Porter. Interior designers at war!

CHAPTER TWENTY-FOUR

Carefully, so as not to make a sound, Honey closed the door behind her and crossed to the wall immediately beneath the two designers, flattening herself against it.

Camilla was yelling. 'Philippe was *my* partner, so *I* take over this contract!'

Julia was equally loud — and venomous. 'He's dead, darling! What is it about the terms of the contract you don't understand, hmm? Get this in between your thick ears, darling. The contract died with him. That's it. All takers are welcome and I've put in a price to complete the project — with a few alterations reflecting my take on Philippe's design. So that's it.'

'Don't you turn your back on me!' Camilla exploded with anger. Honey half expected clouds of flustered feathers to come floating down, as though they were angry chickens fighting over scraps. She guessed they were talking about the St Margaret's Court contract. In all probability it was Philippe's signature on the contract, Camilla viewed only as his assistant. Sniffing the chance to make a fat profit, Julia had barged in.

She perceived the sound of a scuffle, surmised that hair was being pulled and polished red talons were out and ready for action. A cat fight was swiftly developing. Someone less sneaky would go up and try to calm things down, but Honey had got used to being sneakier than she'd ever thought possible. Since acquiring the position of crime liaison officer for the Bath Hotels Association, she had become more and more sneaky. It went with the job. If you wanted to find things out, you had to lie low and listen, not barge out and stick your oar in. It was a pound to a penny that a few home truths might be divulged before the two rivals got to the scratching and slapping.

'You bitch!'

'You cow!'

Other less-than-ladylike expletives came thick and fast, along with the sound of slaps, scuffling heels and ripping cloth.

'Give me that stuff back.'

'I don't have your stuff. I never bloody took it! I've never been near that bloody storeroom.'

Taunts were followed by screeches and the slamming of someone against the railings. They were battling like furies. Honey decided the time was ripe and took two steps at a time.

'OK, girls. The fight's over.'

Taken by surprise, the two women parted, and immediately began to straighten their business suits and smooth back their hair in order to give the impression that nothing whatsoever was happening.

'We were just having a little discussion,' said Julia in her rich, plummy voice, tossing her head.

Honey folded her arms and eyed them accusingly. 'What about?'

'Colour schemes,' said Camilla, jutting out her pointy chin.

'Yes. Yes indeed,' said Julia. She smoothed her blonde-streaked hair back behind her ears. 'We were comparing notes regarding the silk drapes for the honeymoon suite.'

'And I was acting as her sounding board,' added the pert-lipped, glossy-haired Camilla.

'And I'm your fairy godmother,' Honey mused. She wetted the tip of her finger and touched the blood seeping from a scratch on Camilla's cheek. 'So where's the loot, Julia?'

Camilla flinched.

Julia's perfect features faltered like a pie crust sagging in the rain.

'I'm sure I don't know what you mean.'

Honey faced her. 'You bet your sweet life you do. I heard you.' She jerked her thumb in the direction of the steps. 'Quite a little cat scrap. What do you do for an encore? Murder? Sorry!' she said, holding up her hands as though she'd made a genuine faux pas. 'Forget murder as an encore. How about murder being a prelude to this little shouting match? Now, which of you had the most to gain by Philippe's death? Eh, girls? Like to elaborate?'

Camilla looked dumbstruck. 'Are you saying what I think you're saying?'

Julia remained cool. 'I do believe she is, my dear Cammy. She's trying to accuse us of killing dear Philippe.'

'No,' said Camilla, shaking her head emphatically. 'I did not kill Philippe.'

Honey eyed her ruefully. 'Not for all that loot he kept in his storeroom?'

'No!' said Camilla, folding her arms defiantly. 'No, no, no!'

'You inherit everything he left you. You've got to be a suspect in view of that alone. As for you, Julia — well, I'm not sure. You're not mentioned in his will, but perhaps you think you should have been. Wasn't there gossip going round about you two?'

'Her and Philippe?' Camilla looked disgusted, her red lips forming a perfect oval, matched with round-eyed surprise.

Julia blushed. 'It was purely platonic.'

Her salmon-pink blush was enough to belie that little statement.

Honey congratulated herself. She'd taken a stab in the dark and hit the mark. Julia and Philippe had been having a little fling. She'd known for ages that he swung both ways, ever since Philippe had shown her the new bed linens and asked her if she wanted to try them. She was OK with him being bisexual. What she wasn't OK with were liars.

'He promised me some things,' Julia admitted.

Camilla glared. 'You bitch!'

She took a lunge. Honey stopped her, twisting her arm behind her back to hold on to her. Camilla was pretty mad, twisting and turning like a hyperventilating snake.

'Are you saying he promised to leave you some things in his will?' said Honey between the huffs and puffs of trying to keep her grip on Camilla, who was still shouting at the top of her voice.

'The stupid sod! He never listened. I warned him. I bloody well warned him!'

Honey looked up at the windows at the back of the hotel. It was hard to tell if anyone was listening. Round at the front the builders would have been leaning over the scaffolding, a fight between two women brightening their day.

Camilla wriggled. Honey gave her a shake. Twisting the girl around, she peered into her face so she could see her reaction. 'What did you warn him about? Did you warn him to keep the will as it was, leave everything to you, nothing to her? Was he going to change that will, Camilla?'

'Well he didn't, did he!' she spat.

'He couldn't. He was dead. Now, Camilla. If you keep this up you're going to find yourself down at the station with a butch DI asking the questions. How will that suit?'

She felt the girl go limp.

'Fine,' she said, slowly relinquishing her grip.

Honey was about to ask about the missing list of items from Philippe's storeroom, when Mr Parrot appeared. Honey wasn't really surprised that someone had called the battling beauties to his attention. Someone had to be watching out of those blank-faced windows.

'What's going on here?'

He glared pointedly at each woman in turn, eyes unblinking, face as pasty as porridge.

'These women were fighting,' Honey explained. 'I've sorted things out. No need for you to get involved,' she added with a tight smile.

Camilla pouted as she rubbed her arm. 'I could complain about police harassment.'

'No, you can't,' Honey replied breezily. 'I'm not police. I'm a civilian,' she added.

Parrot opened his mouth to comment but merely narrowed his eyes.

Julia Porter, never one to let a lucky chance slip through her fingers, adopted a confident smile for Mr Parrot's benefit.

'I'm here to speak to the project management committee about the interior design contract following the death of the previous contractor.'

Camilla interrupted with all the politeness of a pint-sized rugby scrum-half, elbowing Julia aside.

'I'm Philippe Fabiere's partner. No need to change contractors at all. I'll be carrying on where he left off.'

Parrot arched a thin, fair eyebrow. One corner of his mouth lifted in what might pass for a smile at a convention of grumpy old men.

'I'm sorry. A totally new contractor has been appointed. The owner wishes to bring the building up to date. He favours a Moroccan theme.'

All their mouths dropped open — including Honey's. Those paint pots she'd found were evidence of impending sacrilege!

'Moroccan?' Julia almost screamed the word.

'Moroccan,' Parrot repeated. He looked somewhat bemused by their astonishment. 'Is there anything further I can help you with, ladies?'

Not one of them managed to say a single word. As the eldest, Honey gave it her best shot, but her jaw ached with the effort.

Silently, the three women headed for their cars.

'I feel gutted,' Camilla grunted, her bottom lip pouting further than her upper.

Julia added her disquiet in her own subdued manner.

'I feel quite put out.'

'Shit,' snapped Honey. 'I feel like getting drunk. Either of you doing anything tonight?'

Julia glared. 'Like hell!'

Camilla demurred, then, apparently remembering Honey was still a client, changed her mind. 'That would be nice.'

She forced a tight little smile. Money always had the last say, thought Honey. Likely always would.

CHAPTER TWENTY-FIVE

Leaving her car in the hotel car park, she headed for Cybil's gingerbread cottage just across the road. The old maid opened the door dressed in something violet, teamed with purple mules with black pompoms on the toes. For the first time since meeting her, Honey noticed how tall she was — taller than Honey herself, strongly boned and angular, her shoulders broad like those of an athlete.

'Just getting the logs in from out back,' she said.

The logs were in a wicker basket with a huge handle. It looked heavy. She'd placed them on the floor prior to answering the door.

Two Persian cats, their orange eyes gleaming in a sea of seal blue above snub noses, wrapped themselves around her ankles like hairy leg warmers. She held a third cat in her arms: a Siamese with ice-blue eyes, a sleek coat and a sour expression. The creature seemed disgruntled and yowled at the same time as digging its claws into Cybil's arm. Cybil didn't appear to notice.

Honey offered to carry the log basket through.

'If you can manage it, my dear. It is very heavy.'

Honey smiled and shook her head. She was younger and stronger than Cybil, so of course she could.

The weight of the basket almost pulled her arm off.

Cybil noticed she was struggling. 'Let me, dear. I'm quite used to it.' She picked up the basket with ease.

'I've had a word with the hotel manager regarding the damaged wiring,' said Honey, feeling well and truly put in her place,

'Come in and tell me about it. Shut the door, would you please?'

The door was shut. The cats' yowling accompanied the sound of their footsteps on flagstone floors.

'They don't like Su Ching because she's foreign,' explained Cybil as she led Honey into the parlour. 'It's because she's so terribly different from them. They have long blue coats and orange eyes, and she has blue eyes and a short, creamy coat with chocolate extremities. They regard it as a significant departure from the norm, an alien in their long-coated midst.'

'You'd think that as cats they'd all get on the same,' Honey remarked.

'Why should they?' riposted Cybil. 'Humans don't. We are of many creeds, colours and tongues. There are definite differences.'

Honey had to concede that the old girl had a point. However, she wasn't here to talk about cats. She explained that she'd spoken to the hotel manager and he'd agreed to repair the wiring to her security cameras at the hotel's expense.

Honey handed her the USB stick. 'Here. I expect you'll need that.'

'Not really. I have backups. I keep everything properly organised, you know. Everything is timed and dated so I know exactly what happened and when. It's better than keeping a diary or reading a book. Would you like to see my study and my security screens?'

Screens?

Why would an elderly lady, concerned as she might be about intruders, have more than one security screen?

Honey was suddenly grabbed by a sense of unease. She told herself she was jumping to conclusions. All the same, the feeling of trepidation stayed with her as she followed the old biddy up the stairs.

The floorboards along the landing creaked as she was led to the study, a room with red roses on the wall. More roses bent their heavy heads from what looked to be a fine Sèvres vase — though she couldn't be sure about that, not sure enough to point out that Cybil should not be putting water and mildewing rose stems in it.

Paintings in fine gilt frames hung from the walls. A display of knots hung in a glass-fronted display outside the study door. It stood out from the paintings, a practical subject among sheer works of art.

Honey expressed her inability to tie a decent knot.

'Sailors are very good at knots,' Cybil replied.

Her thoughts were instantly banished the moment she saw the bank of surveillance monitors. At present they were blank, though judging by the winking red lights, they were still receiving power.

'Isn't it a shame?' moaned Cybil. 'I can't watch anything. How can I keep up with day-to-day events without my little darlings here?'

She was not referring to the cats. Honey reached the only conclusion she could. Unbeknown to her friends, Cybil was an inveterate busybody. A nosy parker of the first order. Those screens were more beloved than her cats. Now, wasn't that something!

Honey thought about gently persuading her that spying on her neighbours wasn't such a good idea. After due consideration she thought better of it. Observant people could be very useful. They didn't miss a thing, including all the trivialities that other people failed to notice.

Recalling Mr Parrot's conversation, she decided it wouldn't hurt to do a bit of prying herself. 'Did you go to the village meeting on the night of the fourth?'

'Of course.'

'Were there many people there?'

'A full house! Feelings in this village are running very high with regard to these people wanting to vulgarise our beautiful valley and such a beautiful house. Sir Albert Shaddick would be turning in his grave if he knew what was happening to his beautiful home. He built it in the sixteenth century, you know. His son was lucky enough to choose the right side at the start of the Civil War in the mid-sixteen hundreds and swapped sides in time for the return of Charles the Second. Shrewd lot, the Shaddicks.'

'Very auspicious.'

'Not really. I think a more fitting description would be cunning,' said Cybil her eyes sparkling.

'What did the hotel management have to say about the matter?'

Cybil placed the cat on the mantelpiece, from where the Siamese yowled down at the Persians like some medieval baron locked safely in his castle and taunting would-be aggressors.

'The hotel promised the world, but nothing will come of it. The owner is Russian. His history suggests that he's not the sort to give anything away unless he has to. Such a man will make sure that he doesn't have to. He will not allow the village to dictate to him.'

'How will he placate them?'

It was difficult to read the look in Cybil's steel-grey eyes. Perhaps there was a hint of malice there, perhaps even outright evil. Whatever the look, Honey had the distinct impression that the faded, ugly dresses were hiding a far more nimble mind and body than met the eye.

'He won't. He'll have his own way. He'd destroy this village and everyone in it to get what he wants. The village would rather burn the house down than see it being destroyed by a bunch of foreign peasants.'

The words she used and the way she said them almost made Honey's hair stand on end. It was pretty strong language for a lady who loved cats and wore flowery dresses.

Cabbage roses and violets would never look so innocent again.

'You don't seem to like foreigners very much.'

Cybil eyed her wryly. 'I have met many foreigners in my time. I didn't like them very much back then. I'm a bit like the Persian pussies in that regard. I'm wary of anyone who looks and acts a little differently.'

It was tempting to pry into Cybil's background, but Honey held her tongue. A life behind a typewriter at the Ministry of Defence would prove pretty disappointing — if that was all she'd ever done there.

Honey asked her about the meeting at the village hall. 'I take it the hotel manager was there?'

Suddenly the Siamese swooped down on the other two cats from her mantelpiece perch.

'Warn them, Susie! Show them what your talons can do!'

The cats yowled at each other, one Persian cat diving for cover beneath a chair, the other diving into a coal scuttle from where it peered out like a nervous tortoise.

The Siamese had its claws out and was making its dreadful sound, nothing like your average moggy.

Honey was taken aback.

'Miss Camper-Young?'

The elderly lady appeared not to hear her. She muttered to herself as she placed the Siamese in a cat box and firmly closed the lid. The cat within protested at being left in the darkness.

'Miss Camper-Young?'

The steel-grey eyes blinked from within the folds of flesh that hooded them.

'I wasn't expecting you,' she said accusingly.

Honey shook her head. 'I'm sorry. I came on the off chance.'

The old lady stared back at her as though digesting what had been said.

'You shouldn't walk into people's houses unannounced.'

Honey was about to protest that she hadn't walked in unannounced, that Cybil had let her in.

'Will the cat be all right in there?' she asked by way of diversion.

She indicated the cat box.

Frowning, Cybil glared at her accusingly. 'You had no business to put her in there.'

'I didn't. You put her—'

'Don't be ridiculous.'

She got the cat back out of the box and proceeded to stroke it.

Honey tried to make sense of what had been said but decided she didn't have the skill for that. Instead she decided to backtrack. Again she asked whether the hotel manager, Mr Parrot, had been at the meeting.

The wrinkles in her face deepened as she delved into her memory.

'I don't recall . . . but *he* was there,' she said suddenly, her face lighting up. 'The big boss. The Russian. The criminal. The *oligarch*, as everyone seems to call them these days. KGB, more like. I saw his car outside.'

'He was sitting in his car?'

'Yes, but he knew exactly what was going on inside.'

'What makes you think that?'

'He got out for a cigarette. They still have bad habits, those Russians, you know. Totally unaware that smoking is bad for your health.'

Feeling proud to be British and health conscious, Honey agreed with her.

Cybil carried on. 'I had gone out for a little fresh air — and to take a closer look at him. It is imperative to know who you are dealing with in events of this magnitude. All of them were well "tooled up" — I mean in a technical manner. When the car door opened, I saw the equipment and the Bluetooth in his ear. He was listening to what was going on inside on the outside.' She nodded suddenly. 'That was it. He was outside. The manager was inside and that man Olsen was talking — in fact, the man who was killed was there too for the first half of the meeting. He didn't linger though. I recall he said some things his partners didn't like. They were arguing up there on the platform. He was a strange one anyway — dark skin, blond hair. How ridiculous to have hair like that with such dark skin. It isn't as though it can change anything, is it?'

Honey couldn't quite grasp where Cybil's train of thought was going and didn't want to go there. She was a product of a bygone age and as such had very old-fashioned views. All that interested her was that Philippe had had a run-in with other members of the project team. She'd known how much Philippe had appreciated antiques and historical artefacts, but surely he wouldn't have got caught up in the overall development of a listed building? He certainly wasn't the sort to get embroiled in a feud between his employers and the villagers.

'Do you know the villagers well?' Honey asked.

'Of course I do. I keep an eye on everything that happens in this village and I make sure that anyone who falls out of line is pulled back into it instantly! Here's the proof!'

A pair of large, powerful hands held up a three-inch-wide file that was full to bursting with paper.

Honey eyed the file with grave misgiving. The Cybil Camper-Young of the Laura Ashley rose-covered dresses was turning out to be something of an obsessive. There were letters of complaint to the local planning authority, neighbours and the landlord of the local pub. Yet again Honey fancied a change of direction was in order.

'So! The meeting was useful?'

Cybil's shoulders, as wide and angular as a wooden coat hanger, shrugged dismissively. 'I stayed to hear all that I wanted to hear, and then I went off to continue my observations.'

'Watching the Russian.'

'No. The Martians. They're only around at night. I see them in the north meadow; that's the one behind my cottage, though sometimes they root around in the bushes opposite.'

'Martians!'

The cats purred in response to their mistress's sugary words and slivers of smoked salmon, which she took from a silver butter dish sitting on the table.

'There you are, my beautiful darlings,' she said to the cats, before her attention returned to Honey. 'They're here to kill us all. It's the Martians the police should be investigating. They're allies of the Russians. Wicked aliens all of them.'

Honey felt a tad confused. She'd gone to see the hotel manager with fire in her belly. How could he treat an old lady so? Well, quite frankly she could understand why! Cybil was an old busybody with an odd mind and the muscles of a world-class weightlifter, if that log basket was anything to go by. It turned out that she was also the sort who wrote letters to local authority officials if the neighbours didn't put their rubbish out on time, or if someone installed a new window in a loft without planning permission. It struck her that Mr Parrot and/or his employees were well and truly brassed off with her. Besides that, the old girl was potty. Honey would never again see a Laura Ashley dress without thinking of little green men and strange cats. On the other hand, the timing of the wires being cut was too much of a coincidence.

Cybil was quite the busybody. But like a firework, busybodies could be primed to go off how and when you wanted, as long as you handled it right.

Honey mentioned how appreciative she would be if Cybil were to keep an eye on things. Doherty would be OK with that. She was making enquiries relevant to a murder case. And had she heard about this bunch of morons turning a very grand Elizabethan house into something resembling a brothel in Marrakesh? Hopefully Cybil would repeat it to the planning authority. They in turn would pay a visit and make sure it didn't happen. That would be something positive.

The Siamese cat was back in the cat box wailing its head off.

Cybil eyed the box with a thoroughly distasteful look.

'Your cat doesn't sound happy,' Honey said, purely as an observation. She didn't know too much about cats.

‘She’s not mine,’ snapped Cybil. ‘She wandered in here. She doesn’t belong. Never mind. I’ll soon get rid of her.’

Honey told herself that the deadly intent in Cybil’s eyes was down to her own vivid imagination. The old girl would surely give the cat to the local home for feline waifs and strays, wouldn’t she? Either way, the Persians would rule supreme.

CHAPTER TWENTY-SIX

Sitting inside her car, leaning on the steering wheel, Honey took a deep breath. Well, that was that. She tried phoning Doherty to tell him about Cybil and her security cameras.

Unfortunately, the hills to either side of the valley folded in like two giant table napkins. She couldn't get a signal, so the phone went back into her big leather bag. There was nothing for it but to leave. The two warring interior designers were leaving now too. She watched Julia drive out in her dark-green Jaguar. Camilla followed in her 4 x 4. Why such a small person needed such a big car, she couldn't quite fathom. Maybe it was useful for ferrying interior design stuff around — fabrics, wallpapers, paint charts and whatnot. But that big?

Another vehicle squeezed past them and parked opposite to where Honey waited for the road to clear. A wiry man with fuzzy hair and wearing an orange shirt got out. He'd been attempting to manhandle a whole load of other stuff out with him — bits of material, rolled-up paper that could only be plans of the hotel. His rear stuck out; torso hidden. Swatches of colour fluttered like trapped butterflies on half a dozen pieces of card. One or more of the objects kept falling from his grasp. He looked addled, frazzled and not fit to be out. She was almost sure she'd seen his face before — in an article she vaguely remembered reading in the *Bath Magazine*. The interior designer, Keith Richardson Smythe.

For a moment her gaze fixed on the elegant mansion. Its stonework was dark with age but its lead-paned windows glittered like diamonds each time she moved her head. Philippe must have loved this place, she thought. He'd sometimes said that he'd been born into the wrong age. 'I would have preferred to have lived any time before the death of Queen Victoria, my darling,' he'd said with a casual wave of his long white hand. 'But preferably Elizabethan. I think the doublet and hose would have suited me a treat, don't you think so, my darling? A nice turn of calf and all that!'

Hands resting on his trim waist, he'd done a little pirouette and tossed his elegant head. He was right, of course. He would have made a very elegant Elizabethan gentleman — minus the dyed-blond hair, of course, and the dark skin might have caused some consternation.

Thinking of the manner of his death saddened her. She counted off the list of suspects in her mind.

Camilla Boylan. She stood to gain an inheritance by way of the business. Julia? It appeared that she too could have inherited something, though the fact that Philippe had died before confirming anything cast doubt on her guilt. No wonder the two of them were fighting like cat and dog.

What about the new interior designer? Had he bumped Philippe off in the hope of gaining his contract? It was possible, but she couldn't add him to her list just yet. He was fairly new on the scene as far as the murder investigation went. She'd have to make enquiries.

Next on her list was Ferdinand Olsen. He was a prime mover on the project committee and was having home problems. Husbands with home problems could snap in a minute.

Joybell Peters seemed a hard sort. She served on the management committee and hadn't had a good word to say about Philippe. She'd also been having a relationship with Ferdinand Olsen — though Honey couldn't blame her for that.

Thinking of Olsen's exotic dark eyes, slim frame and tumbling curls brought back the surprise she'd experienced on first meeting him. What the hell was someone like him doing with someone like Deirdre?

She reminded herself that younger men were often attracted to older women. Some found an experienced woman more interesting than a younger one. Mature women also tended to be richer. *Money again*, she thought with a toss of her head. *Does it always come back to that?*

'Think laterally,' she muttered. 'Who else have we got?'

For a start there was the waiter who'd disappeared at the time of the murder. He could not be discounted. No one ran away unless they were running from something. Aloysius Rodriguez had disappeared off the face of the earth. Portugal was his home, but even with the help of Interpol, he had not yet been traced. And what possible reason could he have for killing Philippe? Unless it was sexual — an affair that Aloysius didn't want his wife finding out about.

The shrubs and trees that helped camouflage the car park from the main house and the road began to flutter as a rain-filled breeze stirred their branches. For a brief second she thought she saw someone's hand wave from among them. She looked more carefully before her attention was caught by Mr Parrot coming down the steps behind her in the company of another man. They appeared to be arguing — or rather the other man appeared to be laying down the law. There were two other men just behind them. Although her fingers were folded over the ignition key, she refrained from turning it. The two men she was watching were worryingly familiar. She'd seen them performing on a grainy black-and-white security recording Cybil had shown her. Parrot had lied. It would have been nice to catch him out, but she reined herself in. After all she didn't want him studying her credentials too closely. Best, she decided, to let sleeping dogs lie.

Nosing the car towards the gate, she headed back towards the A4 and Bath.

Halfway there her phone rang. The traffic was heavy, the police out in force directing traffic, so she didn't chance answering it and receiving a heavy fine. Answering phones while on the move was a big no-no. Not until she was parking her car did she return Doherty's call. He didn't answer her right away — not until she found herself on the street and trying to decide whether she should head for home or take a peek at the Spencers' general sale.

Spencers' won. She was perusing the exquisite embroidery running up the sides of a pair of Victorian silk stockings when Doherty returned her call.

'Steve! You are never going to believe this, but a friend of my mother's—'

She heard him groan as though he'd suddenly acquired a toothache; her mother had that effect on her too on occasion.

'Listen! It's not what you think. A friend of my mother's — Cybil Camper-Young — you wouldn't know her, so don't ask. She's built like an all-in wrestler, although she tries to play down the fact, and she lives in Lobelia Cottage immediately opposite the entrance to St Margaret's Court, and guess what . . .?'

'I won't bother. You're going to tell me anyway.'

He sounded resigned. And laid back. And strangely uninterested.

'She has a security camera — or at least, she did have, and guess what . . .?'

'You've already said that.'

Now he sounded glum.

'She's just amazing. According to her some little green men from Mars are responsible for the murder.'

'Great. We won't bother with an identikit picture; we've got hundreds on file.'

'That's not all. Two thugs from the hotel cut the wires to her security cameras just before Philippe was killed. What do you make of that?'

'Interesting.'

He didn't sound like he found it interesting. Honey was disappointed but decided that a little uplifting of spirits was needed and she had just the thing. She fingered the silk stockings, holding one up to the light. My, but they were so, so sexy!

'You sound down, old buddy. Let me take a stab at raising your spirits. What's black and shiny and looks good when worn with four-inch heels and held up with frilly garters? Wanna guess?'

The fact that he didn't immediately bite was a clear message. Doherty always — *always* responded to the sexy stuff. Not this time.

Her spirits sank. She stated the first thing that came into her mind. 'Something bad has happened.'

He confirmed that indeed it had. 'Deirdre Olsen's been trampled to death by her own horse.'

Honey's breath caught in her throat. 'That's terrible. She loved those horses.' She frowned. 'Hard to believe in fact.' It was tantamount to learning that someone had been killed by a close friend.

Doherty made comment. 'Perhaps they didn't reciprocate.'

'I don't think you believe that.'

'No. I don't think I do. Neither do I believe it to have been an accident.'

Honey let the silk stockings drift back into their box. 'I'm all ears. What makes you think that?'

'Olsen's gone.'

'And?'

'A neighbour saw him arrive. Saw him leave some time later in a pretty big hurry too.'

He wasn't too forthcoming about the details of Mrs Olsen's death and why he thought it was murder, but she probed a little.

'So how would he get the horse to kick her to death?'

'To my mind anyone with a strong pair of legs and a knowledge of horses would have been out of there p.d.q.

Even though the perpetrator — a bloody great big horse by the name of Lord John — has a bit of a temper, she was a horsey woman. She'd cope. Women like that know how to handle themselves and handle horses.'

Honey agreed with him and immediately made the comparison with Cybil.

There was a pause. For a split second she was sure he was going to take a detour from work and get personal. She was wrong.

'It's just a gut instinct. I'll wait for the forensic and pathology report.'

She couldn't explain the feeling of disappointment but forced herself to keep on track too. A couple of possibilities occurred to her.

'She could have been drugged — or the horse could have,' she suggested.

He sighed. 'I'll start off with a pathology report on Mrs Olsen and a blood test on the horse.'

She began thinking about the romantic dreams she'd been having of late. Time off. Just the two of them. Seemed that's all they would be until this was over. 'That's your social life curtailed for the immediate future.'

'Long hours, no sleep and no . . . socialising. Never mind, once all this is over . . .'

Keenly sensitive to his mood, Honey opted for sympathy.

'Never mind. We can get together eventually. You bet we will.'

A warm glow seemed to diffuse down the telephone line. She could almost feel him smiling. 'You're part of the hotel world and likely to hear more gossip than I am. You also know the right people to ask. Go to it.'

'I will. Have you found the Portuguese waiter?'

'No. Everyone we've interviewed swears he was in the victim's company on and off. Something to do with art, I believe.'

'I heard the same. Nothing substantial, though I suppose the fact that he's gone missing puts him in the frame. There's no such thing as a coincidence — isn't that the saying?'

'Very much so.' There was a pause. 'Hey, I like anything that goes with four-inch heels. You know that don't you?' It was as though he'd pressed rewind.

She smiled into the phone. The vision she'd painted had hit home. 'A little thought to keep you warm while you work.'

'High heels kill me — one way or another.'

* * *

If he'd had the courage, he would have told her then and there about winning the night at St Margaret's Court. As it was, he decided the time wasn't right, and anyway, the place was still in a state with builders and decorators all over the place. The prize would coincide with the reopening, which shouldn't be too far off. He only hoped that he wouldn't be too busy around that time. He shrugged his shoulders against his jacket, an act of determination more than anything else. He'd make damn sure he wasn't too busy. This was his chance, a chance he'd long been waiting for. He'd take some of the leave due to him. The two of them deserved it. And she'd accept. Of course she would. And soon he would ask her. Despite work and the fear of rejection, he damned well would!

CHAPTER TWENTY-SEVEN

Ivan Sarkov hesitated beside the door of the sleek black Mercedes with smoked-glass windows. His face was red with anger. The planning authority had sent along their listed buildings inspector. He'd insisted that the Moroccan theme and the paints they'd chosen would attract a heavy fine if they went ahead and used them. They'd stipulated traditional, and traditional it would be. The interior designer had been informed and was relieved. He'd told the manager that they wouldn't get away with anything else but traditional and had been proved right.

Turning abruptly, Sarkov took Parrot by surprise. He held a warning finger in front of his manager's face.

'Sort out that Keith character.'

'I'll get him to sort out the paints . . .'

'Do not trouble me with the details! Just do it. Also, the old lady in the cottage opposite.'

'I understand. I will get it done. I promise you won't have the police nosing around again. It won't take long. She's only an old lady.'

Sarkov's eyes glittered and his look hardened. 'She is *not* just an old lady. She is a very *dangerous* old lady!'

'Yes sir. I understand.'

Sarkov stared at him. Parrot really thought he understood about keeping Cybil happy.

Parrot had a pale face at the best of times. It was now a sickly grey colour, like a yellow sky before a fall of snow. It was he who'd given the order to Serge and Orlov to cut the wires. The woman was a definite problem to his little sideline in stolen goods. He'd thought the problem had been dealt with, but the two goons, being Russians, had been slow to carry out his orders. God knows what the old girl had on her security system. Nothing too incriminating, he hoped. If there had been, she would have already informed the police, wouldn't she?

'I'm off on leave shortly, sir,' he added quickly before the door was shut.

Sarkov eyed him with undisguised contempt. Parrot was one of those men who thought the earth would stand still without them around to give it a push.

Ivan's eyes pierced through him. 'I will manage.'

The car door hushed comfortably shut.

Parrot watched the sleek limousine slide away, aware that his armpits were damp and that beads of sweat had broken out on his high, shiny forehead. On the other hand, his mouth was dry and so were his lips. The sight of the car leaving helped him regain his self-control. His racing heart slowed to an endurable level. The sweat chilled on his forehead. He'd come through OK, he told himself, at least for now. Time enough to do what must be done. Tonight he would go round to Lobelia Cottage, make friends with the old girl and gain entry. She'd probably make him a cup of tea and he could pretend to check her security monitors while she went out to the kitchen to boil the kettle. Wasn't that what all old ladies do?

CHAPTER TWENTY-EIGHT

It was bound to happen. Casper wanted a report.

Honey was flipping eggs when the call came summoning her to his office.

Mary Jane was her usual generous self. 'Wanna lift?'

Fearing for her safety, Honey declined. 'I think I fancy a walk! It's not very far anyway.'

She paused at the entrance to La Reine Rouge and checked her appearance. When it came to first impressions, meticulous décor and good housekeeping, La Reine Rouge was second to none. Feeling reasonable enough, she made her entrance.

Sigmund Farley, Casper's new receptionist, was meticulously writing something on a notepad. He had frosty white hair, a tanned complexion and the sort of shoulders only a stint in Her Majesty's armed forces could produce.

His waistcoat was of silver and green brocade. His shirt looked expensive, and he wore a dark-green cravat with a sparkly tiepin. Sigmund believed in blending in with his surroundings. His surroundings were Regency, so he was too. Oh, and he wore a monocle — she glimpsed her reflection in it thanks to the light coming from beneath a pure silk shade.

He looked up when she came in and smiled his professional smile.

'Has Tootsie come to see the captain?'

Sigmund was ex Royal Navy. Why he called her Tootsie she wasn't quite sure, but she looked behind her just in case he was addressing somebody else.

'If you mean Casper, yes. And my name's Honey.'

When he straightened he towered over her by six inches or more and gave the impression of looking down his nose at her; the monocle didn't help.

'Sweetie,' he said in a decisive manner. 'I shall call you Sweetie — seeing as your name is Honey and honey is sweet.'

'What's wrong with Honey?'

He didn't appear to be listening. His face was upturned as he dialled and informed Casper that she was here.

'Sir, this is Farley. Your eleven o'clock is here. Permission to board?'

Bath was a city that attracted eccentrics, so Sigmund's terminology hardly fazed her. Anyway, it was trivial after little green men and old ladies who could give MI5 a run for their money. Sigmund was just another nut in the bar of chocolate that typified her varied acquaintances.

Casper St John Gervais was sitting behind his very big, very expensive and very antique walnut desk. As usual he was immaculately dressed, his shirt blazing white, his tie olive green and his jacket petrol blue. A sapphire and two tiny diamonds glinted from a gold tiepin.

The precious stones were by the by, but Honey envied him that desk — not the piece of furniture itself but the fact that it was so tidy. Casper dealt with one piece of paper at a time. Once it was dealt with it was placed in a neat pile. Once the pile reached a certain height, it was filed away. Thus his desktop always looked incredibly neat and empty. Much as she tried, the top of her desk resembled the *Titanic* after the iceberg had hit it and just before it capsized.

Fixing her with a stony gaze, Casper beckoned her to take a seat. She did so apprehensively. Casper hadn't greeted her cheerily. He hadn't even greeted her miserably.

He eyed her over the apex of his steepled fingers with a searching look, the sort he wore when he wanted immediate answers.

'Have you seen the newspaper?'

She shook her head. 'No.'

'It's decidedly lurid. Bath and the murder of Philippe Fabiere have made the nationals. They're saying that his death is linked to sexual deviancy in the city. Sadomasochism, no less.'

'That's not true,' Honey said hotly. 'Philippe wasn't into any of that. He was a gentleman in every respect.'

Casper's hard expression creased into interest. 'Are you sure?'

Honey gave a curt nod. 'Absolutely. Philippe may have swung both ways, but he wasn't into that scene. He and Julia were an item. She would know better than anyone.'

'That's good. Very good. We need to fight back against the press, publicly.'

'Julia might not like it.'

'The common good outweighs personal preference. She'll have to put up with it.'

Honey opened her mouth to object, but thought that maybe Casper had a point. In any case, it was pretty obvious that the news had surprised him. She vaguely wondered whether Philippe and Casper had been more than friends, though she wasn't really sure whether they were suited.

Casper had turned thoughtful, tapping one beautifully manicured finger on his bottom lip and gazing into the distance. Poor Julia. Honey didn't envy her. She was about to have a horde of journalists lusting for her story. Still, if it set the matter straight . . .

'Talking of setting the matter straight, the refurbishment of the Green River is going fine and Camilla assures me it should be finished on time — two weeks, to be precise. I could do with a few customers around then, and I haven't had any referrals from the association of late.'

'Ah, yes,' said Casper, his head half turned away, his eyes hooded.

His attitude worried her. Something was up.

'I've been thinking you might like a break from your police liaison work. Sigmund is quite interested . . .'

'You can't do this to me!'

This was the last thing she'd expected. She'd put off quite a few bookings, and she'd counted on making up for the shortfall through the association once the work was completed.

Casper's face stiffened. Hands folded in front of him, he outlined what was in his mind.

'Sigmund is very keen to get involved with the police.'

I bet he is! 'I don't think Doherty will be pleased,' Honey growled. 'Sigmund isn't his type.'

Casper became sniffy. 'Doherty will have to conform to modern thinking. If he doesn't, then I dare say the chief constable will replace him with someone who does.'

Honey shook her head in disbelief. 'After all that I've done I'm to be replaced with a Regency dandy? What does Sigmund know about policing?'

'A great deal,' said Casper, fixing her with a warning look. 'He used to be a military policeman in the Royal Navy.'

The revelation came as something of a surprise, though it might explain Sigmund's penchant for dressing up in period costume.

Feeling deflated, Honey headed for the door. 'So how long do I have before he takes over?'

Casper wiped his nose with a lace-trimmed handkerchief. Honey caught a whiff of rose-scented cologne.

'Let's see if you solve this case and we'll take it from there.'

CHAPTER TWENTY-NINE

This couldn't be happening! Casper couldn't mean it. Honey had been far from enthusiastic when first approached about getting involved in crime. But now the thought of it being taken away was devastating.

The sensation of being short-changed stayed with her as she marched towards Queen's Square. Feeling tempted to mumble words her mother wouldn't want to hear, she kept her head down. Because of this, she wasn't initially aware of the car creeping along beside her. It wasn't until the third blast on the horn that she jerked her head up. Doherty was signalling her to hop in.

'You look miffed,' he said as she settled in beside him, hugging her bag for comfort. 'Anything I've done?'

She shook her head. Her lips felt as though they were glued together. How was she going to tell him that she was being replaced as crime liaison officer by a guy wearing breeches and a damask waistcoat? Doherty was basically a tolerant, decent man, but he wouldn't like Sigmund replacing her as his point of contact with the Hotels Association. She was pretty certain about that. Or was she kidding herself?

She managed to part her lips. 'Do you like working with me?'

He was concentrating on steering them out into the traffic, so he didn't immediately answer. When he did, his response was warmly reassuring.

'That's a daft question. You sound as though you need cheering up. How about a short drive?'

'Anything else?'

'Yes. Care for a warm scone and a cup of tea?'

'OK.'

Resting her chin in her hand she stared out of the window without really seeing anything. By the time she came to, they were some way out of Bath and surrounded by open farmland and extensive views. They were parked outside what had once been a toll house on the A46. Built in the decorative Strawberry Gothic style, it now housed a delightful little tea room just off the road which sported a grand view of rolling farmland, the city of Bristol sprouting like a field of mushrooms in the distance.

'We're up here,' she said as though they'd somehow climbed a mountain.

He was holding the door open for her. 'You sound surprised.'

'I thought you might be thinking of whisking me away for a dirty weekend.'

'Would you have come?' he asked.

She thought about it. The disappointment she felt at what Casper had suggested had filled her with gloom. She couldn't help being reticent. 'It's not the weekend. Besides, I'm not that kind of girl.'

If she had been more in tune with the vibes she might have noticed that his smile had frozen for a split second. As it was, she was down in the dumps, and in the dumps she would stay.

'Come on.' Cupping her elbow, he guided her into the tea shop and didn't let go until she was safely seated in front of the magnificent view.

Sitting slightly to her side but opposite, he folded his hands and asked her what was wrong.

Although feeling better, largely thanks to the warmth of the tea shop and the smell of freshly baked scones, she sighed heavily. 'I have to solve this crime — like, today, though preferably yesterday.'

He gave a kind of retreating jerk of his head, as though she'd tapped him on the nose.

'Are you on some kind of bonus scheme?'

Lowering her eyes, she explained the situation.

'Casper has it in mind to replace me in favour of a guy who used to be in the Royal Navy military police unless I show some progress in this case. That means solving it — or I'm out.'

She felt his eyes on her. She didn't like pity of any description. She didn't want him to feel sorry for her, only regretful at the prospect of them not working together again. But she did want him to care. Caring was different from pitying; it was more affectionate. They'd been together long enough for her to know the difference.

It took a full minute for her to meet his look. What she saw there took her by surprise. He was almost laughing.

'This is very serious stuff. You won't like working with Sigmund. He's a nut,' she told him.

His smile stuck.

'And he's gay.'

The smile lessened, but only slightly. 'Does this guy work for Casper?'

She nodded.

'So why would he want a member of his staff to get involved? It's always struck me that Casper likes to keep crime at arm's length. He likes routine. Seems to me that he wants this guy out from under his feet.'

The tea and scones came complete with little pots of Cornish cream and home-made jam.

Honey straightened and she felt brighter. Things were getting better all the time. What Doherty had said made sense.

'You could be right. I'd want to get rid of Sigmund if he worked for me. He keeps referring to Casper as "captain" and me as "Tootsie". How crazy is that?'

‘Irritating,’ said Doherty. ‘How long have you known Casper?’

‘Long enough.’

He was right. Casper *would* find that irritating, but employment laws being what they were, he couldn’t possibly fire Sigmund without good reason. A little respite was the short-term alternative.

With a light heart, she tucked into the scones with far more vigour — and more jam and cream — than she would have previously. Funny how the thought of losing your job ruined your appetite.

She got back to basics. ‘So, how goes it with Deirdre?’

Topped with liberal lashings of jam and cream, the scones slid into her mouth.

‘Traces of belladonna — deadly nightshade — in her stomach. Lots of bruises caused by iron-clad hooves plus one more likely to have been caused by a tyre iron — a very big one.’

Honey frowned as she chewed. ‘Why all this belladonna stuff? Why poison her and Philippe with something as old-fashioned as that?’

The knife Doherty was using to plaster jam onto his cream paused in mid-air. ‘Belladonna is used in herbal medicine for a number of ailments. It can calm people down to the point of unconsciousness, apparently — something I didn’t know.’

Honey’s chewing slowed. She looked into his face as she considered the implications of what he was saying.

‘Read my mind,’ she said. ‘Am I guessing right?’

‘One victim was choked. One was kicked to death. Both had ingested a sedative beforehand — enough to knock them out.’

‘Poison, eh?’

‘The preferred weapon of a woman, they say.’

‘That’s old-fashioned nonsense!’

‘So, who then?’

‘Julia? Camilla?’

'Both women!'

'Coincidence!'

Honey was scraping the last of the jam and cream from the porcelain dishes they came in. Doing it properly took some time, so she didn't at first cotton on to Doherty's silence. She held the scone hovering in front of her lips once she did notice.

'There's something else?'

Doherty turned from staring at the landscape to face her. 'I think there was a witness. I found a couple of stubbed-out cigarette butts in the tack room, which is immediately behind the stall where the victim was found. Mrs Olsen didn't smoke. Neither did her husband. We've put out an alert for Olsen. Either he did it or the phantom smoker did.'

Now Honey turned her gaze to the view without really seeing it. During her visit to the stable with Lindsey, her daughter had remarked that the horse had seemed agitated, rolling its eyes at something that it didn't like. Lindsey had also mentioned that horses were easily spooked by the smell of smoke.

'Horses don't like smoke.'

'Is that so?'

She told him about the day she'd gone riding with Lindsey. 'As you know, my daughter is an expert on a wide variety of subjects. She's been riding since she was seven years old, so horses come pretty high on the list.'

He listened intently as she described the day they'd had, the man Lindsey was sure had been watching them, the bonfire, the horse getting upset and Lindsey mentioning that horses were afraid of smoke.

In her mind she recalled something else about the scene that she hadn't considered too deeply before.

'The lighting at that end of the barn was turned off. I saw Deirdre Olsen switch it off as she led us in. How purposeful was that?'

'Where's this going?'

'She *knew* someone else was there. She knew! I bet it was the man Lindsey saw.'

'The man you didn't see.'

'He must have ducked out of sight just as I got there. It was Mildred's fault. She's no racehorse, that's for sure.'

'And this Mildred. Could she testify to this?'

Honey nearly choked on cream and crumbs. 'Mildred is a Welsh cob.'

Doherty leaned back in his chair and folded his arms. He looked out at the scene beyond the window. The fact that he was biting at his bottom lip made her think there was something he wasn't telling her. 'The husband did it.'

'Are you being honest with me?'

'Of course I am. I didn't say that *I* thought the husband did it, did I? I'm being told that the husband is always the prime suspect, and besides, he's done a runner.'

'Oh. Police politics?'

'The powers that be, namely my superior officers, want the case cleared up and my orders are to go after Olsen.'

'Even though you think he didn't do it.'

Doherty sighed as he wiped his face with his hands. 'I've got a certain budget, a certain amount of manpower and a certain amount of time. And there are other considerations. If Olsen killed his wife — understandable in the circumstances — what were his reasons for killing our interior designer friend? What was the point?'

Both hands cradling the cup, Honey looked at the tea. She enjoyed this amateur sleuthing lark and enjoyed being with Steve. For the first time ever she found herself being made to take it seriously. This was a job Steve Doherty did full-time, and fun didn't come into it. He deserved some free time, and the prospect of being together without work intruding was very attractive, though she wouldn't tell him that just yet. She had to play it cool so he could give his full attention to the job. Still, perhaps she could just hint that she was willing . . .?

'Look . . .'

She was just about to do this when her phone rang.

'My mother,' she said softly.

Doherty buried his head in his hands.

'Hannah? Is that you, Hannah?'

She wanted to say, *Well, if you tapped my number on your cute little pink phone, it must be me*, but she'd only be told not to be facetious. At ten years old, the word had been 'cheeky'. Now it was 'facetious'. Such was the passage of time.

'Of course it's me. Hello, Mother. What can I do for you?'

'It's what I can do for you,' Gloria declared airily. 'This so-called interior designer refuses to hang this Meissen mirror that I've bought for you. She says that it's unsuitable and hasn't been given a place number. Why does a present to my daughter have to have a place number? It's not coming to dine. Only people coming to dine have place numbers.'

Honey rolled her eyes. Sensing the prospect of a verbal tug of war, Doherty looked away. Conversations with Honey's mother embarrassed him at the best of times. She was always right even when she was wrong. He found people like that too difficult to deal with. But Honey was well practised.

'Mother, each decorative item has a place number on the plan originally drawn up by Philippe prior to his death.'

'Then surely my mirror should have a place number. It's Meissen. It cost a lot of money.'

Honey sighed heavily and laid her head back against the wall. She could hear Camilla commenting bitterly in the background: 'I don't have to work here, you know. Fabiere designs are sought after by people of note, and if I don't have carte blanche, I'm out of here!'

Visions of an unfinished refurbishment flashed into her mind. The summer season was approaching, the time of year when room occupancy was at its highest. Everything had to be completed by then. Reception would be a shambles if Camilla walked out of the job.

'Let me speak to Camilla.'

Her mother turned sarcastic. 'Camilla! Do you mean the gangly young woman with the Snow White hairdo and the lips to match.'

Honey groaned. Camilla would have heard.

'Let me speak to her, Mother!' More firmly now.

Gloria did as ordered.

'I will not have the designs of Fabiere Interiors ruined by a second-rate piece of kit,' declared a haughty Camilla Boylan.

The tone of voice of the new boss of Fabiere Interiors was even haughtier than that of the old one. Camilla was feeling her feet.

'Has it got little flowers and cherubs all over it?' Honey asked.

'Yes. It has.'

'I know just the sort. It won't suit reception.'

'Absolutely not.'

'Do you have a mother, Camilla?'

'Yes.'

'Where is she?'

'In Scotland.'

Scotland! Honey was envious and said so.

'You're a long way away and beyond parental control. Believe me, you don't know just how lucky you are. Mine lives close by and still treats me like a ten-year-old. Will you do me a big favour?'

There was a pause before Camilla responded.

'What do you want me to do?'

'I want you in the course of the next few days to drop that bloody mirror. Don't tell her you're going to drop it. Just do it. And make sure it needs substantial repairs. And don't go on to tell me that it's a very expensive item. Remember, she's standing next to you listening to your end of this conversation, so be careful what you say.'

'I understand.'

'Can you do that. A straight yes or no will do?'

Choosing her words carefully, Camilla said that she would do exactly as Honey wished.

'Problem solved?' said Doherty as she closed the connection.

She gave him the gist of it.

He grinned. 'So, what about seven years' bad luck?'

'I'll chance it. So,' she continued, 'where do you think Ferdinand Olsen has got to?'

'We're checking likely places. It shouldn't take too long. He's not the sort to get lost without leaving a trace. Something will turn up.'

CHAPTER THIRTY

Ferdinand Olsen gazed at the sea beyond Star Point. Devon was where he and Deirdre used to come when they wanted to get away from things. He'd opted to stay in the flat they co-owned, the one that she'd enthused about buying back then. As it turned out, he preferred the sea and Deirdre preferred the countryside. She'd also hated being parted from her four-legged darlings, so in latter years she had rarely accompanied him here. He'd never had a problem with that. Her half of the king-size bed had been readily filled by a long line of alternative companions more nubile and sea-friendly than her.

Tonight he was alone with just a bottle of gin and enjoying the view. The estuary shone like silver beneath the moon. Not a wave, not a ripple disturbed its metallic surface. The sight of it made him impatient to leave, but he was cautious. It had taken him all day to stock the boat with tinned food and fresh water, check the rig, change the engine oil and purchase fresh gas canisters. Satisfied that everything was in order, he'd been poring over his charts, marking his course across the English Channel to St Malo. If time and tide permitted, he might take the bull by the horns and strike directly for Santander in northern Spain. Everything was in order. He could do it easily.

He found himself thinking of Deirdre. His hand shook at the thought of her battered and bruised body. But it wasn't his fault, he told himself. She only had herself to blame. She'd loved those horses more than she had him. That's what had soured their relationship. That's what he told himself. He poured another gin over crushed ice and a twist of lemon then added the tonic.

The idea was to leave in the early hours of the morning when the town was asleep and the harbourmaster and customs were not at their height of efficiency. In all probability the police had warned seaports and airports to keep a look out for him. He wanted a new life, one without dreadful Deirdre and all the complications her death would present. No one would notice him slipping out of the harbour.

The stillness of the moon on the water was quite captivating. The sky was clear now, the clouds and rain from earlier in the evening having blown over. The streets were empty, the pavements and roads glistening in the moonlight.

With a sigh of satisfaction, chest heaving with pride, he eyed the thirty-five-foot sailing yacht that would take him off on the adventure he'd always dreamed of — away from these shores, away from his problems. Sail south until the butter melts. Wasn't that the old saying?

'To you and me,' he said, raising his glass in a toast to the waiting yacht.

As he did so he fancied a shadow solidified and moved. Lowering his glass he took a good long stare before realising that the moon had hidden itself behind a ragged cloud. A few seconds and it was shining again. All was well with the world.

At three in the morning he quietly slipped the lines. In order to maintain absolute silence, he avoided starting the engine, using the boat hook to push himself away from the quay.

Luckily the wind was blowing off the land. The boat eased away without too much effort.

For a brief moment he thought he smelled gas but decided it was a trick of the breeze. Someone else on some other boat had a leak in their gas line. How stupid was that? If it sunk into the bilges, one spark and boom! All over.

On clearing the boats berthed to either side of him, his finger hovered over the engine start. He paused on hearing the sound of a small inboard engine chugging along the fairway at the end of the pontoons.

Olsen ducked just in case he was seen. It was pretty certain that it was the customs vessel doing its nightly round — a little later than usual. The last thing he wanted was them stopping him and asking questions. So far he'd been incredibly lucky. It would take a while yet before the police traced his Devon address or the fact that he had an independent means of getting away.

The sound of the launch faded. Olsen breathed a sigh of relief. It was all over. He was on his way.

It was the last thought in his head before he pressed the ignition. The engine ignited, and so did the rest of the boat.

One almighty explosion split it from stem to stern. Flames leapt nearly twenty feet into the air.

Despite the lateness of the hour, a host of dazed onlookers appeared on the scene.

Nerve-jarring alarms courtesy of the emergency services sounded in response to hurried calls on mobile phones. Mouths gaped and spines shivered in response to the scene.

'Must have been gas,' someone suggested.

Not much comment was made. All eyes stayed fixed on the pillar of flame and the choking smoke coming from what was left of the boat and the man on board.

CHAPTER THIRTY-ONE

The evening out with Camilla Boylan had not been as useful as Honey had hoped. With hindsight, she told herself she should have known better. Having taken over the task of refurbishing the reception area of the Green River Hotel, Camilla was bound to try and make the most of it. She started off by trying to persuade Honey to use more luxurious fabrics, by which she meant much more expensive fabrics. 'We could go a little away from the French theme and turn a little medieval. How about a wonderful Italian Renaissance–style painting? Pride of place over the fireplace?'

Honey considered how it would look — that was before she reminded herself that she didn't have a fireplace.

'We can get a really decent marble one from a reclamation yard,' gushed Camilla, undeterred by the mere fact that a fireplace was sadly lacking in Honey's reception area. 'I saw a real beauty out at Frome Reclamation. It came from a Bavarian castle somewhere in Eastern Europe.'

'I thought that Bavarian castles were usually situated in, well, Bavaria!'

Camilla shook her glossy bob. 'Nope! Not all. This one was in Romania. The locals burned it down.'

Quite frankly it sounded like one of the tallest stories she'd ever heard, though of course Mary Jane told some that were out of this world — quite literally, in fact. She sensed that Camilla was out to build her reputation and her bank account post Philippe Fabiere. It made her feel like a guinea pig.

'Did you tell my mother this?'

Camilla swigged at her glass of Chardonnay, emerging from behind it looking disgusted before she remembered she was sitting opposite her client. She recovered her smile.

'Your mother was just trying to be helpful.'

'Like hell she was. My mother likes to be in control of her life, my life and the life of everybody around her. That includes my hotel.'

'Well, that being as it may—'

'Look. Can we stop right there? You're here to increase your fee on my project, and I'm here to ask you some questions that you may very well have been asked before.'

Assuming that Honey was on the same wavelength as she was — in other words, paints, carpets, swatches and cushions — Camilla dived into her bag and took out pen and pad.

'Fire away! Where shall we start? Marble fireplace? Or the painting? Something solid and dramatic in a gilt frame? Caravaggio would be nice. A view of the Grand Canal in Venice . . .'

'Let's start with where you were on the night Philippe was murdered, and where you were the night before last.'

The air of businesslike camaraderie turned sour. Camilla's pen hovered above her notepad. Her face visibly paled and thick mascara flaked into dust as she blinked and blinked again.

'I've already told the police where I was.'

'Tell me.'

Camilla's response was preceded by an exasperated sigh. 'I was at a fair. I told them. They've verified that I was.'

'Where was this fair?'

'In the Victoria Rooms in Bristol.'

Honey presumed it was a fair featuring the latest in interior design.

'Was Julia there?'

Camilla's jaw dropped before she brayed like a donkey. 'Julia? What would Miss Paint and Paper want at a health and homeopathy fair?'

'I'm sorry?'

Camilla presumed that Honey's shocked expression had something to do with her take on Julia.

'Julia slaps on the paint and paper like there's no tomorrow. And I'm not talking about the walls of a house . . .'

'I know,' said Honey, raising her hand, palm outwards. Her insides had turned to blancmange. This was a connection! She piled in. 'I'll concede that Julia does indeed wear a ton of makeup, but we're not talking about Julia. We're talking about you. You say you went to a health and homeopathy fair?'

'Yes.'

'And you're interested in that kind of thing?'

Camilla frowned. 'If you mean by "that kind of thing" that I prefer natural remedies to the drugs piled into us by an overzealous medical profession, then yes. That's me.'

It was difficult to speak with a dry mouth, but Honey did her best. 'How about belladonna? Do you have any?'

'Not on me. Do you want some?'

She fancied Camilla was being sarcastic.

'Look,' she said, reaching across the table and grabbing a chunk of Camilla's hair. 'Someone doped Philippe with belladonna before throttling him with a decorative Victorian lavatory pull handle. Someone also did the same to Deirdre Olsen before throwing her beneath the most agitated of her four-legged friends.'

'That's nothing to do with me!'

'I don't believe you!'

Honey held on despite Camilla wriggling like a fish on a hook. Other people in the Firsty Fish bar looked round to see what the noise was all about. There was no option but to let go of Camilla's hair and leave her to slide down into her seat. She began throwing her belongings, including the pen and pad, back into her bag.

'I will not be treated like this! I suggest you get somebody else to finish your contract. I certainly will not!'

'Camilla . . .'

'Get lost!'

'Camilla! If you don't finish it, I won't pay you. Besides, you still have some responsibility for the missing things that I ordered and paid for.'

Camilla pursed her bright-red lips, and Honey got the impression that something else was bugging her.

'We'll come to some arrangement. Anyway, I'm not keen to ever set foot in your establishment again.'

'Because of my mother? Look, I can have a word with her . . .'

'Not her! The ghost! I don't like ghosts!'

There was no point in trying to persuade this silly girl that Sir Cedric and her earthly intermediary, Mary Jane, were harmless. Besides, she didn't have the time for that. The bit was firmly between her teeth and she was out for a gallop.

'OK. I'll accept that. But I still need you to answer a few questions about the death of your business partner.'

Camilla settled down. 'OK. I'll tell you what I know.'

'Was Philippe into health food and herbal cures?'

Camilla frowned and wriggled as though her tights were too tight.

Honey repeated the question. 'Did Philippe use herbal medicine?'

Camilla nodded. 'Yes.'

'Did you know he was taking belladonna?'

Camilla shrugged in a casual manner. 'So? It's not illegal and it's not just a poison. It can be quite beneficial in small quantities.'

'Quit the lecture. I've read up on it online.'

Actually Lindsey had done the research, but that was a mere detail. Camilla didn't need to know that.

'Would Philippe have carried the belladonna around with him?'

'What the hell has this got to do with his death? He was choked to death with a lavatory handle, for God's sake!'

'But doped up first. I understand that, taken in certain amounts, belladonna can do that. Yes?'

Camilla squirmed and her pert red lips parted, revealing snow-white teeth. 'Oh my God. Do you think he took too much?'

'Yes, but was it voluntary?'

'He never could hold his drink,' Camilla blurted.

Honey thought about it. If it was true that Philippe couldn't hold his drink then that was the time when someone could slip him too much belladonna, or he could take far more than he should because he was drunk.

She put the question to Camilla. 'Had he ever done that before — got drunk and taken too much?'

Camilla nodded. 'When he was in the right company, yes.'

'What was the right company?'

'Anyone with an artistic bent. Or just plain bent,' she added with unguarded venom.

The missing waiter sprung easily to mind. 'Did you know Aloysius Rodriguez?' Honey asked.

'Who?'

Honey decided that Camilla's puzzlement was genuine. It wouldn't have troubled her too much if Camilla had throttled her ex-partner. To be guilty she would have had to have an accomplice. After all, it required strength to choke Philippe, and someone capable of pushing or pulling Deirdre's body under the hooves of the horse.

'Do you like horses?'

'Not particularly.'

'Do they frighten you?'

Camilla frowned. 'What's this about? Are you a psychiatrist or something?'

OK, it did sound like a pretty mad line of questioning. Honey shook her head. 'Never mind.'

The legs of Camilla's chair grated on the wood-block flooring as Camilla got up. 'Perhaps it might have been better if Philippe had come to the fair with me, but he didn't. We had time for a quick bite and then he was off. He had to meet someone later.'

Honey had visions of him meeting some love interest, someone he didn't want Camilla to know about. 'Do you know who?'

Camilla shrugged.

'Why didn't you mention this before?'

The place setting on the Irish linen tablecloth held Camilla's attention before her gaze shifted to the left. She shrugged again. 'It slipped my mind.'

* * *

The trucks waiting for the ferry that would take them from Felixstowe to Zeebrugge wound like a segmented snake from the customs offices all the way back to the transport terminal entrance that dealt exclusively with heavy goods vehicles.

The night was dry, and the water beyond the harbour entrance was oily black and just as still.

The customs men were armed with clipboards and pens. They referred to each other after each truck was waved through, once licence plates and paperwork had been thoroughly checked.

Behind the wheel of a German-made truck, the Russian driver sucked on his burning cigarette and pretended not to be alarmed. He'd left his window open in the hope of catching a word or two of what was being said. This wasn't the first time he'd gone in and out of England via the port. From Zeebrugge he would cut into Germany before heading north to Moscow. There had never been any problems until now. The trips had proved lucrative; there were buyers waiting for what he had locked away in the huge trailer he dragged behind him. Apart from the odd security alert following the 7 July attacks in London, he'd never been held up before.

The ramp onto the ferry rattled with each new truck passed by customs and driven aboard by its relieved driver.

The Russian threw his cigarette away even though it was far from being burnt out. He felt the sweat patches grow beneath his arms and break out beneath the dirty corduroy cap covering his thin hair. He smelled his own fear.

He was now sixth in line from the ramp. Soon it would be his turn. His fingers drummed on the steering wheel. His eyes flickered. He'd been driving non-stop for forty-eight hours since leaving Moscow. Forcing his sore eyes to stay open wasn't easy. If he could just keep going he could get on board and sleep there — in the cab of the truck, if he had to.

His eyes flickered.

Keep going.

Not long now.

His eyelids were heavy as lead.

He counted between blinks.

Five trucks, four trucks, three trucks, two . . . SMASH!

His skull smashed against the windscreen. He heard his ribs crack as he struck the steering wheel. He gasped for air as the truck's cab shot forward at an angle onto the ramp, one wheel hanging off in mid-air over the water, the cab toppling to one side. The truck hit the trailer in front then bounced off at an angle and ended up with one wheel off the ramp.

The trailer fell onto its side with an almighty crash just yards from the water.

The Russian's world turned black. He no longer saw or heard the uniformed men taking charge of things, arresting the driver in the truck behind. He wouldn't have known the guy was Polish and that he too had been driving for days non-stop — totally illegal on British roads.

Tired and disorientated, the Polish driver had fallen asleep over the wheel. His foot had been as heavy as his eyes. It was resting on the accelerator. The Polish truck had smashed into the back of the Russian truck. The Polish trailer and its cargo were undamaged. The Russian vehicle was lying on its side, cab smashed, trailer in danger of tumbling into the water.

CHAPTER THIRTY-TWO

The last thing Honey had expected at nine thirty that morning was that she would be receiving a call from customs officials in Felixstowe regarding the identity of two people found bound and gagged in the back of a truck on its way to Russia.

'They say they are staying with you and that they left their passports at your hotel. Though, on checking, it seems the gentleman concerned was mistaken about this. He was carrying his passport on him and hadn't realised. Their names are Mr and Mrs Hoffner and they are German tourists. Can you confirm this?'

Once she'd retrieved her chin from somewhere around her navel, Honey responded that, yes, they were staying with her. What the hell were they doing trussed up in the back of a truck?

'Can you explain exactly what's happened?' she asked the official on the other end of the phone.

The voice on the other end was courteous but curt. 'I'm sorry. We cannot possibly divulge any information at this time. As soon as they've finished giving statements, we'll put them on a train back to you.'

'Are they all right?'

'A little stiff. They've been bound and gagged for quite a while.'

'The knitting should help,' Honey blurted. Funny how she looked forward to seeing Frau Hoffner sitting in her favourite spot, click-clacking away, now there were no worries about being sued.

The customs official didn't get it, so his response was slow, as though he wasn't quite sure what he was agreeing to.

Honey realised she must sound like an idiot. Under the circumstances, it didn't matter very much. Stunned, she hung up. Everyday, run-of-the-mill tourists were not in the habit of being abducted. Only very rich tourists ran up against that particular problem. Abduction around the Bath area was practically unknown. Things changed, of course, if you ventured into Wiltshire, where this particular practice was said to be carried out by little green men who made crop circles. Nobody in Wiltshire seemed to mind very much about either of these unexplained phenomena, with the exception of the farmers, of course. Flattened crops were difficult for the combine harvester to deal with. However, the people of Bath would not tolerate such behaviour. They had quite enough with the foreign exchange students every year, without having to cope with Martians as well.

The moment she'd hung up, the tinny sound of 'Spring' from Vivaldi's *Four Seasons* alerted her to another call coming in.

'Have you heard the news, hen?'

There was no mistaking Alistair's Scottish brogue.

'Wallis Simpson's wedding stockings are up for grabs?'

'You should be so lucky, hen! They're probably in the hands of Her Majesty's Government along with a signed copy of the articles of abdication.'

Honey's grin was coupled with a powerful desire to know why he'd phoned. He never rang her unless he'd heard some juicy gossip on the antique trade's grapevine. In the past the grapevine was entirely word of mouth. Now it operated via email and social media. Gossip travelled quicker that way.

'An item of interest,' Alistair went on. 'A truck leaving the country turned over at Felixstowe following an accident. You'll never guess what they found in the back.'

It landed inside Honey's head like things do when you least expect them. It was as though someone in the back room — that is, at the back of her head — was working some kind of mental abacus and making everything add up as it should. 'The contents of Philippe's storeroom.'

'You've already heard?'

Honey winced. It vexed her to think that Alistair had heard about it before she did. She reminded herself that she was first and foremost a hotelier. Antiques were merely a hobby. Looking at it positively, the reception area she'd envisaged and which Philippe had designed would now be finished exactly to the design Philippe had planned — depending on the police, that is.

Anger burned in her stomach. This theft was personal. She wanted her stuff back, but the more she thought about someone stealing her bosomy oil paintings — small but expensive items among the vast amount Philippe had stored — the more questions there were to be answered. Felixstowe! Why Felixstowe? The answer came swiftly back. She'd always been good at geography — her top subject at school. Felixstowe had great ferry links with the continent. From there roads led everywhere.

Alistair confirmed this. 'The truck was on its way to Russia when another truck smashed into the back of it, cannoning it into the truck in front. The cab went crabbing over the side of the ramp and ended up hanging over the harbour wall. The trailer it was hauling went over onto its side. Incredible, don't you think? Like something from James Bond.'

It was indeed. *From Russia with Love*, perhaps? Then something dawned on her.

'The truck turned over! How could I be so insensitive? The poor Hoffners! Here I am worrying about my paintings when they were nearly killed . . .'

She was rabbiting, her words following the thoughts in her mind as surely as a cat chasing a mouse. This event had unnerved her.

Alistair calmed her down.

'The two people they found trussed up in the back are fine. I don't think they would have been by the time they got to Russia though. That was a sealed unit they were in. Must be terrible struggling for a last breath in pitch darkness, not even able to hug each other.'

Alistair couldn't have painted a more frightening picture if he'd tried. Honey felt full of remorse that she'd already packed up the Hoffners' belongings and let their room.

'Thanks for letting me know,' she said to Alistair and hung up.

'Anna! Anna!'

At the sound of her shouting, a loud wail rose like an air raid siren from the linen cupboard.

Anna's face appeared from behind the door. 'Shhhh!' she hissed angrily. 'I have only just got baby off to sleep.'

'Sorry.' Honey's voice dropped to a whisper. 'We have to put the Hoffners' things back in their room.'

'They are coming back?' asked Anna, sounding surprised. 'From where have they been?'

'Felixstowe.'

Anna looked puzzled. 'I would rather be dead than spend a holiday in Felixstowe. It is very draughty and the sea is very grey. You cannot walk on it.'

She meant cannot walk *in* it, of course — in other words, paddle. Other than that, her description was pretty accurate. Anna had used that particular ferry crossing a number of times; she was speaking from experience.

'The Hoffners weren't stopping, though I'm sure they wished they were.'

'They were going somewhere better?' Anna busied herself alternating pillowcases and sheets.

Honey was too het up to explain in detail.

'I doubt it, and the trouble is they only had one-way tickets.'

CHAPTER THIRTY-THREE

Honey's mother was sitting quietly at a table in the conservatory, confronted by a tray of tea and shortbread sitting on the table in front of her. Honey eyed her from the doorway. It wasn't often she saw her mother looking so thoughtful, worried even. Her finely pencilled eyebrows were drawn into a deep frown. The tea and shortbread remained untouched. Usually she would have been nibbling by now.

Honey became aware that Lindsey had joined her.

'I've never seen Grandma sitting so still and so quiet,' she whispered. 'Do you think she's ill?'

Honey shook her head and whispered back. 'No. She wouldn't allow it.'

They both stood there for some time, watching for some idea of why Gloria Cross was looking so nervous. She didn't usually do nervous. She usually did straight in your face, laying the law down.

'Go on, then,' whispered Lindsey, elbowing her mother's arm.

'What?'

'She came here to see you. What are you afraid of?'

'She looks so shifty.'

'No. Nervous. Just nervous.'

Her daughter was right. Honey took a deep breath. What was she afraid of? 'I haven't seen my grandmother looking so disturbed since the day she thought I'd told her I was considering becoming a lesbian.'

Honey looked at her daughter in surprise. 'You never told me that!'

'I didn't tell her that either. What I actually said was that I was going to become a thespian. A friend of mine had got me a small part in an amateur dramatics society play. I think Grandma had a cold that day and her ears were waxed up. She stated there and then that she'd never let her ears get waxed up again. She always wanted to know what I was up to, no matter what. And she came along to see the play.'

'OK,' said Honey, and took a sharp intake of breath. For a moment it seemed her bosoms had risen into her throat. 'Here goes.'

Her heels made a light tapping sound as she swept over the pretty stone floor, recently laid with russet-coloured tiles imported from Spain.

'About time!'

Her mother threw her an accusing look.

Honey noted that, concerned as her mother might be, it did not prevent her from laying on the red nail polish and being her usual impeccably presented self.

She was wearing a floaty turquoise outfit with gold jewellery and pale bronze shoes with matching handbag.

'It's Cybil,' gushed Gloria without giving her daughter time to ask what the matter was. 'You know I told you before that she has this head problem. Well, I think it's getting worse. I do believe she's going gaga!'

'I see.'

Honey really did see, or rather, had seen. However, she didn't let on about Cybil's conversation regarding the cats and the fact that she hadn't seemed to remember inviting Honey in.

Anyway, she'd been in the company of older people, notably her mother, long enough to know what 'gaga' meant.

It meant awkward, opinionated and possessing a devil-may-care attitude towards family, friends, men and the world in general. Old folk pushed the boat out when they knew damned well that time was running short.

'Old folk do get forgetful. You can hardly hold that against her.'

Her mother was not fooled.

'I can see you're only humouring me. Don't. This is serious. She's becoming a meddler of the first degree. She makes it her business to interfere in other people's lives.'

'You mean yours, Mother?' Honey raised her eyebrows in what was meant to be a sarcastic manner. The effort was lost on her mother, who appeared to be taking this very seriously indeed.

'Certainly not,' she said indignantly. 'She's not interested in the likes of me. She's after people who break the law. And foreigners. She's got a thing about foreigners. You know what she's like.'

Yes, Honey conceded, she did know what she was like. Cybil was a nosy parker. She was old, lived alone and was probably lonely. It was par for the course.

'She likes to know what's going on around her,' Honey offered. 'She seems quite involved in village life.' It wasn't necessarily true, but it sounded right.

Her mother was having none of it. 'Hannah, I am old but I am not obtuse! Cybil thinks she's some kind of Robin Hood. She steals things and gives them away.'

'A kleptomaniac.'

'Admitting to having a condition has got her off the hook a few times. And she reckons that the owners of the hotel opposite are in league with some characters from *Star Trek*.'

A vision of Cybil wearing Lincoln green and toting a bow and arrow came to mind. So did a few way-out creatures from the Intergalactic League. Television had a lot to answer for. Both scenes were funny enough to bring a smile to her face.

Her mother noticed.

'Hannah! This is no laughing matter. I am very much afraid that Cybil is going to land herself in a great deal of trouble. Perhaps Robin Hood is not the right person to make a comparison with. Zorro might be better.'

Honey bit her bottom lip to keep from laughing out loud. Zorro? Could she really see Cybil wearing a black cape, big hat and leaving her initials etched with a sword point? She could not. Cybil was very, *very* Laura Ashley.

Hiding her smirk by pouring the tea, she asked her mother how come she knew all this.

Her mother leaned close in a conspiratorial manner. 'She told me herself. She said that she intended righting a few wrongs before she dies. Especially against people who dislike cats.'

All things considered, Honey decided that it wasn't really a bad idea. Some kind of superhero could do a lot of good if he — or she — put their mind to it. She told her mother this.

'No, Hannah. I know Cybil's not quite all there, but that doesn't mean she can cast aside responsibility and go out there armed with a gun that she picked up in East Berlin somewhere around 1969.'

'Mother, you're telling porkies,' said Honey, unable to stop the smile from spreading. 'Cybil doesn't *really* have a gun.'

'Oh yes she does. And she's a crack shot.'

She looked at her mother's face. Honey had always hoped that she'd inherit her fine cheekbones and youthful, sparkling eyes. At this moment Gloria Cross was wearing a look Honey had rarely seen before. She was looking seriously concerned and a little confused.

'You mean it?'

Gloria Cross nodded.

Honey gaped. A woman in her seventies was walking the streets of Bath with a concealed weapon. If they'd had street gangs — which she didn't think they did — the punks would be wise to watch their step. Otherwise, *bang!*

'You *do* mean it!' she exclaimed, her expression disbelieving.

Her mother nodded slowly. 'I wouldn't say anything about it if I didn't know it to be true. She showed it me.'

This was surreal. Elderly ladies did not fit the mould of vigilante types. OK, Cybil was well built, but she wore rose-printed chintz. How could anyone who wore stuff like that go round packing a Luger, or any other gun for that matter?

She consoled herself in the hope that the gun was purely a replica or, failing that, so old that it did not work. Even better, she might not have any bullets. However, wishing and hoping wasn't enough.

'You must tell her to keep it out of sight or she'll be arrested,' Honey told her mother after she'd considered the matter.

'No,' said her mother, setting the cup and saucer firmly back on the tray. 'I can't seem to get through to her.' She frowned. 'She never used to be like that before she went into the service. Only when she came back. And only sometimes. She was very insecure.'

'Well, there you are. Go and have a nice talk with her.'

Her mother glared. 'Don't be so ridiculous, Hannah. I know nothing of that kind of thing. You're the professional! *You* must have a talk with her.'

CHAPTER THIRTY-FOUR

The Zodiac Club was heaving as usual. The blue smoke and rich smell from the sizzling steaks hung thickly in the air, confined by the barrel-vaulted ceilings of the subterranean premises.

The club was approached down a set of wooden steps and stretched out beneath North Parade, exiting onto North Parade Gardens.

The air hummed with the chatter of those who worked in the hospitality trade. Usually it wasn't this busy until the witching hour, but even in the fair city of Bath, Tuesday night was slow for business. Especially in what Honey always thought of as 'the shoulder months'. April was a shoulder month: neither the height nor depth of the season, and the weather neither here nor there. Folk were making the most of it.

Doherty had phoned earlier asking to meet her at their usual place. He'd said he had something important to tell her. 'Something about you and me.'

There was something about the way he spoke that pulled her up short. She tried to recall exactly what it was, besides that his tone of voice was kind of cute. She'd been expecting their relationship to step up a notch. This could be it.

Dressed to the nines with a hip-hugging skirt, a plunging neckline and an itch she hoped Doherty would get round to scratching, she waited at the bar. And waited. And waited. Having a drink. Getting angrier. Having another drink.

Folk around her were having fun, drinking, dining and laughing together. A guy she knew pushed through the crowd to get to her. He asked if he could buy her a drink and perhaps they might have dinner sometime. She told him she was waiting for someone.

Now she was wishing she'd accepted. Damn Doherty! Her good opinion of him worsened with each passing minute. Now why the hell did she want to get involved with somebody like him? For a start he only shaved every three days or so. And he dressed casually, even scruffily — faded jeans, black leather jacket, black T-shirt straining over a surprisingly well-honed body . . .

She shook her head. The bad opinions were warring with the good, or her good sense with her hormones. The fact was that she'd never seen him in a smart lounge suit or tuxedo. Come to that, she'd never seen him in his birthday suit either . . .

Then her phone rang. Well, he'd better have some pretty good excuse.

'We've found Olsen. In Devon,' he went on. 'Well, we've kind of found him. He's got a weekend place here and *did* have a yacht.'

She ignored the past tense regarding Olsen's weekend boat. This could be it! Olsen was caught. 'Does he admit killing them both?'

She could understand to some extent why he'd disposed of his wife, but Philippe was a different matter. OK, they'd been members of the same project team, but that was their only connection and there wasn't a whiff of rivalry between them. There seemed no reason for one to murder the other.

She became aware that Doherty was saying something about bits and pieces. Her phone connection had been playing up so she didn't catch it all.

'Can you repeat that?'

'Olsen's not admitting anything. He's been blown to bits. A gas canister on his yacht leaked and it got into the bilges. The whole thing blew up. I'm told it could have been a leaky gas canister or somebody could have left the tap on. Are you at the Zodiac?'

'Yep! This is where we were supposed to meet.'

'Ah! Yeah! Is it busy tonight?'

The way he added such an incongruous comment to the more serious one regarding Olsen's demise threw her, until she realised the reason why.

'I'm OK,' she murmured, eyeing the action going on around her, the liaisons, the laughing, the press of people up against the bar. 'Any leads?'

'None. We have to surmise that Aloysius Rodriguez had something to do with it and yet he seems so unlikely. Interpol and the Portuguese police have checked his home address. He's vanished without trace. His wife hasn't seen anything of him and enquiries point to a family man with three kids working abroad to get the best for them.'

There was sympathy in his voice. Rodriguez had a family. Neither of them wanted him to be guilty. Absence could equal guilt in some cases.

Honey told him about the Hoffners, the truck and the contents of Philippe's storeroom. 'Can you believe it? The Hoffners trussed up among boxes of Dresden and architectural artefacts!'

She sensed his surprise and felt elated that she was the one to inform him.

'I'm not up to speed on that one yet. I'll catch up when I get back,' he responded.

He sounded tired. She imagined him rubbing his face with his hand in a wiping motion designed to perk him up a bit. All it seemed to do was rearrange the bags beneath his eyes into more manageable portions.

'Will you be long getting back?' she asked.

'Hell no. I'm so sorry about this. Tonight of all nights.' He sounded severely disappointed. He paused then said, 'There's still something I need to discuss with you. It's a surprise. I think you'll like it.'

'Sounds intriguing.'

'It is. It's a proposition.'

'Not a suggestion?'

'That too.'

She sensed his tiredness had receded and that he was smiling. *I know that because I've got to know him so well,* she thought to herself. That's nice.

His suggestion for the time being was that they catch up just after lunch on his arrival back in Bath. She told him that would be fine. It fitted in with her schedule. First job was to work out the guest list for the opening of their newly refurbished reception area. Most were members of the Bath Hotels Association, plus a few radio and local media magnates for good measure. Anything for a bit of publicity.

Once the decks were cleared, including welcoming Dumpy Doris back with open arms onto the breakfast shift, it was off to visit Cybil Camper-Young and suggest that she hand in her gun to the police. That way she wouldn't end up with a criminal record for keeping a gun without a licence. It was only a historic gun after all. It was probably rusty from disuse, she thought to herself, and smiled. Yes. That was it. It was just a rusty old gun in the hands of a rusty old woman.

CHAPTER THIRTY-FIVE

Mary Jane bubbled with excitement.

Honey was dealing with a caller with hearing difficulties and had to speak rather loudly.

Anna had plonked baby and carry cot behind the reception desk and was heading for the door, a packet of cigarettes clasped so tightly that her knuckles were white.

'I won't be long,' she called over her shoulder.

The baby began to cry.

Honey made signs for someone to pick it up.

Mary Jane did the honours, but only until a taxi arrived to take her out to the American Museum at Claverton Down.

She bundled the child into Doherty's arms. 'Here you are.'

'I don't . . .'

He didn't have a chance. Mary Jane was older than him and thus had greater experience of how to pass on big and little bundles. He found himself holding the baby.

Over the reception desk and the baby's head, they discussed where they were on the case.

'We have to accept that Aloysius Rodriguez was the last person to see Philippe. Find him and we could have our murderer. I say *could* because it still wouldn't explain Mrs Olsen's death, though the modus operandi are very much alike. However, Mr Olsen is a different matter. I'm pretty certain it was an accident.'

Doherty took a deep breath and downed his black coffee without really tasting it, while jigging the baby up and down.

Honey eyed him from beneath veiled lids. A smile haunted her lips. 'You're good at that. Had much training?'

He eyed her back. 'Never had the chance.'

She read something of a promise in his smile. Doherty was possessive about his personal history. Honey didn't know whether he had ever been married and had children. Watching him with the child found her wondering and even feeling a little jealous. Her emotion was surprising. She hadn't felt it so intensely before.

The generalities of everyday living were carried out automatically, without really noticing you were doing them. As for enjoying what you were doing — well, that didn't really come into it.

Honey's thoughts were floating and she had no control over the dreamy look that came to her eyes. The index finger of her right hand tapped her bottom lip.

While Doherty cooed over the child, she began reciting details of the case as if it were a shopping list.

'Mrs Olsen loved her horses. Mr Olsen had loved his boat and Philippe had loved . . .' She shook her head. 'I don't really know. He was in a bathroom and was killed by having a porcelain lavatory handle shoved down his throat.'

'An antique lavatory handle,' Doherty added.

Honey stopped tapping her lip and looked at him wide-eyed.

'That's it!'

'That's what?'

'All three of them were killed by something they loved. It's a kind of pattern.'

'Rubbish. They were killed by someone involved in the health food game. It's nothing but a big scam in my opinion.' He took a bite of his bacon sandwich and gave some to the baby.

Honey raised an eyebrow.

Doherty ignored her.

'The way I see it is this,' he said, placing what was left of his sandwich back on the plate. He began counting items off. 'Olsen was blown up. Philippe got his belladonna from a practitioner of homeopathic medicine . . .'

'And Mrs Olsen the same?'

He stopped. 'No. I don't think so. We've checked. She wasn't taking anything like that.'

Honey couldn't help the triumphant smile.

'*She* wasn't. Her horses were. I've heard that people with pets or who work with animals sometimes take veterinary medicine if there's no prescribed stuff to hand.'

'Philippe had been drinking crème de menthe. Perhaps he merely drank too much and got confused with his dosage.'

'Possibly.' Honey cupped her chin in her hands. 'It might have been accidental with one person. Not so with two.'

Doherty looked thoughtful as he munched the last of his bacon sandwich. 'Oh. I forgot to say. Pathology found a bruise on the back of his neck. A very professional job according to them.'

'What does that mean?'

'Army training. Something like that.'

'Russian army training?'

His eyes met hers. 'I see where you're going. The hotel owner is Russian.'

Honey narrowed her eyes. 'Poor Philippe. The most dangerous thing in his life before this was a clashing colour scheme or ugly lampshades.' She sighed. 'Still, back to business. We're forgetting the locked bathroom door. We know how it was done, but why was it done?'

Doherty wiped the grease from his lips one-handed with a paper napkin. 'To gain time before the body was discovered.'

Honey's dreamy look came back, outward evidence of her thoughts. She recalled the scene. Anyone trying the locked door would have assumed that the person on the inside wished for privacy — for whatever reason. Could it be that Philippe had not been alone in there?

'Philippe was in there with the waiter,' she blurted suddenly.

'And he killed him.'

Honey shrugged. Until they found Rodriguez it was all supposition.

Anna came back for the baby.

'Oh. She is wet,' she said, casting an accusing look at Doherty. 'You did not change her?'

'No,' he said, wiping his hands on the paper napkin. 'I only do bacon sandwiches, not baby changing.'

CHAPTER THIRTY-SIX

The mechanic whistled as he backed the coach into the workshop. A colleague waved him in until he could stop straight and true above the inspection pit. The coach had been hanging around for a while waiting for a new differential to be delivered. The owners had also requested that the vehicle be thoroughly cleaned inside and out while it was being repaired and given a full service.

The mechanical requirements took up most of the day, but there was enough time left before five thirty. The coach was moved into the area reserved for cleaning interiors with vacuum cleaners and upholstery sprays.

The team of young men charged with the cleaning work weren't greatly enamoured of the task they had to do. It was steady work but not well paid. Nobody moved quickly to get started.

One of the youths was talking on his phone. His girlfriend was on the other end. She'd popped out from her office for a smoker's break. The youth, whose name was Ahmed, didn't mind a bit; he wasn't looking forward to crawling into the cavernous luggage bay. Time wasting suited him far better.

He was leaning against the back of the bus, unseen by Rod, the foreman — or so he thought.

'Oi!'

A stout finger stabbed at his shoulder, almost causing him to drop the phone. He was jolted forward as the rear luggage door jerked open. Rod had used the remote.

'Christ!' exclaimed Rod, and stepped back as a foul odour wafted thick and strong from the rear opening. 'Something's dead in there.'

Ahmed wrinkled his nose. He could hear his girlfriend on the other end of the phone asking him what the matter was. Hand shaking, he raised the phone to his ear. 'Something's happened. I'll phone you back.'

Resting his hands on bent knees, Rod was peering into the rear of the coach. Ahmed stooped and did the same, but warily, half guessing what Rod was going to ask him to do.

'Get in there and take a butcher's.' He gave the Asian lad a push.

Ahmed stooped and leaned as though he were going to, then reeled back as the full impact hit him.

'Not bloody likely.'

He didn't care if he did lose his job. That sickly sweet smell told him something was bad — very bad.

'Soft sod,' Rod grumbled. He got out a small torch. The luggage area took up around two thirds of the bus, immediately beneath where the passengers sat. The other third was taken up by the engine.

Covering his mouth with his hand, he put one knee onto the rubber seal that stopped the hatch from rattling, took one look then retreated.

A few others, sensing that something was going on, had gathered round. Ahmed was still at the front of them.

'What is it?' he asked, as if he didn't already know.

Rod took a deep breath, though the smell of decay lingered in his nostrils.

'Something's dead in there all right. It's a bloke and he stinks something rotten!'

CHAPTER THIRTY-SEVEN

Wandering around the auction rooms and Bath's many and varied antique shops helped Honey think. For the second time in two days she was accosted by Doherty.

'We've found Rodriguez.'

Doherty was sitting in his sports car with the top down. The sparkling chrome dazzled Honey's eyes.

Doherty had pulled in on double yellow lines, but he wasn't staying long enough to incur the fury of a traffic warden. A look of enlightenment was in his eyes. He was off somewhere — and in a hurry.

'Where did you find him?'

'At a bus garage near Slough. He was found in the luggage compartment of a tourist bus that was in the workshop. Judging from what I've heard so far, he's been in there a long time. The differential went AWOL on the bus some time ago on its way back from Bath to London. SOCO are doing their stuff. I'm up there to poke my nose in.'

'Is there any chance . . .?'

'If you're asking to come along, I think you already know the answer to that. Let's not tread on the Forensics boys' toes. I'll come round to see you the minute I get back.'

He waved as though this brief conversation had been a very casual interlude in his professional life. And yet he'd taken the time to stop. She appreciated that. Yet again it set her to wondering. Was she reading more into their relationship than she should? Or was she on the right track? Were his quips sincere, although spoken in jest?

Never mind that, she told herself. Stick to the job in hand.

The crime scene was all very well and good, but she was unsettled that it was so far away and she was here, feeling as though she were holding the threads to it all. There could be some hard evidence right under her nose. You could never really tell about things and people unless you dug deeper. It was like her mother's friend, Cybil. Who would have thought that the old dear kept a gun handy? She hadn't yet mustered the courage to go out and see her about it, to try and persuade her to hand it in to the police.

Yes, she needed to snoop a little more on a local level. Anyway, it wasn't enough to depend on forensic science to prosecute. Motive and some idea of how the waiter had ended up where he did would also be helpful.

'Excuse me!'

A young woman pushing a double buggy pushed past, almost knocking her into the road.

'These pavements aren't wide enough,' cried the young woman when Honey dared to cast a glance in her direction. 'I'm going to write to the council about it. You're my witness, Trace! OK?'

The young woman's companion enthused agreement. She would back her friend.

Once they'd passed, along with the rest of the shoppers and tourists, Honey stepped back onto the pavement. Home was where the heart was, or in her case a never-ending list of chores and staff who sometimes seemed more capable than she was. She was too soft with her staff, too willing to jump in and help out. She would always run it in 'one man and his dog' mode. However, though she might not always shine in the catering and hospitality trade, her mind was doing whiz-bangs on the crime scene.

An aspect of the brief communiqué between the two young women stayed with her. Having a witness was useful to the buggy pusher. Not so to whoever had murdered Philippe Fabiere.

'Yes!'

She stopped dead in the middle of the street. A host of French students piled in behind her.

'*Pardon, madame!*'

There were a few more apologies as she was tugged to her feet and brushed off. A man with dark-brown eyes and the sort of face one might dream of alongside chocolate cake and a magnum of Bollinger smiled at her.

'*Mademoiselle*, are you injured?'

He was using both hands to hold her up, one arm wrapped around her back so that he held both elbows. His palms were warm. So was his voice. He might just as well have said, '*Mademoiselle*, would you like to come to bed with me?'

'Yes,' she gulped. Then, realising she was answering the imagined question rather than what he'd actually asked her, she altered her reply. 'No! I'm fine. Really I am.'

'Are you quite sure? I would hate to think that you have been bodily injured by my students' enthusiasm to get to the abbey.'

'That's nice.' Her voice was as wobbly as her legs. That voice! Did it come mail order? She'd love one, preferably on a CD so she could play it throughout the night.

'Would you like to come with us on a tour of the abbey? I am presuming you are a local, *Mademoiselle*, so your input would be very useful to us. You would be most welcome.'

The question came out of the blue and took her completely unawares. She realised her mouth was hanging open and soundless, and she had to catch her breath. As she did so, she took the opportunity to notice a few other nice things about him. His hair was thick and dark, grey streaked from his temples in two thick seams. There were wrinkles at the corners of his eyes. His mouth was wide and sensuous — and was opening and closing again. He was saying something. Gathering her senses, she fought to listen.

'It is a recital. Bach,' he was saying.

The last thing she'd had planned for today was to spend lunchtime sitting in Bath Abbey listening to a Bach recital.

'Yes,' she replied, her body outmanoeuvring her common sense. 'I'd love to.'

He took her by the arm. What a gentleman.

'I am Jean-Claude, by the way.'

'Hannah. But call me Honey.'

The abbey had a hushed aura about it. The organ was playing softly. *What the hell am I doing here?* she asked herself. As it turned out it was quite the thing to do. Listening to music helped her focus on the job in hand. It was also quite nice to feel the heat of Jean-Claude's thigh against hers. And contrary to first impressions, he wasn't here to listen to music. He informed her that he taught at an architectural academy in Lyons and was here to study Bath's fine buildings, while also attending a workshop on interior design. The recital and her company were added extras.

The course on interior design caught her attention. She asked him the names of the workshop leaders. They turned out to be Camilla and Julia. He explained that it would have been Philippe Fabiere, but that he had met with an accident.

'We would have preferred a Frenchman. It would have given us greater insight. We would have been viewing the city and its interior furnishings through privileged eyes. Philippe Fabiere was ideal.'

She didn't enlighten him. Whatever Philippe had told him was OK by her; neither did she tell him that Philippe's 'accident' was anything but.

As the lilting music rose to the apex of the arched nave, she considered what to do next. It wasn't for her to go to St Margaret's Court asking the staff and management for the last date and time they had seen Aloysius Rodriguez. That was Doherty's job. Still, it would be good to know what was going on. A burning curiosity smouldered inside, growing steadily bigger as the performance progressed.

At the close of the recital, Jean-Claude asked her if she would care to accompany them to Café Rouge.

'Allow me to recommend something to make you glow.'

'I would love you to make me glow!'

His voice and those soft brown eyes urged her to go with him. It would be interesting to hear more about the workshop, but even more fascinating to go snooping at St Margaret's Court and at the Olsens' place. At least the crime scene boys had more or less finished with the latter.

It was tough, but she had to take a rain check.

'Look,' she said, hardly believing she was turning down an opportunity to accompany such a good-looking man, 'I'm going to have to decline your invitation. How about if you come along and have morning coffee with me tomorrow?'

She didn't say, *How about you and your students coming along?* She purposely kept things pretty general. The students looked a nice group, but she'd prefer him to be there by himself.

She gave him her business card.

'Say, about eleven?'

Her eyes sparkled when she smiled and her fingers lingered on his as she handed over the card. Hopefully he'd get the message.

'I will check my diary and if I can, I will be there.'

Her feet felt as though they were encased in lead as she dragged herself away, groaning deep in her throat and not daring to look back. All being well she'd see him tomorrow. Duty called. Or was it pure curiosity, or even a determination to crack this case before Doherty did? Or was it much, much more? Did she want to impress him? Did she just want Sigmund Farley out of the picture? She sorely wished for the latter. Whichever way, first stop was St Margaret's Court for questions, then Lobelia Cottage. There was still that little talk with Cybil regarding a gun.

CHAPTER THIRTY-EIGHT

Purple trailing lobelia added to the freshness in the air outside its namesake cottage. Spring was in the air, though a chill breeze still nipped at people's noses. Birds were twittering as they gathered items for their nest building, and the earth smelled fertile. Before long there would be a lot of reproduction and growing going on.

The cottage stood silently in the warm sun, creaking as its old joints woke up to the growing warmth just as it had done for hundreds of years. House martins had arrived early this year, darting in and out of the eaves, busily building their nests. The swallows would follow.

Honey turned her face towards the sun before rapping at the old front door. She waited a while before pressing her ear up against the warm paintwork. Not a sound.

She rapped again. Out of the corner of her eye something moved. One of the blue Persian cats had leapt up into the window. She could just about hear its plaintive meow through the single-glazed pane. The other Persian jumped up too and settled immediately opposite its identical companion. They resembled a couple of bookends.

No one came to the door. Bearing in mind that Cybil was pretty spry for her age and would have opened the door by now, it occurred to her that the aged spinster might be in the back garden. According to her mother, Cybil was very fond of her sweet peas and her beloved peonies. 'She digs at all hours of the day and night,' her mother had said with a dismissive look. 'I couldn't be like it myself. Especially at night. I can't imagine what she plants at night.'

'Unless she digs something up.'

'Don't be ridiculous,' her mother had retorted. 'Only grave robbers dig things up at night.'

There was no way in the whole wide world that Gloria Cross would *ever* blemish her beautifully manicured, polished nails in the pursuit of growing green things. Her priorities were different.

There was nothing for it but to make her way back to Bath, check in at the Green River to ensure everything was running smoothly, then take things from there.

The dishwasher was having one of its off days, so it was all hands to the pump — her hands, as it happened. As she dunked dishes and pots, she thought things over.

Aloysius Rodriguez had witnessed the killing of Philippe Fabiere. Goodness knows how the horses were involved, but there had to be something out at the stable to throw light on the subject. It was worth a trip. Once the dishes were done she headed straight out to her car.

The sight of the rush-hour traffic beginning to build up threw cold water on the best of plans, but still Honey's enthusiasm persisted. She puffed out her cheeks as she attempted to cross the road. It was getting busier by the minute, the buses and cars revving and turning out fumes. No way could she get to her car, get it out of the car park and drive out into this. She needed her car here! Now!

In the process of attempting to cross the road, she heard a car horn. Not just any car horn — Mary Jane's.

Looking over the roof of the French Peugeot that was close to running over her foot, she espied Mary Jane behind the wheel of the pink Cadillac coupe, a sight that was beginning to become quite familiar around Bath.

Her mother was sitting in the passenger seat. They both waved.

'Wanna lift?' Mary Jane shouted.

'Only if you're going my way.'

Mary Jane gestured for her to come over.

She wove around the back of the Peugeot and explained where she wanted to go.

'Hop in.'

The cars were pressed so close that all she could do was hop in.

'It's pretty busy,' said Honey, eyeing the traffic presently surging like a wave around them.

Mary Jane laughed. 'I'll just wave my magic wand.'

Her long spindly arm was about as close as she could get to a wand. She waved it, at the same time making eerie noises.

Honey's mother looked over her shoulder. 'We've had such a great day.'

For some obscure reason — perhaps it was the odd sparkle in her mother's eyes — Honey had no wish to know exactly how their day had been so great.

'I gave your mother a palm reading. I've only just started studying how to do palmistry, but your mother was a willing guinea pig, so we went for it.'

'I'm going to meet a tall, rich, handsome stranger.'

'Right!'

Honey's reply was intentionally noncommittal. Her mother would always and for ever be a romantic at heart.

'So! Direct me,' Mary Jane ordered as the traffic magically began to thin and heave forward.

The good thing about rush-hour traffic was that it didn't just slow things down in the city, it did the same on the open road. When it came to the race between the tortoise and the hare, Mary Jane would be cast as the hare. It was a miracle she had yet to receive a speeding ticket. In her estimation it was something to do with being looked after by her guardian angel. In Honey's estimation she guessed the police didn't want to bother with all that paperwork — and dealing with someone who depended on a spirit guide to take her safely along Somerset's highways.

The Olsens' place was, as expected, in total darkness. Honey directed both her mother and Mary Jane to stay in the car while she went to investigate.

They didn't seem to mind. They were giggling together and cracking jokes she couldn't quite understand.

'Send in the cavalry if I'm not back within thirty minutes.'

She wasn't sure whether they heard her or not. They didn't seem to. Resigned to the situation, she headed around the back of the house.

The trees surrounding the place threw long shadows over the gravelled courtyard, the vegetable gardens and the paddock beyond. The stables looked especially gloomy.

Resisting the urge to creep low like some kind of top-secret operative made her feel stupid. There was nobody to hide from. She straightened. The gravel crunching underfoot sounded so loud. She began going forward on tiptoe, thinking it was more stupid than creeping forward like a praying mantis.

The latch on the stable door was fastened only with police tape. She understood from Doherty that the horses had been removed by a charity organisation — the very one she suspected Mrs Olsen had been fundraising for at the car boot sale.

The door opened smoothly. The interior still smelled of horses, damp straw and fresh hay. It was very dark. She fumbled for the light switch, found it, flicked it on . . . the lights failed. The darkness remained.

She stood at the entrance. *Shall I go on?* she asked herself. *Yep. You bet.*

The darkness couldn't purely be due to the lack of sunlight. She realised shutters had been pulled across the windows that ranged the length of the building around ten feet above the ground. Doubtless someone from Crime Prevention had come along to ensure that the property was left as secure as possible.

Reaching out tentatively to her right, she followed the line of stalls, not sure what she was looking for but feeling she had to go down to the end. It was in the last stall that Deirdre Olsen had been found. That was also the place where she'd imagined seeing something or someone move and disturb the horse.

She did what she could, walking around the stall, kicking at the ground, not sure what she expected to find. She looked up to see a dim light at floor level. If she remembered rightly, there'd been a tack room right opposite this stall. Slowly, placing one foot carefully in front of the other, she headed across the concrete runway between stall and tack room.

Heart hammering, she reached for the door handle. Just like those of the main door, the hinges had been kept well oiled, so when she pushed it opened silently and smoothly.

A small night light had been left on. Her heart returned to beating at a healthier level. Any kind of light, no matter how dim, was better than none at all. She made herself a promise to get her blood pressure checked.

There was nothing in here she wouldn't expect in a tack room, including a medicine cupboard. Horses became ill too. At present it was hanging open and empty. She guessed the police had taken away whatever had been in there for fingerprinting and such like.

The tack room smelled as tack rooms do: linseed oil and leather polish. Shiny leather saddles lined the walls behind her. A long bench ran the full length of the wall beneath them. Hay covered the floor beneath the bench, scattered like straw across a stable floor. Honey frowned.

Hay?

She went down on all fours to check that it really was hay. Picking up a handful and taking a good sniff confirmed it. Why spread hay over the floor? Horses ate hay. They lay on a bedding of straw. And why spread anything at all beneath a workbench?

There was only one conclusion she could draw from that. The straw had been spread out to hide something like a secret trapdoor leading to stolen loot — or something else.

'Curb your imagination,' she warned beneath her breath.

Burrowing further beneath the bench she began scraping the hay away, throwing it behind her like a dog digging for a bone.

Her knuckles hit against something hard and metallic — a safe! A combination safe! She tugged at it. It opened.

Amazing! Someone had left it open.

The light was dim, but she could just about make out several rolls of cash . . .

Her nose hit the floor as strong hands gripped her ankles, yanking her out backwards, knees scraping on the floor.

'Hey!' Someone hit her on the back of her head and sent her sprawling onto her face. Something hard was pressed into the nape of her neck.

'Don't move or I'll shoot.'

It was a male voice. She didn't need to ask what he was here for. The safe was already open. Someone had come in shortly before she had. She'd disturbed him.

'You've come for the money?'

She winced at another jab to the neck.

'Shut up!'

Being brave and sticking up for herself was not an option. International guests beefing about a hotel bill were easy to stand up to. She could do it any day. Guns were more dangerous and best avoided.

Be a coward, she told herself. She closed her eyes, gritted her teeth and waited for him to go.

There was a scuffling of feet on the hay she'd scattered around as he grabbed what he wanted.

The gun jabbed her again. 'Count to one hundred before you get up from there. Poke your nose out any sooner and I'll blow it off. Understand?'

Of course she understood. She was very fond of her nose. Neat and unobtrusive, it sat perfectly in the middle of her face. She nodded.

A slight scuffling and then silence. Taking no chances, she was slow to raise her head just in case she received another jab in the neck. It didn't happen. The likelihood was that he was gone, but she wanted to be sure. Rolling over onto her back, she paused for breath and listened. She heard nothing but the scurrying of a mouse and the cooing of a pigeon, taking advantage of the extra living space now the horses and the humans had moved out.

Her mother and Mary Jane were still in the car. They looked up when she came puffing and panting with bits of hay sticking out of her hair.

Her mother got out so she could get into the back seat. 'You're sweating. And the scarecrow look isn't big this season.'

'I appreciate the concern.'

'Find anything out?'

'Yes.'

Her mother looked expectantly at her. 'Well? What did you find out?'

'I hate guns!'

Her shouting like that caused both of them to swivel round like wooden tops.

Breathing now normal, Honey found her voice. 'Did you see anyone run out here while I was gone?'

They shook their heads.

'Nobody came out this way,' remarked Mary Jane.

That fact was no big surprise really. Honey could have kicked herself for not charging into the paddock and the field beyond. She recalled the day she'd gone riding with Lindsey, when they'd seen a man burning rubbish and watching them. When they'd discovered that whatever had been in the cardboard boxes he'd been burning had come from France. When they'd guessed that some of it must have come from Philippe's storeroom. She hadn't been so sure before being held down on the floor with a gun in her back. Now she was. The Olsens had been involved in some kind of antiques scam. Philippe had found out. Now they were all dead.

She recounted all this to her mother and Mary Jane.

Mary Jane screwed her face up like an overripe crab apple and shook her head.

‘If they’re all dead, that means someone else is involved, that’s if there really is an antiques scam going on.’

‘Well, I think the game plan goes something like this. Philippe’s stuff was stolen. Philippe discovered what they were doing and . . .’ Honey flapped her hands to emphasise how elementary this all was.

The two older women looked at each other.

Honey knew what they were thinking without them saying a damn word. Philippe may have discovered that the Olsens were stealing from him, but he couldn’t possibly have killed them. He was already dead.

Mary Jane shook her head forlornly. ‘In all my years of experience, I’ve never come across a ghost who killed anybody, even if they had done them wrong.’

Honey hated finding herself in a cul-de-sac, though she had to admit it wasn’t as bad as being on the end of a gun barrel.

‘So who do you think the guy was with the gun?’ asked Mary Jane.

Honey shook her head. She didn’t have a clue.

‘How about we take a look round? I’ve got a pretty pistol myself.’

Much to Honey’s surprise, Mary Jane opened her glove box and fetched out a long-barrelled gun of some description.

‘It’s a Colt forty-five,’ Mary Jane explained cheerfully. ‘Quite a museum piece really, but it does still work.’

She’d totally misinterpreted the looks on the faces of Honey and her mother. Gloria pointed out that it was against the law to carry a gun.

Honey corrected her. ‘It’s against the law to own a weapon without a licence. Said weapon is supposed to be broken down and kept under lock and key. It’s a major offence to carry one around in your glove compartment.’

‘I haven’t told a soul about it,’ Mary Jane said earnestly, as though that made it better.

‘Put it away!’

Mother and daughter both breathed a sigh of relief once the weapon was out of sight. Now there were two armed and dangerous old ladies running around, thought Honey.

'We could have gone after that guy and shot his ass,' Mary Jane muttered. She sounded severely disappointed.

'Did that guy really pull a gun on you?' her mother asked.

'You bet he did,' Honey responded.

Her mother gave a curt nod of her head. 'Your father pulled a gun on me once. He said he'd shoot me if I didn't stop spending more than my allowance.'

Honey failed to make a comment, and not just because she had some sympathy with her father. Her mother was still a clothes horse in her seventies. It stood to reason that she'd been lethal when she was young.

But it wasn't just that. Honey was still a little numb and bruised from her ordeal. Besides that, she was trying to fathom what the hell was going on. Who was the man with the gun?

CHAPTER THIRTY-NINE

The Hoffners spilled across reception, throwing their arms around Honey and showering her with kisses.

'It is so good to be back,' trilled Frau Hoffner.

They said the same thing in both languages over and over again — and who could blame them?

Honey invited them to join her for a glass of champagne.

'Tell me all,' she enthused. 'Who did it and why?'

Frau Hoffner picked up her knitting, leaving it to her husband to explain.

'Go on, Wilhelm. Tell Mrs Driver all about it.'

'Please, call me Honey. Most of my friends do.'

The old couple beamed broadly.

'That is so nice of you,' said Frau Hoffner.

'It was like this,' Herr Hoffner began, his eyes shining with delight at the prospect of being able to recount his story all over again. Apparently they'd already signed a deal with a national newspaper, but they decided that the exclusivity of the contract did not preclude them from telling her.

Wilhelm Hoffner told it from the very beginning, when the other painters had asked him if he was able to do the job.

'Warren and Peter dropped me off at the hotel — St Margaret's — to do some painting. It wasn't too bad a job, although the corridor was very dingy and I never saw a soul there. Anyway, there I was . . . doing my work. I take great pride in my work, you see.'

Honey intimated that, yes, indeed she did know. Pride beamed all over Herr Hoffner's face.

He carried on explaining. 'I work hard. I get hungry. I get thirsty. I go to kitchen, but I get lost. Then I find a secret door. I push. There are steps downwards. I go down steps and find myself in a room full of treasure!'

He went on to describe the things that were in there. Something heavy and sickening curdled in Honey's stomach. He was describing the things she actually *knew* were in Philippe's storeroom, things that were on the list Lindsey had downloaded.

'Have you told the police this?'

He nodded. 'Of course.'

'I take it you took your wife back there to show her what you found.'

He nodded again. 'They were things in storage — that's what I thought. Gerda likes beautiful things. There were some very pretty pieces of Meissen. She likes the little cherubs and the pretty flowers on Meissen statuettes and candlesticks. I thought she might like to see them, but I could not do that openly. People might not like it, so I found her some overalls . . .'

Honey felt a great sense of relief. The Hoffners had acted innocently, and luckily the police had a copy of the list and had deduced exactly what they'd found.

Frau Hoffner interrupted. 'While there, we saw the truck being loaded and heard someone coming. We didn't want to be caught, but we were. They didn't know what to do with us at first, so threw us into the truck. Told the driver to get rid of us.'

'Those articles were stolen. You were in great danger. You should have known that.'

They shrugged. 'One more chance at adventure. It was worth it.'

'The people who discovered and tied you up — they weren't Russian by any chance?'

Herr Hoffner shook his head. 'Definitely not. I have seen some of those who work at the hotel on security. They are very broad and big. The person who knocked us out and tied us up was tall but slim.' He frowned. 'There was a smell the person had — a definite smell . . .'

Honey waited while he strained to remember.

'No,' he said at last. 'I should know what the person smelled of, but I cannot quite name it. I am sorry.'

It was a great shame, but Honey was loath to push him. He'd been through enough.

'Let's finish this champagne,' she said with gay abandon. 'I'm so relieved to see you safe and sound.'

'We are relieved too,' said Frau Hoffner. 'And I so missed my knitting.'

'I expect you did.'

'Cats,' he said suddenly. 'One of them smelled of cats. Not the man who tied us up, but someone did.'

Peering past the happy Hoffners she saw a shadowy Mary Jane listening around the door. She was wearing a less-than-welcoming expression, symbolically stuffing wads of cotton wool into her ears.

CHAPTER FORTY

The smell of French perfume always preceded the appearance of Gloria Cross.

'Have you spoken to Cybil about handing in that gun yet?' she asked.

Honey was checking the wines and spirits order against the racks in the cellar. Her response to her mother's question was muted. Just a kind of 'Hmmm?'

'That gun should be put out of her reach. Her mind's not what it was. She's acting very strangely.'

Honey cocked an eyebrow in her mother's direction. She looked immaculate, as always. Gloria Cross *never* left the house without painted nails, lipstick and a colour-coordinated outfit. And she never wore flat shoes. If ever *Vogue* published a magazine for septuagenarians, she'd most likely make the front cover.

'Do you think it's dementia?' Honey offered.

'No! Cybil's decided to be a cat. In her opinion the cat world is far more civilised than the human one.'

'She could have something there.'

Her mother was less than pleased with this answer. 'Don't be facetious. It's ridiculous. Whoever heard of a woman wanting to be a cat?'

Honey didn't mention Catwoman. Cybil in tight-fitting spandex was not what this was all about. Something had gone *ping* in Cybil's mind. OK, in her case it was a bit unusual, but in old people in general it was not entirely unheard of.

'I've been talking to Mary Jane about it . . .'

Alarm bells began to ring in Honey's mind. She stopped counting the bottles of Chateau de Rieu. Her mother was looking very serious.

'And?'

'She reckons hypnotism might work. Mary Jane is very good at hypnotism.'

So that was the reason for the sudden increase in elderly camaraderie — that and Mary Jane's venture into palmistry and the forecast for her mother's love life.

'Mother, how are you going to achieve that? I know nothing about it, but I have heard that in order for hypnotism to work the subject has to be willing to be hypnotised. I can't see your friend Cybil being very willing at all. You'd have to tie her to a chair.'

Her mother looked indignant. 'She should be very pleased that she's got good friends to help her. I wouldn't dream of tying her to a chair. Anyway, she's stronger than me.'

Honey sighed. Her mother had made up her mind and there was nothing she could do about it. For the moment she had other fish to fry. Doherty had sent a team round to the tack room to check the safe for fingerprints. What with the body in the tour bus and checking out the Hoffners' report regarding the stash that they'd found in the deep cellar at the hotel, he was having a busy time. Honey was desperate to get involved but sensed this was becoming something big and that she should stand back and leave it to the professionals.

Ordering wines and spirits, dealing with clients and checking bookings took up most of her day. A sales rep from a soft drinks firm took her out to lunch. He was young, boastful and fancied his chances with an older woman. He was also after her soft drinks order. In an effort to clinch a deal he began bragging about the places he supplied with his upmarket and rather expensive bottles of tonic water, pineapple juice and ginger ale. All this while his knee brushed against hers — by accident, of course!

St Margaret's Court Hotel came up in conversation.

'Excellent cellars,' he reported. 'Stretching the length of the building. They've got their own sommelier, of course. He told me that there were some cellars they'd never found their way into from inside the building, though they knew there were outside entrances. They don't bother with them, of course. They don't need to. They've got plenty of storage room.'

'Sounds intriguing.'

Detecting her increased interest, he leaned forward and gazed into her eyes. She felt his knee press more firmly against hers. His voice dropped to a whisper.

'They suspected that someone was using those cellars without their permission. The big boss — the Russian dude that made his money from copper smuggling, so I hear — gave orders to confiscate whatever was in there. What a crack!' He began chuckling. 'Imagine the surprise of whoever it was using the place. All their gear gone in one swift move.'

He chortled.

She smiled.

'So, what kind of things were stored there?'

'Paintings, antiques . . . that kind of thing. Stolen, I shouldn't wonder.'

'Very likely. And what happened to it?'

'It got loaded onto a truck and taken away. The Russian's got a palace back in Russia. Well, he would do, wouldn't he?' he added, grinning at his joke. 'He's Russian.'

Honey fingered the fork she'd been using to eat her salad. It was tempting to dig the prongs into Mr Smug's knee, but on reflection it was a bad idea. Keep all informants on board. Be nice to them.

Once lunch was over she checked things back at the hotel. Lindsey was behind the reception desk looking agitated.

'Grandma's in conference with Mary Jane. They've asked not to be disturbed.'

'You look disturbed.'

'They were talking about drugging somebody. I overheard them. Do you think Grandma's going a bit gaga, or do you think Mary Jane has something to do with it?'

Honey checked through the mail as she answered. 'I'm not sure which one is nuts and which one is crackers.'

'You're distracted.'

'Hmmm.'

'You've looked through that mail seven times. They're bills. You can see they're bills. Oh, and a Frenchman called in to have coffee with you. I told him you were out and wasn't sure when you'd be back.'

'Oh! Too bad.'

Honey slapped the lot down. 'I'm not concentrating. I'm trying to decide whether to interfere at St Margaret's Court or not. The police are out there making enquiries. I don't wish to intrude, but I wonder . . .'

She told Lindsey about her conversation with the soft drinks' salesman.

'Slippery Sid told you that, did he?'

'Slippery Sid? I thought his name was Errol.'

Her daughter had an expressive face. She could *talk* with it. No need to open her mouth at all. This particular look said, *Come on. Are you that stupid?*

Honey conceived that her daughter was wise beyond her years. 'OK. I get your point. Slippery Sid suits him down to the ground. Have you heard that my mother and Mary Jane are on a mission?' It wouldn't hurt to get Lindsey's opinion.

Lindsey rolled her eyes. 'Has it ever occurred to you that my grandmother and Mary Jane are very alike?'

The question brought Honey up short. Her mother had exquisite taste in clothes, a questionable taste in men and a very healthy respect for money. Mary Jane on the other hand wore anything that came to hand as long as it was pink or pistachio, thought men were a useful appendage to the female race and only spent what she needed to spend. The clothes were usually bought from charity shops or car boot sales. It was colour and the way she threw things together that mattered, not the source of the items.

This gave Honey pause for thought. When it really came down to it, she supposed they were alike in having their own point of view on a multitude of subjects. They both adhered to their own particular image: her mother's straight from the catwalk, Mary Jane's courtesy of the Cats Protection League.

'You could be right. They're both set in their ways.'

'Just different ways,' added Lindsey.

Honey eyed her lovely, logical daughter. She'd grown her hair long of late. It was presently tied back in a ponytail at the nape of her neck. This month's colour was red streaked with blonde. It matched the red-and-white-striped Regency wallpaper in the upstairs corridor.

'Everyone has a point of view of the world, but can come together on common ground. For instance, Grandma is very worried about Miss Camper-Young's behaviour, and Mary Jane, although harbouring differing views to Grandma, understands her concern.'

'So you think it's a good idea to hypnotise good old Cybil?'

Honey couldn't help worrying about the fallout. Mrs Hoffner's 'away with the fairies' expression was still fresh in her mind.

'Certainly not. I think the poor old dear may very well be a bit off her trolley, but that doesn't mean they should intervene. She might very well enjoy being a cat for the remaining months of her life. If that's what she wants to be, then so be it. Who are we to intervene?'

Honey's attention was drawn to one particular aspect of her daughter's statement.

'Months? Cybil has only months to live?'

'You didn't know?'

Honey shook her head. 'No. What's the matter with her?'

'A brain tumour.'

'The poor woman.'

'Indeed. Do you know she's had a very adventurous life? That's what Grandma told me. She was a secret service agent in the Cold War. She spent a lot of time in Moscow and Berlin and she speaks German and Russian fluently. Did you know that?'

Honey nodded silently. It was very interesting but had nothing to do with the case.

Lindsey went on to list the other things Cybil had done. 'Grandma reckons that Cybil was trained as an assassin. Besides that she's sailed, and flown aeroplanes single-handed, and driven racing cars . . . there's nothing that woman hasn't done. She must feel pretty fed up with her lot at present. I know I would.'

Honey grimaced an agreement. No, it couldn't be easy, but her thoughts were elsewhere. It didn't do to barge into St Margaret's Court and start asking questions about the antiques found stashed in the disused cellar. But there was nothing to stop her from asking Cybil what she knew about it. With a bit of luck the security cameras would have been blinking in that direction on the night everything was loaded into the truck. It could even be that they had recorded an image of the person who had knocked out the Hoffners, tied them up and booked them a one-way ticket to Russia.

CHAPTER FORTY-ONE

Lobelia Cottage glowed like a large slab of honeycomb. The sun had deigned to come out from behind a smattering of gilt-edged clouds and spring flowers were dancing in the breeze. Clinging to the trellis work forming an arch around the front door, an early clematis waved a fragile welcome.

Lobelia Cottage was a ripe subject for a chocolate box; it was pretty and untouched by the modern need to insert double-glazed windows and a plastic-framed conservatory. Miss Cybil Camper-Young preferred the older styles and ways of doing things.

Honey lifted the cast-iron knocker and gave a swift tap with it. In response two flat feline faces appeared at the window to her right. Yellow eyes glowed and small mouths opened, making sounds she could not hear. She briefly wondered where the other cat was lurking, possibly skulking on a mantelpiece. Like Cinderella it was unwelcome in the Persian sisters' household.

She bent and made cooing noises and tapped her fingernails on the windowpane before giving another rap with the knocker. As she waited she glanced back up the winding path to the gates opposite, a shivery feeling creeping down her spine. Doubtless she was being watched. That was when it struck her that Cybil and the Russian owner of the hotel were like gunfighters egging each other on, each watching what the other was doing. They were spying on each other, though goodness knows what could be so interesting — or threatening — about Cybil.

A trembling wisteria, its buds bright green, caught her eye at the end of the cottage where the terracotta paving disappeared around the side to the back of the house. Honey had seen the creepy bits in enough horror movies to know that she shouldn't go in that direction. Yet it was broad daylight and this was St Margaret's Valley, three miles from Bath. The chances of meeting a mad axe murderer were virtually nil.

She followed the path, which narrowed and funnelled beneath a trelliswork arbour supporting the ancient wisteria. Leaves brushed her face. She wondered about spiders. Her voice echoed when she called out. The tiles beneath her feet were green with moss. She thought that odd. Cybil always seemed such a fastidious person, the sort who was good at gardening. Not like herself. One word to a plant and it died.

She was pondering the whys and wherefores of this when the leaves to her left sprang open. Something brushed her face. She cried out. She raised her hand. The perpetrator had already gone.

She paused for breath, hand on breast. 'Be still, my racing heart.'

It was a blackbird. Just a blackbird leaving its nest.

She came out of the arbour into a clear space where the practicalities of life overrode the prettiness. A washing line was strung from a fixing in the back wall, down along another path and across to a tree. A few coloured plastic clothes pegs clung to the green wire line.

The apex of a shed roof poked out from beneath a tangled canopy of some sort of climber that was only just coming into bud.

There was no reason why she should go on; it was patently obvious that Cybil was not at home. But she couldn't help herself. Lobelia Cottage was the land that time forgot. It was a delight, pretty and practical, guarded by hi-tech security cameras, yet possessing the silence of the centuries, its small windows squinting warily at the outside world.

She would have liked to wander around the cottage itself, peering at the wealth of old things gathering dust inside, things that would fetch a good price at auction. With that in mind, she tried the back door. As expected, it was locked. Her attention turned to the shed.

She tried the rusty-looking key but found it wasn't locked. She peered inside, fully expecting to find only a lawn-mower, a pair of shears and perhaps some potted geraniums waiting to be transplanted to a hanging basket.

Excepting the geraniums, everything one expected to see in a garden shed was there. A roll of garden hose bumped her on the head. A number of items were hanging from nails set into the roof: a watering can, a hoe, a garden rake and a piece of rope looped neatly into a figure-of-eight. She recalled the framed knots hanging on Cybil's wall.

Honey closed the shed door behind her. At the back of the house she peered into a small window. Next to it was a small wooden door set at the bottom of some steps. She concluded it probably opened into a cellar.

Peering through the small window produced no results except that a lot of spiders lived in webs suspended from the frame.

But no Cybil.

She found it odd that the elderly resident of Lobelia Cottage was not in residence. A worried thought sprang immediately to mind. Had Cybil's Russian neighbours lost patience with her snooping and done away with her?

She stopped at the garden gate. A cloud covered the sun as she raised her eyes to the ornate gateway across the road. She shivered. They weren't easily detectable, but she was pretty sure that pinhole security cameras were watching her. They were probably inserted in the red eyes of the gilt dragons sitting atop the gateposts. The possibility angered her; she clenched her fists, wanting to go over there and kick the pristine gravel of the drive out into the road.

Cybil could be in deep trouble. Enquiries had to be made and the sooner the better. She considered contacting Doherty, but St Margaret's Valley wasn't mobile phone friendly. A bit of foot slogging was in order. Questions needed to be asked.

Honey got back in her car and headed for the village pub. If there was one place where she might get answers, it was there.

She pulled in. The lunchtime trade was in full swing. A few old-timers sat drinking cider in the corner next to a huge inglenook fireplace. She could tell they were drinking cider by the colour and shape of their noses: raspberry red and bulbous. A few workmen hunched over their lunch. Two were eating something with chips to be washed down with what looked like shandies. The oldest was tucking into a prawn salad accompanied by an orange juice.

A bespectacled man was standing behind the bar wiping glasses and looking decidedly fed up. He beamed on seeing another customer coming through the door.

'What'll it be?'

Information was valuable but didn't run to a full three-course meal. She ordered a diet drink.

'Nothing to eat?'

There was a hint of accusation to the way he asked the question, as though merely coming into his bar warranted more than a meagre drink.

'A ham sandwich?'

'If you like.'

She paid him. He had a cocky assurance about him, without the good looks to match. Lank greying hair that hadn't seen a barber for years was swept back from a thin face. His body was bony and had about as much shape as a lollipop stick. His pallor was symptomatic of the pub trade: hours spent behind the bar, the only outing being a trip to the wholesalers to stock up on snacks and frozen chips.

If there was one thing the hotel trade taught a girl, it was when to butter up and when to pounce. Having buttered him up by buying a drink and a sandwich, she figured the time had come to pounce.

'I wonder if you could help me . . .'

Adopting the fragile female face wasn't easy, but she did her best. The pub landlord looked up from polishing yet another pint glass. The eyes behind his thick spectacles were not exactly friendly — more cautious, as though he were afraid she was going to ask him for the loan of a twenty-pound note — or a free drink.

'An old relative of mine lives in Lobelia Cottage. I've knocked on the door but I can't seem to get an answer. You don't happen to know where she might have gone, do you?'

'Ah!' He held the glass up to the light, brought it back down and proceeded to polish at a perceived smudge. 'Well, Lobelia Cottage and the elderly lady who lives there! Now what do I know about her?'

His tone gave her the impression she was about to get a lecture or receive some pearl of wisdom that only he possessed.

'Her name's Miss Camper-Young. She has cats.'

Too much information! Why had she added the comment about cats? It was totally irrelevant. The pub landlord seemed to think the same too, one eye narrowing as though he were using a microscope and she was the microbe.

'I really don't know about the cats. All I know is that she didn't come in here to take a drink or sample our culinary offerings. She wasn't a customer. I don't take much interest in people who do nothing towards maintaining village life, like supporting local businesses.'

Honey felt obliged to defend the old girl. 'I don't think she drank. You know how it is. One schooner of sherry and old folk tend to fall asleep or fall over.' She added a light laugh. A means to an end.

The landlord wasn't impressed.

'A drink or two never hurt anyone. In fact, the latest medical findings stipulate that it can, in moderation, do the heart a power of good. I can personally introduce you to seniors who'd swear by having a drop a day.'

His look veered to the two elderly men with the cider-inflated noses.

'Women are different.'

The scrutinising eye swung back to her. 'I've noticed,' he murmured, one side of his mouth curling into a sneer.

A middle-aged blonde woman came out with her sandwich. She had a pleasant expression, soft brown eyes and was wearing an overlarge white apron. It was safe to assume that, besides being the cook, she was also the landlord's wife. She shot Honey a friendly smile.

'Hello, dear. Just passing through, are you?'

'Sort of . . .'

'She's visiting a relative,' explained her husband.

'In the village? That's nice. Who might that be, then?'

'Miss . . .'

'The old dear in Lobelia Cottage.'

It was like being at a tennis match. The questions and answers were batted back and forth at speed.

The landlord's wife looked surprised.

'She's been there a lot more of late than what she used to be. Nobody seems to 'ave seen her for years. We all thought she'd died and that the place was in probate or something. Then suddenly up she pops like a Jill in the box. Some reckoned it was the first time they'd *ever* seen her.'

'She likes to keep herself to herself, and she does have cats,' Honey explained.

The landlord stated the obvious. 'You can't hold much of a conversation with a cat.'

'I think she likes peace and quiet,' Honey offered.

'Like this bloody pub,' the landlord snapped gloomily, his eyes following the three workmen who'd downed their food and drink and were off out the door.

Having no wish to hang around in unfriendly company and left wondering about Cybil, Honey started on her sandwich.

The landlord went to the cellar to change a barrel. The old men with the bulbous noses wanted another round.

The landlady poured herself a glass of soda water.

'Are you the lady's niece?' she asked.

Honey said that she was. A little lie wouldn't hurt.

'It's quiet here,' she added.

The landlady shrugged. 'Always the same on a lunch-time. Hardly worth opening, dear. Everyone's at work in Bath or Bristol or whatever. If I 'ad my way I wouldn't bother, but my Les, well, he's a stickler for form and wanting to please everyone. Won't 'ave it, he won't. Got to be open for the regulars, he says.' She leaned forward with a secretive look on her face. 'As if the likes of them two old buggers is going to put much in the till. Look at 'em. Tweedledee and Tweedledum. It's different on a night, of course, when people are 'ome. People come in then, though not as many as my Les would like. Never is enough for 'im.'

The last sentence was muttered bitterly. The pub trade was known to divide more couples than it ever brought together. Not surprising, really. They were working and living together twenty-four hours a day, enough to make anybody murderous.

'Do the Russians ever come in?' Honey asked. She knew it was highly unlikely but was keen to avoid hearing about matrimonial troubles.

The landlady pouted her lips in disgust. 'Not the Russians themselves, but people who work there sometimes pop in.' Again she leaned close. 'I've heard some rum things are going on up there, but what can you expect? They're all foreign criminals if what you read in the papers is anything to go by.'

There it was again! Everyone viewed the Russians as gangsters.

Now it was Honey's turn to lean close and act secretive, in true gossip style.

'So tell me, does anything juicy go on up there?'

The landlady frowned and looked puzzled. 'They're always changing the staff. Not just one at a time, but the whole caboodle. The manager stays the same, though. He comes in sometimes for a quick one and sits over there in the corner reading a paper.'

'Always alone?'

'I think so . . .'

'Not always.'

Les the landlord was back.

His wife looked surprised to see him. 'You done that quick.'

'I done it right.'

Honey sensed he wasn't one to be criticised.

'As I was saying,' he went on. 'He weren't always alone — mind, I think he preferred to be.'

Honey was dying to know who the manager had met, but she refrained from leaping on the landlord and beating the details from his body. Her remit as crime liaison officer didn't come with a licence to kill. She also controlled the urge to sneeze. Ham and English mustard, a lethal combination.

'What makes you think he preferred to be alone?'

'I don't stand behind this bar without ever learning anything. If looks could 'ave killed, that fella that came to see 'im would 'ave been stone dead. No sir, he didn't look too pleased at all.'

Les the landlord smacked a bar towel down onto a brass spill tray.

'I wonder why that was,' said his wife.

Honey was wondering the same thing.

She put in her own comment. 'They obviously knew each other.'

'Definitely,' said Les.

His wife frowned. 'What makes you think that?'

Les began pouring pints of cider for his two remaining customers.

'Loretta,' he said in a measured fashion. 'He didn't look happy to see the bloke. Now it stands to reason that he 'ad to know the bloke in order to not look 'appy to see 'im. Right?'

His wife jerked her chin in a curt nod of understanding.

Although still wondering whether Cybil had been kidnapped and/or murdered, Honey was intrigued.

'So you don't think he was a friend.'

'Not sure.'

'Some kind of business acquaintance, perhaps?'

Les was now pulling the second pint of cider. He looked upwards as he considered the question.

'Could be. He had something wrapped in newspaper.'

'It was an ornament.'

Husband looked at wife in disbelief.

'You said the bloke always drank alone. Now you're saying that this other bloke — the one you didn't see — was flashing an ornament.'

Recalling what the Hoffners had told her, Honey's ears pricked up.

'What kind of ornament?' she asked, her heart in her mouth.

'Well . . .' Loretta considered, her eyes rolling to one side, up and down and then to the other.

'Well, go on.'

It appeared that her husband was as impatient as Honey to know the contents of the newspaper.

'A small dish. I think it had flowers on it.'

Honey did a quick calculation. 'Meissen perhaps? Dresden?'

Loretta looked at her blankly. 'It looked pretty.'

First an item at the car boot sale, then the stash beneath the hotel and now this. Honey began putting two and two together. The man they were talking about had to be the link between the stash beneath the hotel and the item Smudger had bought at the car boot sale. Obviously the manager also had something to do with it.

She thanked them for their hospitality before leaving. Once outside the door she phoned Doherty and told him what they'd told her. He promised the manager would be questioned. The arrow of suspicion regarding all the deaths was now pointing directly at him.

Doherty suggested they meet up. 'I'll phone you when I'm free.'

She didn't tell him what was going on in her head and that she was only down the road from him, enjoying — or was it enduring? — the hospitality of the local innkeeper. He wouldn't approve of her intentions — namely, breaking and entering if Cybil didn't come to the door. Such a deed was strictly illegal, but no matter how often she told herself that, the thought wouldn't go away. The security camera at Lobelia Cottage might possibly hold a very important clue to all this. There had to be a record of the truck being loaded with items stolen from Philippe's storeroom, that and the Hoffner couple being manhandled, trussed up like Christmas turkeys and bundled aboard.

Would she let the fact that no one was at home in Lobelia Cottage get in her way?

No, she decided. No way!

CHAPTER FORTY-TWO

Honey drove further along the valley. She wanted time to think. Pulling in at a gate, she got out and stared at the cows while she thought things through. The cows stared right back, chewing as they considered her.

Breaking and entering! It's breaking and entering, for God's sake! She grimaced with the pain of it all. Guilt was like that — a right pain. *But think of Cybil,* she reminded herself as she chewed on a straw. There was no getting away from it. Her mind was made up. She would break in if Cybil didn't answer the door. There was no guarantee that the dear old soul had come to any harm, but what else was she supposed to think?

The guilt kicked in again but curiosity kicked it right back out. *Do you want to see that security recording or what?* whispered the voice of curiosity. *Go on! You know you want to. Go for it!*

By the time she got back to Lobelia Cottage — having parked a discreet distance from the door — the sun had made a sudden decision to take an afternoon siesta, having disappeared behind a cloud.

She stole a glimpse across the road at the imposing entrance to the St Margaret's Court Hotel. Between the foliage she could just about make out police vehicles parked outside. Doherty was leading the investigation, probably asking for their security recordings while enquiring who was the last person to see Aloysius Rodriguez alive.

There was no point in barging in there. Besides, Doherty deserved to have centre stage in this. He'd worked hard on the case, and although at times he was stressed to breaking point, he'd never lost his rag with her. In fact, quite the opposite, almost as though the upmarket hotel had given him a once-in-a-lifetime opportunity to further his career. She hoped that was the case. He certainly deserved it.

Leaving the car unlocked and the keys still in it, she retraced the steps she'd taken earlier to the cottage's front door. No longer glowing in sunlight, the ancient property had a chill, almost haunting feel about it, like the gingerbread cottage in the fairy tale of Hansel and Gretel.

Things rustled about her. OK, there were a lot of leaves to rustle and, very likely, little creatures living within the flowery jungle were aware of human footsteps approaching and were scuttling away. A mouse ran across her path — a lucky mouse, seeing as the cats were not allowed free range in the garden.

When she lifted the knocker the front door swung slightly ajar. She paused. A door that was ajar presented something of a dilemma. Earlier it had definitely been shut.

The security recordings from the old girl's cameras beckoned like a birthday present tied with gold ribbon and with Gucci stamped all over it. If someone else was inside, someone dangerous . . . Well! She'd just have to deal with that particular booby prize when she came to it.

The first thing that struck her on entering was that no four-legged friends came out to curl their bodies around her legs. Neither had the animals appeared at the window when she'd knocked at the door. Odd then that the door was ajar; the expensive creatures were not allowed out to roam and forage like other cats. The door should not have been left open at all.

She wondered if they were locked away somewhere. On the other hand, an intruder wouldn't have cared if the cats got out. Her feet turned to lumps of lead at the bottom of the stairs. She looked up to the tight corner at the top. Should she carry on and risk meeting whoever was up there, or turn and run?

This was one of those moments when she wished she'd travelled in Mary Jane's Cadillac. Mary Jane kept a tyre iron beneath the front passenger seat. A modern VW like hers didn't have that particular facility.

Taking a deep breath, she went upwards. Halfway up, a stair creaked beneath her weight. Heart racing, she paused and listened. No one leapt from the shadows. It had to be safe. Didn't it?

She went bravely on, passing several bedroom doors before coming to the one with the display of nautical knots hanging on the wall outside. Inside, the grainy grey images on the screens flickered hesitantly. The room was dimly lit by them and an Anglepoise desk light.

On checking the images on the screens, she saw they were all firmly fixed on the hotel entrance across the road. By using the toggle she could swivel it around to take in areas of the garden, the front gate, the arbour and the path running alongside the house. It struck her that these were the areas the cameras should focus on if Cybil was worried about intruders. So why was she so obsessed with the hotel?

She reminded herself that the resident of Lobelia Cottage was a very old lady suffering from a terminal illness. Age alone was enough to send her dotty without having to cope with that extra burden.

There was a small desktop computer sitting next to the bank of screens. Reassuring herself that she could handle the equipment, she moved the mouse, bringing up a screen of folders. Cybil, being a methodical person, had labelled each one with dates and start times. Honey was duly impressed. She herself went along in a muddle with such things, for the most part depending on her memory to remember what was what. If it wasn't for her daughter, Lindsey, she'd get into a right mess. Lindsey was a lot like Cybil, Honey thought with a smile, though perhaps she wouldn't like to hear that. Honey began her search for the recording of the night the Hoffners had been bundled into the truck.

'Gotcha!'

She'd found the right one. Before double-clicking the file, she glanced over her shoulder. Being too exuberant could land you in trouble, she admonished herself.

The screen flickered, before showing an image of the night when a truck was being loaded with all manner of luxury goods, including antiques and paintings.

Only one of the men seemed vaguely familiar; it had to be the hotel manager. The other she didn't recognise, no matter how much she narrowed her eyes and tried to focus.

Once the two men had disappeared, there was movement in a nearby bush. Out popped the Hoffners, creeping towards the truck, checking the direction in which the two men had disappeared.

Mr Hoffner appeared to have a camera slung over his shoulder. He began taking shots, both he and his wife leaning into the truck.

Unseen by the Hoffners, another figure suddenly joined them.

She gave a little gasp as the third figure reached forward with both hands. The Hoffners collapsed like sacks of wet barley. The figure heaved both of them up into the back of the truck. Whoever it was carried a length of rope and scrambled up into the truck after them. Honey decided that this must be the third of the thieves, though somehow . . . there was something different about this one.

She frowned and clicked on the 'rewind' icon.

The figure appeared again, long and lean and wearing . . . a skirt.

'What are you doing here?'

The room was flooded with light.

Honey spun round.

Cybil was standing in the doorway. Her eyes glittered. She had a length of rope over one shoulder and was carrying a cat basket in one hand and a Luger in the other. Honey gulped.

'Miss Camper-Young! Thank goodness it's you.' She hoped she sounded convincing. 'I knocked at the door. I thought you'd had an accident or intruders. I didn't see the cats.'

The old girl's face was as hard and rutted as a plum stone. Mrs Gullible she was not, but there was hope.

'My mother thought you might be in trouble, and with all the worries you've been having about the place across the road . . .'

'They had to go.'

'They?' She hadn't a clue where this was going, but Honey decided to play along. 'The cats? Do the cats have to go?'

'The foreigners. They should all go back.'

Honey blinked. If what she was hearing was true, Cybil did not approve of the German couple and was sending them back to where they came from. She ached to point out that a pair of air tickets would have been more appropriate but didn't have the guts to say so. And then it clicked. They'd been barking up the wrong tree. What was it each of those murdered had in common? Mentally she ran through the list. A Portuguese waiter and a dark-skinned interior designer. Ferdinand Olsen, who was half Norwegian, half Spanish, and Mrs Olsen. OK, she wasn't of foreign extraction, unless you counted being upper-middle class with a preference for horses over human beings, but that could have been a mistake. The rest were all foreigners. As for the Russian owners of the hotel opposite . . .?

'I don't like foreigners. I'm using the skills I learned in MI5 to bump them off. It was easy to get in and dispose of that annoying black man with the blond hair. Seeing as he liked antiques so much, I forced one down his throat. He'd been with the waiter earlier — another foreigner. I watched what they did. Disgusting!'

It was hard to know what to say to a gun-toting septuagenarian, harder still to accept that this woman had been trained to kill. One of the cats yowled in its box.

'Your code name wouldn't have been Octopussy by any chance?'

Cybil tutted in disgust. 'Ian could never keep his mouth shut.'

'And you don't like Russians.'

Icy blue eyes narrowed over the barrel of the gun. 'I hate them most of all. They killed Leonid.'

'Your lover? I see . . .'

'No! My cat! I loved that cat. He lived with me in a luxury flat in Moscow. I was working undercover. Mikhail was my lover. He worked for the KGB. He said I had to prove my love for him by killing the cat, his only rival for my love. Little did he know! I didn't love him at all. I was merely doing my job. But I couldn't let him know that. I had to . . .'

Her bottom lip began to quiver so much that Honey was tempted to rush across the room to give her a cuddle. She took another look at the gun and held back.

'I had to shoot my beloved Leonid!'

Honey wasn't usually one for putting her foot in it, but when she did, she did it big time.

'It was only a cat, after all . . .'

She said it lightly. Too lightly for Cybil.

'You! You're just like the rest,' she shouted, raising the gun and aiming it dead centre between Honey's eyes.

Realising her mistake, Honey backtracked big time.

'Look, I know you love cats . . .'

'None as much as Mikhail!'

She was in love with a foreigner, though to hear her speak you'd think she was talking about a cat. Cybil's getting very confused. It's part of her condition. A confusion verging on madness, thought Honey. The wild stare in Cybil's eyes was enough to tell her that. Old women didn't glare like that — not unless they were totally mad.

The Russians in the hotel opposite had been incredibly tolerant about her. They'd known she was spying on them and although they'd initially found it necessary to cut the wires to her security cameras, they'd later relented. She found herself asking why. The reason could be that they knew she was dotty, and even more so, knew who she was. Knowing he was at risk, the new Russian owner kept away from the mad old woman.

So why had she spared the Hoffners? She decided it wouldn't hurt to ask.

'The man helped me get Su Ching down from the tree the other day. He was very kind to me, so I was kind to him. Anyway, I thought they'd probably suffocate eventually without me having to do anything else.'

Charming!

'And Mrs Olsen?'

'The horse woman!' Her attitude changed, her mouth screwing up into a spiteful grimace. 'She was out here riding one day. One of my Persian queens got out when the hunt was out. That blasted woman rode right at her. Said she had run out in front of her. My darling queen broke her leg. I couldn't forgive her for that.'

So that was it. Cat haters and foreigners were one and the same thing as far as the resident of Lobelia Cottage was concerned. She'd killed them for being what they were while her mind was unhinged. Probably she wouldn't even go to prison, merely a high-security hospital. It wouldn't hurt to reassure her of that.

'Cybil, you won't go to prison for this because you're not well, dear.'

Cybil blinked. 'Of course I won't go to prison. I was acting on orders.'

Whoops. It was not wise to continue. There had to be another way to get out of this.

Honey went over the facts in her mind. Somehow or other Cybil had got into the hotel opposite without the security guards seeing her. She'd been heading for the Russian. Philippe had got in the way. Mrs Olsen's death was self-explanatory.

It amazed Honey that an elderly woman had managed to evade the broad-shouldered guards.

'The guards are stupid,' said Cybil in response to her unasked question.

‘How many times have you managed to get into the hotel?’

‘Not enough. First the dark guy got in my way, though not so much as that man Olsen. He specifically kept a look out for me. I had to get rid of him.’

‘And the waiter?’

‘He saw me coming from the bathroom and followed me out. I was nearer to the tourist bus than to the hotel, so I thought a little ride might do him some good.’

All this explanation was making Honey’s head spin and her mouth dry. Somehow, she had to cut through all this and get the gun-toting grandma back down to earth.

‘What about the poison? Did you know that they took poison?’

Cybil shook her head. ‘Tonic. They were health freaks, and when I stuck the labels on the bottles I upped the dosage a little — ten times the recommended dose, in fact. It wouldn’t have killed them, only made them a little woozy.’

So here she was sitting and exchanging pleasantries with Bath’s equivalent of the Wimbledon Poisoner.

She had to try again.

‘I think we should get help,’ she said. ‘You couldn’t help doing what you did. You’re not very well.’

Outwardly she sounded calm and totally under control. Inside she was screaming for help.

A slow, crazy smile spread across those wrinkled lips.

‘You don’t fool me, Mrs Driver. I know you’re working for them. I know they’re trying to take me aboard their spaceship and away from my darling queens.’

Right! Cybil’s mind was back with the Martians.

If she hadn’t believed that the woman was crazy before, she certainly did now. Anyone would!

‘Now look . . .’ she began hesitantly. It crossed her mind that being the representative of little green men was a capital offence in Cybil’s eyes. ‘You know who I am. I’m Gloria’s daughter. You’ve known my mother for years.’

‘She’s one of them!’ Cybil snapped, now steadying the gun with both hands.

'No,' Honey said, adamantly. 'I can categorically state here and now that my mother is not of Russian descent.'

'Not Russian! Of course she's not *Russian*! She's from another planet.'

That particular comment almost made Honey want to laugh out loud. She at least took it a little more lightly than she should have.

'You might be onto something there!'

'Don't be facetious! Put up your hands!'

This was getting worrying.

'What are you going to do with me?'

Cybil swung the length of rope from off her shoulder.

'Tie you up.'

Being restrained she could cope with. It was what might come after that worried her.

CHAPTER FORTY-THREE

Doherty sat on the corner of the hotel manager's desk. Reginald Parrot was pretending not to be rattled. A tic beneath his right eye indicated otherwise.

'Want to tell me about it?'

The man glared.

'I don't know what you mean.'

'Don't play smart. I know your beef. Come clean and I'll make it easy on you.'

The man looked amused. 'I take it you watched last night's late movie. Philip Marlowe?'

Doherty was admitting nothing, but it was true that he'd been watching late-night television. He distinctly remembered falling asleep halfway through *The Big Sleep*.

'I want names,' Doherty persisted.

The man shrugged and stayed silent.

Doherty persisted. 'We've got the Russian driver. He's pointed the finger at you. Now let's see, stealing and smuggling priceless artefacts . . .'

He wasn't at all sure how valuable the contents of the truck had been, but Honey had assured him she'd had a few thousand invested in some of it. That was good enough for him.

'I'm not taking the blame all by myself,' the manager blurted.

'Who else do I blame?'

The man's mouth hung open. His coal-black eyes stayed fixed on Doherty's face. They both knew that this was the chink Doherty had been waiting for.

'So tell me,' urged Doherty, walking round the desk, hands clasped behind his back. 'Give me a good reason why I shouldn't throw the book at you.'

Crikey! He really did sound like a TV detective. He swallowed the urge to laugh. This was neither the time nor the place.

'Gilbert! Gilbert Godwin!'

Doherty frowned. 'I recognise that name. Am I right in thinking I might find his dabs on file?'

Mr Parrot's boot-button eyes looked at the floor. 'I suppose so.'

'Where do I find him?'

It was a matter of minutes after giving the order to look for Gilbert Godwin that a return call followed from another officer.

'We've found a bloke getting drunk and throwing money around. The bloke's name is Gilbert Godwin and he's got form. But listen to this. He reckons the money is his and that him and his ma were in business together. Get this! His mother's name was Deirdre Olsen. Apparently he's her illegitimate son. How's about that?'

'Arrest him.'

'Charges?'

'Theft and smuggling stolen goods.'

He ordered the same for the hotel manager, who was led away by two of his officers.

'I feel like a celebration,' he exclaimed, stretching his arms because he felt so good.

A young lady with blonde hair and a sweetheart expression informed him that the owner wished to speak to him. He was taken to a very smart apartment on the first floor.

Ivan Sarkov rose from his chair as Doherty entered and offered his thanks.

'I've won a night here in a raffle,' Doherty explained. 'How about making it even more special?'

'Anything you want,' said the Russian.

Doherty was jubilant as he started his car and headed for the Green River Hotel, feeling sure Honey would not turn him down, not after all this. A little of the old Doherty charm and she'd be hot and panting for an evening of good food, excellent wine and unfettered passion.

CHAPTER FORTY-FOUR

Honey was anything but unfettered at present, what with Cybil having hog-tied her in the basement with her hands and feet behind her.

'What are you going to do with me?'

Cybil patted her purple lips with a skinny finger and rolled her eyes upwards to the arched stone ceiling.

She sighed deeply. 'I don't know. You're not foreign, so it wouldn't really be very fair to kill you outright. I mean, even a secret agent has to have a good reason to kill somebody. And then, that's only in response to a specific order. It's always for a cause. The end justifying the means and all that.'

Great, thought Honey. *Here I am with a mad old lady who thinks that anyone who isn't a cat is a spy. How do I get out of this? Negotiation! That's the key. Develop a rapport with your captor. Appeal to their better nature.*

'This is very uncomfortable,' she said, jerking her head at the knots around her wrists and ankles.

'You'll get used to it, dear,' said Cybil with a watery smile, the sort grandmothers use when dealing with a grandchild who refuses to eat their greens.

'Do you like cats?' she asked suddenly.

'Oh. Yes! I love them!' Honey couldn't have shown more enthusiasm if she'd tried.

'I'm glad to hear it.'

Cybil placed the Luger across her lap. Honey gulped. In her mind she returned to the negotiation lifeline, searching frantically for any little tip she'd picked up about dealing with hostage takers. Number-one rule, make friends with them, take the relationship to a very personal level. Gain their sympathy. Well, she had already tried that, but a second try was most definitely on the cards.

'It's very cold down here.'

OK, it wasn't the most original line, but everyone has to start somewhere.

Cybil didn't appear to hear. She sat back in an old Windsor chair that was dusty and the subject of much wear — a bit like Cybil herself.

Honey asked herself whether she might be imagining things, but the old face looked paler, and it seemed that, before her eyes, the thin frame that had surely touched five feet ten at least now looked to have shrunk.

'Miss Camper-Young? Are you OK?'

The old eyes closed. She shook her head. 'You won't get away. I've locked the door.'

Honey called her again.

'I'm not feeling very well . . .'

'My mother said you weren't. Perhaps if we went upstairs and made some tea, or better still a cup of hot chocolate each.'

Anything — just don't shoot me or leave me down here.

Cybil was unmoved. Her eyes were still closed. Her jaw hung open and she gave a languorous sigh.

'I can come with you and make it if you don't feel up to it.' Last ditch attempt.

Honey paused. By the look of her, Cybil didn't look very up to it at all.

'Miss Camper-Young? Cybil?'

There was no response.

Panic rose in her stomach like a swarm of wasps.

'I don't believe it. I don't believe you've died on me! Hey!'

A low-pitched death rattle cackled from Cybil's throat.

'Shit!'

Honey pulled at the binds. Great! What a situation to be in. She was tied up hand and foot and lying on her belly. The exit was up a set of stone steps to her right. The door at the top was locked.

Seeking signs that she might have been wrong and her companion was merely asleep, she shouted, 'Cybil, you mad old bat! Wake up! I'm hungry. I want to go home!'

Not a whisper. Not the slightest movement. Miss Cybil Camper-Young, a woman who had worked for the secret service and led a quite extraordinary life, was as dead as dead could be.

Honey looked up the stairs to the firmly shut door and shouted for help. A cold chill fell over her like winter mist, the sort that seeps right through to the bones. One shout for help would not be enough. She had to keep on and on shouting and hope that someone would hear her. If they didn't she was likely to end up as dead and cold as Cybil.

CHAPTER FORTY-FIVE

Lindsey looked up to see Detective Inspector Steve Doherty breezing through the door looking very pleased with himself.

'You look as though you've found a fifty-pound note.'

'Better than that,' he said, giving her a quick peck on the cheek. 'I've found the mastermind behind the theft of a large amount of antiques and valuables, including those belonging to the lately deceased Philippe Fabiere.'

'Good for you,' said Lindsey, sounding genuinely pleased for him. 'And the murders?'

'Ah!' He frowned. He was finding it perplexing that Gilbert Godwin had a useful alibi for each of the nights in question. He was a scoutmaster and had been at meetings on each occasion. He told Lindsey just that. 'He didn't do it.'

'Do you believe him?'

'Scout's honour.'

He could see by Lindsey's expression that she wasn't sure where this was going. However, he was in no mood to explain further. A little more checking once Godwin had spent more time in the cells might change things. He *needed* things to change. Most of all he needed a break. Godwin and the hotel manager both had alibis for the times of the murders. He was feeling all at sea. Only Honey accepting his invitation to a night of unbridled pandering and passion could bring him back to shore. He was well and truly in the mood for all of it.

'And where's your lovely mother?'

'I'm not sure. She was speaking to the Hoffners earlier, asking them about their abduction. They were trying to recall exactly what happened. She asked them if they could remember anything else apart from what they'd told the police already.'

'And did they?'

Lindsey shook her head. 'No. They were a bit traumatised by their ordeal, but Mary Jane has offered to help.'

Doherty raised his eyebrows. Mary Jane was a doctor of the paranormal, not a psychiatrist. He pointed this out.

'Hypnotism,' said Lindsey laughingly in response to his questioning expression. 'Apparently, Frau Hoffner is a natural subject for hypnosis as long as there are no meddling spirits around. By the way, I think by meddling spirits she's referring to my grandmother. She's been banned from the premises.'

One side of Doherty's mouth lifted in a grin. 'I can see that her presence might cause some problems. So, when is this taking place?'

'Right now. They're up in Mary Jane's room. That's Mr and Mrs Hoffner and Smudger. Smudger is there to witness the event — and to lean against the door to stop my grandmother barging in.'

In Doherty's estimation, gleaning any further information from the Hoffners while they were hypnotised was a long shot. Long shots sometimes came romping home, he told himself. Give it a try.

Lindsey gave him the room number. He told himself this was important, more important than asking Honey out. Actually it wasn't. He was merely putting off the fateful moment when she said yes, or more worryingly, no.

'Let me in,' he said after knocking at the door of Mary Jane's room.

'No can do.'

'Smudger, it's me. Doherty.'

There was a sound of a bolt being drawn. Smudger's face appeared, pink-cheeked and blue-eyed. On recognising Doherty he opened the door wider.

'All right, mate?' Smudger had a bouncy way about him. Corn-coloured hair flopped over his brow. Doherty attempted to get through the door. Smudger stopped him. 'Got to ask you to be quiet, mate. OK?'

'Sure.' Doherty nodded and strolled in, apprehensive as to what he would find. The fact that Smudger had been brought in as a witness was a bit of a mystery, but there again so was Mary Jane. It was pretty easy to imagine her wearing a pointed hat and bending over a cauldron with a book of spells in her hand. He didn't believe in this stuff, so what the hell was he doing here?

Frau Hoffner was sitting upright in a chair knitting. Having seen her around the hotel before, knitting away as though her life depended on it, Doherty saw nothing odd about it now — until he saw her eyes. There was a faraway look in them, certainly not the look of a woman concentrating on her knitting. The needles were click-clacking away as though being driven by a piston engine. Like an automaton.

Mary Jane was standing in front of her swinging a silver pocket watch from side to side.

'That watch used to belong to my grandfather,' whispered Smudger.

Doherty nodded in acknowledgement. Smudger had a silver watch. That explained why he'd been brought in to witness the event.

'Now,' said Mary Jane. 'I want you to set your mind back . . .'

The room was a little warm and Doherty found his attention waning. The swinging watch didn't help. Neither did the monotonous tone of Mary Jane's reed-like voice.

'So what happened exactly . . .'

Herr Hoffner was sitting in an armchair, hands clasped tightly together. His eyes, brimming with affection, were fixed on his wife. Doherty presumed he hadn't been a good subject for hypnotism. Mrs Hoffner appeared to be exactly the opposite.

Bits of information filtered through, though nothing that he hadn't heard before. Every so often Mary Jane referred to Frau Hoffner's knitting. With each referral the knitting needles slowed their unrelenting rattle.

Doherty didn't get what that was all about, so he paid no mind to it. Shit, what was he hoping for anyway? Everyone knew Mary Jane was a sandwich short of a picnic. As for Mrs Hoffner, he didn't know her well enough to pass judgement, though he couldn't help thinking that her continual knitting must get on Herr Hoffner's nerves.

Mary Jane's voice droned on like a short-tempered bluebottle. One key, one tone, one goal, interspersed only with Frau Hoffner's responses. The sound of the knitting needles was not quite so resonant nor so persistent.

'So what else do you recall? Was there anything specific you noticed when the police came to your rescue?'

Doherty yawned. That they were surrounded by broken bits of crockery, probably. Some of the stuff had got broken. A painting had fallen over and landed on Herr Hoffner's head. His head had gone straight through and out the other side. The restorers would have a field day with that one!

'Knots! I remember thinking how professional the knots were. As good as any round-the-world yachtsman might manage.'

Mary Jane accepted what she said, then began to trail back into the thing about the knitting.

Doherty was no longer listening. He was remembering Honey telling him about a display of knots and how athletic she was, plus having a secret service background — if that was to be believed, of course. Old people could be a little over-imaginative.

He shook his head in disbelief. His suspicion was too crazy to be true, but he had to check it out now. Right now!

'Something wrong?' asked Smudger.

'I need to go.'

'There's one in there.'

Smudger pointed to Mary Jane's private bathroom.

Doherty ignored him. He didn't need the bathroom, but he did need to ask a few questions of the one person who might help with the crazy suspicion that was hurtling through his mind like an express train.

CHAPTER FORTY-SIX

Gloria Cross, Honey's mother, eyed the man in front of her with undisguised wariness. He was good looking in a rough-diamond kind of way, and although with hand on heart she couldn't really say she'd never fallen for a rough diamond in her time, she'd usually saved herself with a bit of common sense. Men like him inflamed the passions, but when it came to domestic bliss, a steady Eddie won the day. There were a few other provisos — like a decent sum in the bank, preferably Switzerland or the Cayman Islands — but a little dalliance never hurt anyone.

That's why she'd never protested too loudly about her daughter's friendship with Steve Doherty, a mere police officer. She'd told herself he was a passing fancy, one that Hannah would pass by if Gloria had her way.

The fact that he was standing here on her doorstep looking very scruffy, handsome and intense was a surprise. The fact that he wished to ask her a question filled her with fear. A marriage proposal?

'What sort of question?' she asked him, narrowing the gap in the open door just in case he might force himself in.

'It's about your friend, Cybil Camper-Young.'

'Oh!'

Gloria felt relief flood over her that he hadn't come to ask for her daughter's hand in marriage. He'd come to ask about her old friend Cybil.

Her smile was broad enough to span the Grand Canyon.

'Why didn't you say so, officer? I'm always willing to help the police in whatever way I can.'

She showed him into her lounge, a place of cut crystal, gilt-edged occasional tables and an off-white carpet.

She indicated that he be seated. 'So, what is this about?'

Noting that the sofa had cushions piped with gold silk and that the tassels on each corner were carefully and identically positioned to sweep to the right, he perched nervously on the edge, knees tightly together.

'I'd like you to tell me all you know about her. I understand she served in undercover ops in the Cold War.'

'Yes. Basically she was a spy. She used to tell us that Ian Fleming based his books on her but turned them into men. I'm not sure if she was telling the truth.' She tutted and shook her head disapprovingly. 'Imagine, a friend of mine with a licence to kill.'

'Imagine,' said Doherty, smiling weakly. 'But she was younger then.'

'Yes. About twenty-six, I think. Perhaps a year or so older. I'm better preserved than her,' she added primly, patting her hair and obviously seeking a compliment.

'Enlighten me. Exactly what was she involved in?'

Gloria looked at him as though he were stupid. 'She was stationed in Russia. It was all very hush-hush. She never used to talk much about it, but of late she did let a few things slip. She wasn't supposed to, of course, but her mind is going.' She frowned. 'She's got dementia. It's linked to a brain tumour. It's purely a matter of time.' She shook her head. 'Her mind's not what it was.'

Doherty decided that he didn't need to ask anything else. He needed to speak to the old lady out at Lobelia Cottage. All through this case he'd dealt confidently with the procession of suspects. They'd all thought themselves cleverer than him. Who would have thought that an old lady in her late seventies really was so, but also slightly mad?

He took his leave of Honey's mother and headed back to the Green River Hotel to see if Honey had returned. She had not.

'She's probably bumped into an old friend,' Lindsey declared brightly.

She didn't add that he was possibly French and over here on the French exchange scheme. Her mother had wowed her with a description of the gorgeous Gallic dish.

Honey had not been able to make their date but had confided to Lindsey that she was hoping they'd run into one another other again. The exchange scheme went on for quite a few weeks. There was plenty of time.

Doherty frowned as he thought things through. He didn't have time to wait around. There were other things requiring his attention, but which came first? Should he give Gilbert Godwin a thorough grilling, or take a leisurely drive out to Lobelia Cottage?

The city streets were getting busier by virtue of the approaching Easter holiday. He pulled in on Queen Square with the intention of giving himself a minute to think, congratulating himself on being so lucky as to find a gap. How should he handle the old girl? he asked himself. He couldn't barge in there and accuse her of anything really, except for tying up the Hoffners, and it was hardly as though she was likely to do a runner. She was old, for goodness sake!

A figure came into focus in his rear-view mirror. A traffic warden with menace in her eyes. That's when he realised he was parked on double yellow lines. He promptly pulled out again.

Finding another space around the other side of the square, he pulled in again. Immobility helped him concentrate. Could it really be that Miss Camper-Young had killed all those people? It might work in fiction, but surely not in real life?

It was a few minutes before he spotted the traffic warden again. Having seen him pull into another space on double yellow lines, the minx had trotted all round the square, pen poised and ready to write out a parking ticket.

He grinned, started the engine and pulled out again, leaving her standing there with a look of utter dismay on her face.

Feeling sunnier and decisive, he headed along the A4 towards the turnoff to St Margaret's Valley.

By the time he pulled into the space outside the old cottage, he was feeling more than confident enough to handle Bath's resident Mata Hari.

The door was ajar, but he knocked anyway. A slight breeze pushed it open a bit further. He looked down expecting the old girl's cats to come sliding out around it, their tails upright like the mast of a yacht.

No cats came out. No old lady either.

Unlike Honey, he decided that even old ladies who have worked for the secret service don't venture out much in the chilly spring weather. He took the view that she'd accidentally left it open.

Being a courteous sort of chap, he called out to her. 'Anybody there?'

Nobody answered.

The cottage echoed with emptiness from its stone-flagged floors to its low, bumpy ceilings. It should have echoed with silence too, but Doherty was aware of a low sound, like a humming in the ear, yet not a hum. It occurred to him that the sound could be coming from the upstairs room housing the security monitors.

He bounded up the stairs, taking them two at a time. He no longer cared whether the house was empty or not, though he was certain nobody was at home. He focused his mind on the job in hand, going into the room, studying the screens.

He spotted the computer, and out of pure curiosity flicked through the history of the few hours before he'd arrived. The pictures mostly covered the comings and goings across the road at the hotel. Tiring of watching plumbers, builders and the flamboyant Keith Richardson Smythe arrive, he fast forwarded — and there she was. Honey Driver marching up the garden path.

He did the same thing with the other cameras. Honey was walking around the back of the house. At first she was all alone. And then she wasn't. He started at the image of Miss Camper-Young. She was tall, athletic and of a no-nonsense disposition. She was also jabbing the barrel of a gun into the small of Honey's back.

Leaving the screen frozen on that image, he raced out of the room and around to the back of the house.

On the screen he could see that Honey was being taken to a small wooden door surrounded by ancient stone. There were steps leading down to it and a small window to one side full of cobwebs.

Bounding around the back of the cottage, he found the door. It was locked. He also heard the faint noise he'd heard upstairs and realised now that he was hearing the cats.

He hammered on the door. 'Honey?'

* * *

What would Houdini do? wondered Honey. She'd wriggled and squirmed in her efforts to loosen the rope, but nothing had worked. Her host was dead and the cats were yowling for their dinner.

'We're all going to die here,' she said out loud.

The cats looked at her expectantly from behind the wire doors of their carrying baskets.

'Sorry, pussies.'

How should I prepare myself to die? she wondered.

The old voice of common sense and reality told her not to be so stupid. Easter was coming. Menus had to be prepared, rooms made spick and span for the avalanche of visitors. She couldn't afford to die. She had too much to do.

And yet . . .

Her attempt at high spirits faded away. Unless someone came looking for her or called by chance, she was as good as dead. Here she would die with an old lady and three cats.

Suddenly there was Doherty.

'Honey? Are you in there?'

'Of course I am!'

'Can you unlock the door?'

'Do you think I'd stay in here if I could?'

The door shuddered. In Hollywood films a man only had to shove his shoulder hard against a door to send it into smithereens. But this was English oak. It didn't fall to bits on being hit by a masculine shoulder. Only boxwood did that.

Doherty hammered on the door again.

'I'll get help.'

She presumed he'd go and get the special coppers who smashed through doors with a ramming device.

Suddenly he was back again.

'How far are you from the door?'

She wasn't good at judging distance and had failed her driving test first time because of it. You needed to be able to judge distances if you were trying to park between two other cars. She'd misjudged and scratched the pair of them. But she made an effort to gauge the distance.

'About fifteen feet.'

'Is there anything you can hide behind?'

What the hell was he doing?

She was lying beside a large oak barrel.

'Yes,' she shouted back.

'Make yourself as small as you can and wait there until I say you can move.'

She did as he said, then paused. The cats were beyond the barrel.

'What about the cats? Are they likely to get hurt if you do what you're going to do?'

'Don't worry. They'll be fine.'

She wasn't sure whether to believe him.

* * *

Outside Doherty had phoned for assistance, but in the meantime he was trying to recall his knowledge of basic chemistry.

So far he'd rounded up the equipment he thought he needed. This consisted of a grow bag, an old stocking, a small amount of diesel and a light bulb. If the special unit with the ram didn't get here within the next fifteen minutes, he would go ahead and blow the door off its hinges — hopefully!

On the other side of the door, Honey was reading his mind. 'Doherty!'

'Yes,' came the muffled reply.

'You're not doing what I think you're doing?'

'I'm just amusing myself until help comes. By the way, did you see what direction Miss Camper-Young took off in?'

'She didn't. She's in here with me.'

He couldn't quite work that out. He'd definitely seen the old girl poking Honey in the back with something wicked and lethal. Perhaps he was barking up the wrong tree after all.

'Is she OK?'

'No. She's dead.'

Had Honey killed her? Surely not. He went back to making his explosive. Luckily the special unit and the ram arrived before he finished it.

There was a lot of dust as the door went down and the policemen strode over it making their grand entrance.

It would have been nice if Doherty had swept her up into his arms and kissed her passionately, but he didn't do things like that. Instead he stood there with his fists resting on his hips, grinning like a Cheshire Cat.

Honey glared back up at him. 'What's so funny?'

'I think I've got you exactly where I want you.'

'Is that so?'

He nodded. 'Yes. It is.'

CHAPTER FORTY-SEVEN

It was always going to be a bit unbelievable that a little old lady had gone off her rocker and run around killing people. On checking the forensic evidence, it turned out to be true.

But despite his apparent innocence, Honey still had reservations about Ivan Sarkov, the new owner of the St Margaret's Court Hotel.

'He might not have been behind the stolen goods, but I think Cybil was onto something with that guy.'

Doherty wasn't really listening. Like her, he'd been surprised at the outcome of this case, but it was finished now.

Sarkov had to be up to something, and according to some members of staff, he was too free and easy with his fists. But the only way to get any evidence was to appear as innocent guests and have a snoop around.

'That's it! That's what we have to do.'

Doherty looked at her askance. He knew deep down that he had to come clean and explain that the plans he had were nothing to do with crime. A sticky situation.

Honey was full of exuberance. She almost danced. Her eyes certainly did.

This was not at all what Doherty had had in mind. The type of undercover work he was interested in took place in bed . . .

'I just thought that if we booked in as guests, chances are none of the staff would recognise us. Once we were washed and brushed up, that is.'

'I think it's a brilliant idea,' Honey enthused, her eyes sparkling. 'How about Saturday night?'

Doherty told himself that he wasn't really taking advantage of her exuberance, but hey, a guy had to make the most of things.

'How about tonight? A romantic meal followed by . . .'

'Why not?' She whooped with joy. 'What a fluke that you won that raffle. They can hardly refuse us entry, can they?'

'No. Of course not.'

If Honey noticed he was a bit subdued about all this, she didn't say so. Spending a night at St Margaret's Court was supposed to be a red-letter day for them. He'd been looking forward to it. Now he was kind of fifty-fifty about the whole thing.

He consoled himself with the hope that it might not all be work. They might fit in some fun.

The vibes were good. Caspar was pleased with the outcome. Sigmund, her possible replacement, had fallen in love with a bloke who installed zip-wires in adventure centres and gone off.

Love was in the air.

* * *

'So we're finally here.'

Honey pretended to be interested in the décor. The ceiling was a mass of what could only be termed plaster-cast stalactites dripping downwards. Each one was crowned — or perhaps bottomed might be the right word — with a beautifully crafted example of a Tudor Rose, the amalgamation of the Houses of York and Lancaster, symbol of the Tudor dynasty that had ended with Elizabeth I.

The corner posts of the bed boasted richly carved, bulbous protuberances of indeterminate period. Crewel-work bed coverings glowed with bright reds, vivid greens and rich blues.

Honey's heart skipped a beat when she looked at the bed. She'd spent many nights lying alone and thinking of this moment. Would she and Doherty ever get it together? Well, the time had arrived. The decision was up to her.

'Did you bring your pyjamas?'

He said it jokingly.

'Did you bring yours?'

His smile was lopsided and his eyes twinkled. He always had that look when he had certain thoughts in his mind. His hands were clenched slightly too, as though he were thinking of squeezing something not a mile away from his fingertips.

'I never wear them,' he said.

She smiled back. 'Neither do I.' It was an outright lie. Sometimes when the nights were very cold and the heating had gone off, she'd opt for the flannelette and a pair of bedsocks. Add a nightcap and she'd be a dead ringer for Wee Willie Winkie — except for the candlestick, that is.

'Shall I open the champagne?'

For all his bravado, she sensed he was nervous. It had taken a desperate situation and a near-death experience for him to work up the courage to ask her here. She was feeling nervous too. They'd been a bit like an old banger of a car for a long time now. Three speeds: slow, stop and all get off and push.

She watched him, the subdued way he was doing things, the slight shake of his hand as he picked up the magnum of champagne.

'This is nothing to do with the investigation, is it? This is about us.'

'Well,' he said, holding the champagne bottle in one hand, the fingers of the other flexing in preparation for unfastening the wire and pulling out the cork. 'You don't have to stay.' His manner was more commanding now, nervousness consigned to the waste bin.

His sensitivity had touched her. The feminine side of her was bursting to come out. He was making her feel young again.

'I know I don't have to stay, but I will.'

'That's good,' he said.

The champagne cork came out with a pop. Allowing it to make that sound was strictly a breach of etiquette, but Honey didn't care. The stuff in the bottle was still the same. They'd enjoy it, and everything else with it.

THE END

ALSO BY JEAN G. GOODHIND

HONEY DRIVER MYSTERY SERIES
Book 1: MURDER, BED & BREAKFAST
Book 2: MENU FOR MURDER
Book 3: WALKING WITH MURDER
Book 4: THE JANE AUSTEN MURDERS
Book 5: MURDER BY LAMPSHADE

Thank you for reading this book.

If you enjoyed it please leave feedback on Amazon or Goodreads, and if there is anything we missed or you have a question about, then please get in touch. We appreciate you choosing our book.

Founded in 2014 in Shoreditch, London, we at Joffe Books pride ourselves on our history of innovative publishing. We were thrilled to be shortlisted for Independent Publisher of the Year at the British Book Awards.

www.joffebooks.com

We're very grateful to eagle-eyed readers who take the time to contact us. Please send any errors you find to corrections@joffebooks.com. We'll get them fixed ASAP.

Printed in Great Britain
by Amazon

31217345R00151